Payton Edgar's Agony

M.J.T. SEAL

TO CHRISTOPHER

.

CONTENTS

PROLOGUE

Payton's Plate
The London Clarion.
February 9th 1962

An acquaintance in a rather loud and unattractive jumper recently advised me to attend 'Humpty's', a somewhat poky little joint just off the Shaftesbury Avenue.   In future I shall think twice before taking on recommendations from overly enthusiastic associates with dubious tastes in knitwear.

Our experience was questionable in every sense of the word.

"What on earth are bread and gristle rissoles doing on a modern menu?" was one of the first queries to pass my lips.   Another more immediate question one is forced to ask when studying the pitiful menu in the window was *"am I sure that I really want to eat here?"*

This I asked of my companion Mr Spence as we studied the unclean windows and stained net curtains within.   But in the interest of public service, your intrepid culinary adventurer braved the threshold.

Humpty's appears to be aiming for a nostalgic feel, of pre-war good times and simple home cooking, however this should never be an excuse for poor class and – regrettably - even poorer hygiene.   Our plates were clearly strangers to hot soapy water, and there was crusty evidence of some unidentifiable malt-based substance upon the prongs of my fork.   Such disorder extended far beyond the tableware; the service received was haphazard at best and the standard of our meal lower than an ant's ankle.

Mr Spence is a lover of soups, and yet even he struggled to finish the tepid pond water that was the mushroom and chestnut broth.   I risked the potted pig's cheeks in the interests of journalism.   This tasteless pulp was served with one measly slice of Hovis and was, inevitably, returned to the

1

kitchen barely touched.

For the main course Mr Spence opted for the rissoles and - just as I had predicted - regretted this choice greatly. I plumped for the lamb shank which appeared with much promise (perhaps the only bonus of the pre-war approach lies in the generosity of the portion), but which delivered nothing more than stringy and flavourless disappointment. Dessert was a pauper's choice of tough spongy jam pudding or a dull fruit crumble, and although Mr Spence braved the sponge I am ashamed to say that I did not have the stomach to continue.

I believe the establishment is run by a retired police chief. Ironic that one should turn from fighting wrongdoing to committing the worst kind of culinary crime as I stood witness to that night.

In future I will not be accepting recommendations from acquaintances in shapeless and distasteful knitted jumpers, of which this dining experience was surely the culinary equivalent.

Payton Edgar

PART 1

CHAPTER 1
In which Payton Edgar receives an offer

There are number of standard responses to everyday situations that one expects to be said in polite English society. Of a newborn baby; "*such a beautiful child!*". This being said despite the dry blotchy skin and the face puckered like a malformed turnip.

Of the newly-weds; "*such a perfect couple!*". This being said despite the bride's dismal choice of wedding attire and the groom's evident wandering eye.

And then of death - there are only choice number of suitable lines one can use in the face of unexpected death. With this in mind, sitting opposite a complete stranger - a man who had just been made a widower, I said what should be said. I said it gently and with great care.

'I am so sorry for your loss.'

There is, in polite society, only one suitable response to this; a grateful and solemn "thank you".

'Don't bother,' came the gruff reply. 'My wife was murdered, Mr Edgar. *Murdered!*'

Inappropriate in the extreme!

I would soon become accustomed to such ideas. In time, I would find it only natural to talk of murder, motives, suspects and so forth, and yet at the beginning such ideas were entirely alien. Death and drama was simply something that happened to other people. The majority of my days were spent uneventfully moseying through London's parks or contemplating the boutiques of Savile Row or, on a quieter morning, dear old Bond Street.

Every morning without fail I dressed in one of my well-pressed signature blue suits and Italian brogues, the uniform of a true gentleman. Each day I would venture out, using my stick as my guide, stepping carefully as I went and taking shelter from the rain to ensure minimal risk of staining or scuffing. My weeks were routine and pleasingly predictable, beginning with my Monday morning finances and ending on a Sunday evening by the fire in my pleasingly soft leather slippers. My months were patterned by the demands of my role as restaurant critic, being punctuated with the occasional delightful dining experience - or even more delightfully substandard dining experience - and nothing more.

In short, I led a very comfortable life but by no means one tainted by personal drama, trauma or tragedy.

As one looks back on the years, however, it is the occasional times in which the Grim Reaper played an unforeseen part that are the most memorable, and an observer would be forgiven for considering my experiences to be somewhat exclusively macabre. I'm sure I have had many positive and happy experiences (and perhaps even some dull and uninteresting ones) however these do not spring to mind as readily as the dramatic and the deadly.

Were I asked to write a book of my life, I would not find it difficult to pass over my formative years, nor would I wish to dwell on the influence of my warring parents. Father, an eminent but entirely ineffectual geologist, stemmed from fine stock as he was prone to remind us all at any given opportunity. For my the majority of my upbringing he was either away on trips to various digs or pits, or immersed in matters of stratigraphy behind the closed doors of his smoky study. Mother, whose parents had not been so thoughtful as to be neither eminent nor affluent, was happy to live her life almost entirely detached from spouse or offspring and gallivant around town with her sister.

Father had passed away just after my eleventh birthday, his estate only encouraging Mother to party on, unencumbered by debt or financial responsibility.

One is given to believe that a life indebted to alcohol and medicinal stimulants is a short and troubled one. On the contrary, Mother lived to a ripe old age before passing away suddenly at one of her ghastly house parties in the spring of 1961. This death marked the beginning of a fresh chapter in my life, one which brought a number of unexpected deaths to my door. And not only unexpected deaths, but also deliciously unnatural deaths.

Murder, it seems, rather likes me.

The nonsense all started at Thistle House, Fleet Street; the home of the London Evening Clarion.

My workplace is a peculiar building. Conceived in the swing of the twenties, it is now a rather shabby place, draughty and cluttered on the inside despite its box-like magnificence on the outside. The building is impressive in an industrial sense, housing both a myriad of offices and the thundering printing presses all underneath one roof. Its offices sweep upwards from around the basement in a horseshoe formation so that, on most floors, it is possible to stand and grasp the iron fencing and peer downwards to the rumbling presses below.

I have always found the vast dungeon of printers and sorting machines to be most imposing. When combined with the dizzying buzz of social interaction within the offices surrounding them, this quagmire of people and machine is a daunting environment. It is for this reason that I rarely ventured into my workplace.

I would have perhaps spent more time there should I have had an actual office space to myself instead of being boxed in alongside four others who I have never felt it necessary to get to know. Instead I opted to scribe my missives in the comfort of my homestead and to deliver my finished piece by hand well in advance.

It pays to remain fastidious when it comes to deadlines.

The five storeys of offices are mainly used for news and politics. Mine, for what it is worth, is situated on the top floor under the ambiguous title of "leisure", sharing our space with home wares, gossip, fashion and, much to my dismay, sports. The cigar-chewing men in sports often single me out as a fellow male of the species and attempt to enter into a casual discussion on the dismal football league tables or baffling golf tournaments, leaving me agreeing blindly to their comments and, if asked a question (heaven forbid!), forcing me to stammer some broad riposte into my collar before swiftly excusing myself.

I avoid the office entirely during the dreaded Wimbledon fortnight.

Most of the upper floor is given over to 'Dear Lady' magazine, one of the Clarion's more successful business ventures. With an atmosphere not unlike a beehive, I always did my best to avoid the offices of Dear Lady magazine almost as much as those of the sportsmen. I need not describe these offices further, for I have said beehive, and this is surely enough.

Rather unusually, on this particular morning in question, I had been called to the offices of Temple Bilborough.

Billy, as he is more commonly known by his devoted underlings, owns the lion's share of The Clarion from its printers to its people, and since buying in to the business at the start of the decade had made himself into a very visible and approachable leader. I think that I am right in saying that he is the youngest in his position on Fleet Street, and being just over the forty-year mark with a youthful face and a winning smile must have served him well in matters of business.

Despite the fact that the man was only a mere decade younger than myself, I still saw my chief as something of a whippersnapper, such was his approach. It has always appeared to me that young Bilborough has a tiring and relentless energy, and he has, in my opinion, done a far better job in moulding the newspaper and its unruly workforce in two years than most managers could have done in a lifetime.

Where others sit barking orders from behind their desks, Bilborough had made his presence known in all areas of the building, approaching problems with a rather unusually human touch. He was no slave to the unions, either.

More to the point, the man was keen to improve the general class of the newspaper, and it is a discernible fact that agreeing to take me on as restaurant critic - an undeniably innovative step within the British press - had proven to be one of the more successful of his actions. My presence in the Evening Clarion added a fresh element of sophistication into the journalistic mix. The employment of Payton Edgar at his hands must surely have been one of his crowning moments during his stewardship of the paper.

'Mr Bilborough,' I said as I entered his office, forcing a smile, for I cannot deny I was suspicious. He looked, as usual, fresh faced and content.

'You requested to see me?'

The young man beamed.

'Mr Edgar, good morning! Come in, come in! And call me Billy, please!'

I would do no such thing.

'Do sit down,' his eyes sparkled brightly, 'I have a proposition for you.'

The proposition, when it came, was undesirable in the extreme.

'Mr Edgar,' the man began, 'I must start by saying how much I enjoy your piece each month.'

Naturally.

'And I keep meaning to tell you how much I enjoyed your festive entry - had me in stitches, I must say.'

Quite what he meant by this I am unsure, for I am no comedian.

'Now then, an opportunity has arisen for you to extend your talents, as a personal favour to me, of course. One of our Clarion workers, Miss Betts, has unfortunately been forced to take some considerable time off for, how shall I put it? Let's say - a ladies' operation. She could even be absent for as much as three months. As you can imagine, this leaves me at something of a loose end.'

Honoria Betts was a strong candidate for the most undesirable person in the building. Grey in pallor and with a mood to match, she had the grace and style of a discontented bull. There would never be a civil greeting in the corridor as one passed her, barely even a grunt. As she slumped on through the building, her heavy-lidded eyes were inevitably cast downwards to accompany her frown. Thick grey hair sat restrained severely by an Alice band atop her head, pulled back to reveal an ever-furrowed brow. It seemed as though she carried her own personal storm cloud with her wherever she went, and I was glad to have had very little to do with the woman.

Honoria was a key player on 'Dear Lady' and had been for some years, and, for some unfathomable reason, her journalistic ineptitude had bled through to the pages of The Clarion, for she fronted the dire 'Peggy's Problem Postbag' column. I knew all about this because for a short period some months back Peggy's ragtag Postbag had been positioned adjacent to my sublime restaurant review, squashing my piece to the corner of the page - much to my horror. Thankfully this pointless wittering correspondence piece had later been relegated down into the bowels of the newspaper where it belonged, nearer to the "*lost and found*" section.

'As I said, Mr Edgar, I have long been a fan of your prose, and am looking for a wordsmith such as you to take over her Clarion article in her absence. I-'

'Peggy's Postbag!' I spat, despite myself. I clasped the smooth brass head of my walking stick in both hands, my knuckles whitening. The young man fell silent, clearly unused to being interrupted.

'You want me to take over Peggy's Postbag?' I asked, incredulous.

He had the temerity to smile.

'Indeed! Quite a challenge, I know. I am aware that it is significantly more work for you, being a weekly, and-.'

Although he continued, I had stopped listening.

The man was obviously under the impression that his proposition was a good offer in some twisted way or another; something decent to which I would have even a smidgeon of an inkling towards. The poor man was gravely mistaken, for Payton Edgar had no such inkling.

I could tolerate his misguided babbling no longer. I gave my stick a forceful thump on the floorboards, at which he abruptly stopped his speech mid-sentence. I loved my stick. With a stamp against the floor or a forceful and well-placed tap to the person it carried with it the power to control any given situation. I had purchased this myself some years back at Petticoat Lane, getting a fair drop on the price after outwitting a particularly bothersome salesman. The stick was of exceptional quality, a fine dark mahogany fixed with a gleaming brass owl motif atop of it. I had decided to ignore the fact that I had once associated such accessories with the feeble elderly.

And, once again, my beloved stick didn't let me down as it made a pleasingly sharp crack against the dusty boards at my feet.

'A challenge, Mr Bilborough? A challenge?' I snorted. 'That piece writes itself! I cannot believe that you are asking me, Payton Edgar, culinary trend-setter and restaurant critic, to become-' I could barely say it,

'Peggy with her ridiculous problem postbag. To take on the mantle of a fictitious fishwife? Offering soggy advice to even soggier whingers?'

Bilborough wasn't smiling any longer, and yet still he persisted.

'Now, I know that you are a proficient writer and that we have a small backlog of your reviews, Mr Edgar, so we could run with these. Or you could rest your own column if you liked. Call it a holiday from your restaurant review, so as not to snow you under-'

'That would be doing our readers a great disservice, do you not think?'

'Well-'

At this point he left just too long a pause for my liking.

'I cannot quite believe that you are asking me, Payton Edgar, to write for Peggy's Postbag!'

Bilborough persevered,

'It would, of course, be paid work, let's not forget.'

'You could pay me in gold doubloons from the seabed of Atlantis and my answer would be unchanged, Sir. It is not a job for me.'

I stood.

'I take it you are not a fan?' my superior said, not without a twist of sarcasm.

'Peggy's Postbag is a trite piece of journalistic fluff, and is far, far beneath someone of my talents.' I issued my statement without hesitation as I felt the beginnings of a knot of anger in my gut.

'So I take it that is a no?'

'Yes indeed it is a no. A very big no, most certainly. I am a restaurateur, Mr Bilborough, and a serious writer. I am no grey-haired gossip-monger, dribbling trite advice into my embroidery! I am sorry, Mr Bilborough. I remain loyal to you and to The Clarion, but at this I have to draw the line.'

As I left the office I felt the little knot of anger inside me tighten. This little knot was to follow me home.

CHAPTER 2
In which Payton Edgar is invaded

Dear Peggy's Postbag,
I am convinced that my dear friend, who comes to embroider and knit with me, steals from me behind my back. On numerous occasions I am missing a cotton thread bobbin or two after she has left, and I have taken to counting my needles where there are often discrepancies.
What shall I do?
Worried knitter, Tower Hamlets

Dear worried knitter,
This is a certainly a quandary as you do not wish to upset your friendship, of course. I suggest that you pop the kettle on, sit down with her and have a jolly good chat about it. Perhaps quote some Matthew from the bible. I'm sure that she will come around and you shall have many more happy harmonious hours knitting together.
Love from Peggy

It has rarely been known for Payton Edgar to allow female company into his neat bachelor pad, but that is exactly what I had been forced to do back in the autumn of 1961. A man's home is his castle, I had once believed.

Not any more.

The female invasion began with my Aunt Elizabeth.

My aunt and I shared a curious history, and not an altogether pleasant one. My mother and her sister had been frustratingly close. It is normal for sisters to develop a healthy relationship of mistrust and deceit, however my Mother and Aunt Elizabeth were, unnaturally, the very best of friends.

I need not go further into a detailed account of the character of my Mother, suffice to say our relationship survived my childhood years in an air of cold indifference, growing ever frostier over the years, with a chill that was never to thaw out before her sudden death in the dying days of the previous summer.   Many of my earliest, not to mention scariest, memories involve my mother, ever ready with a clip around the ear or a sharp pinch to the upper arm if I so much as spoke a word.   It was little wonder that I had grown up to dislike the woman so much.

It was to this end that, over the years, I developed rather a blinkered view of my Aunt Elizabeth.   I do not consider myself to be inclined towards hostility to others; rather the opposite.   I am a charitable soul, and try to do my best to see the good in people. Again and again, over the years, I would find myself turning to Aunt Elizabeth for the attention my Mother had failed to give.   I would, inevitably, be disappointed.

One particularly memorable episode regarding a beautiful cake stood as a case in point.

I had suggested to my mother that we surprise her sister with a cake on a milestone birthday that was looming, only to be informed that if that was indeed my wish then I would have to save and spend from my own meagre pocket money.   This I foolishly did, relishing the fact that accountancy had come naturally to me from an early age.   Besides sweets from Mr Allen's poky little shop on the corner there was little else of worth to spend my meagre fortunes on, and this was some years before I developed my unbridled fondness for lemon sherbets.   Soon the day in question rolled around, and with great care I positioned the towering sponge that I had ordered in pride of place upon our dining room table.   The cake was slathered with rich fondant icing and adorned with floral sugar work which had been produced by a hand showing some considerable skill.

It was *beautiful*.

'How much?' was all that my Aunt Elizabeth had to say upon clapping eyes on the thing.

'Sorry?' I had squeaked.   "I mean, I beg your pardon?'

'How much did you spend?'

Wrong-footed by her stark lack of delight, I had stammered out my price.   Aunt Elizabeth snorted.

'I hate cake.   Do you know what that would do to my waistline, Payton? If you have to waste money on me then make it gin in future.'   She abruptly left the room, and the cake went untouched.

I was twelve years old.

The war and adulthood had brought a welcome distance from family and I had kept this distance without difficulty ever since.   Christmases and birthdays passed by without as much as a thought.   We were as strangers.

And then, suddenly, the malevolent manifestation of my dear old aunt had appeared at my doorstep like a deathly spectre, bringing with her unwanted family truths and, even worse than that, a sentence of domestic misery.

I had avoided any involvement in settling Mother's affairs. It was only natural that my aunt should deal with her estate. It turned out that the inconvenience of her sudden death had revealed dark matters of addiction that had been unknown to all, resulting in Aunt Elizabeth losing the roof over her head to Mother's legacy of debt.

It was apparently to go without question that Aunt Elizabeth should stay with me. I first heard about this only two days before her appearance, by a quick scrawl on a postcard. This despite the fact that the sly old crone had shown no interest whatsoever in her sister's only child in the five decades before she was made dispossessed and desperate.

My initial reaction was, of course, irritation, but then those old feelings of warmth for my aunt crept back into mind, and I made haste in decorating my spare room in preparation. I had a man in to re-paper and add a lick of paint to the skirting boards and I even went so far as to place one of my favourite items, a sleek and tasteful Doulton vase, upon her windowsill.

It was the birthday cake scenario all over again. My aunt had taken one look at the room, grunted a few times, and then complained bitterly about the wallpaper.

Against the will and determination of Aunt Elizabeth, I had little strength. She had very speedily made it clear that she believed herself to be the head of my household, despite being somewhat restricted in physical action and entirely empty of pocket.

At first, I had spent two horrendous weeks avoiding her shadow as she stalked through my gorgeous little townhouse complaining about the decor and moving things about without consent or the slightest consideration for aesthetics. It was akin to housing a groaning somnambulist with no eye for ornamentation, a creature that was intent on turning my beautiful abode into some sort of personal junk shop.

The only agreeable item I was to inherit out of this turn of events was a baby grand, an echo of my mother's good-time-girl youth. The piano, once tuned and polished, was a beautiful addition to my living room. The rest, however, was inelegant junk.

Chipped glassware appeared here and there, and the odd Victorian floral vase, fat and garish, cropped up to clutter my surfaces. And the very worst of all; four or five ancient dead-eyed porcelain dolls appeared, dressed in dusty and discoloured frilly frocks. At least two of these had ominous cracks about the skull. These were evidently as antique as my aunt herself, not to mention just as unwelcoming.

I freely admit that I am not the most tolerant of people when faced with such blatant disrespect, but I really did my best. Suffice to say, as the beady eyes of the porcelain dolls seemed followed me everywhere I went, I prayed for salvation.

A temporary respite was granted to me on a Tuesday afternoon in October, when Aunt Elizabeth suffered a stroke.

Upon my return from the hospital, and having the place to myself at last, I have to confess that I floated through each room in a silent cloud of bliss.

I was granted two glorious weeks of peace and freedom as she was institutionalised very much against her will at King's, before being discharged suspiciously early to resume her reign of terror. I can only assume that my aunt had run rings around the medical staff and they had been only to glad to hurry her to discharge, for, in many ways, the stroke had only made matters worse. Aunt Elizabeth's already unreasonable demands had become ever more unreasonable and demanding than before. She was more or less restricted to her bed in my gloomy downstairs back room at the foot of the staircase. This chamber had become her lair, and she only occasionally ventured to the wheelchair beside the bed on what she considered to be her stronger days.

I had taken this opportunity to enforce an embargo on the vile ornaments scattered about the house. Having gathered up the majority of these distressing trinkets from my shiny surfaces I had arranged them around her bedroom, only too pleased to remind her of how important it is to have her own things around her.

My aunt had declared herself bedridden and chose to fix herself to the mattress and cry out orders like a particularly severe headmistress. And yet it soon became apparent that she toured the house when it was otherwise vacant, the tell-tale signs of snooping becoming more evident with each passing week.

My post often looked just a bit too neatly stacked on the doormat. Cushions moved without explanation. One morning I almost leapt out of my skin as I saw that one of her pallid wide-eyed dolls had reappeared on my mahogany what-not. On one occasion one of the Royal Albert teacups in my cupboard had its handle facing in the wrong direction, suggesting that bony old fingers must have been exploring.

And yet if she could get about, the wily old goat wasn't about to let on. Instead she would holler and groan from her room and ring her little hand bell constantly until attention arrived. She was, of course, in need of some practical nursing care, and to this end I kept my distance; Payton Edgar is not cut out for nursing care. Not that she would have let me near her with a sponge. So far as she was concerned, nursing is a female occupation, one of the few opinions of Aunt Elizabeth's with which I wholeheartedly agree.

And so, inevitably, more women were to invade my town house, bringing the alien scents of lavender and antiseptic into the rooms. In yet another failed attempt to please and pacify my aunt, I had insisted that she have a live-in nurse, and I had taken time to clear out my box room at the top of the first staircase, dust it down and suitably kit it out to serve as servant's quarters.

No less than two doomed nursemaids had braved our threshold. First there had been Alice Jameson, a neat young woman who I had found through a carefully composed advert in the window of Boots. It soon became clear that the woman struggled to cope with my aunt's more obnoxious side.

Miss Jameson was a sweet natured girl, who unfortunately lacked the strength or experience to counter the impossible behaviour she was presented with daily. Towards the end of her short spell as Aunt Elizabeth's handmaiden, young Alice Jameson was clearly struggling under such conditions. The girl appeared more pale and worn with every passing day, and dark rings appeared at her eyes. In the end, showing a previously un-displayed sense of perception and calculation, the timorous Miss Jameson took the opportunity to steal away into the night without word.

One couldn't blame the girl. I understood her fear only too well.

I advertised immediately in the personals and, on a soggy Thursday afternoon, Mavis Sayer moved into the box room.

Mavis was an unusually short and portly woman with tight dark curls plastered around her crown and more than a hint of a moustache on her upper lip. Her cheeks were always heavily rouged, and I had been amused to see that her tongue peeped through her lips just a little when she concentrated.

Our initial interview had been brief, as the applicant was clearly well qualified, and I had soon welcomed her into my house. I was careful to give no illusions as to the perilous nature of my aunt's behaviour, and was gratified by Miss Sayer's reply. Indeed, the woman had seemed cheered at what she referred to as "*a challenge*". Mavis certainly had the maturity and strength that had been lacking in Miss Jameson, and within days I was delighted to hear her holler back at my aunt's loud groans in equal volume with stubborn and cheery replies. Aunt Elizabeth clearly despised the small sweaty nurse. I, on the other hand, could not have been happier with her work.

There were, however, a number of difficulties brought about by Mavis Sayer's presence.

Her ripe body odour would not have been far down on the list, not to mention the rotating collection of thick brown stockings which she hand-washed and dotted around the bathroom to dry. At times I cursed what this forest of nylons did to what was once one of my favourite rooms in my lovely townhouse. It was almost as bad as the porcelain dolls.

However, despite these shortcomings, all-in-all she was a dedicated nurse and a tremendously hard worker. Having her around the house was more like harbouring a mute, industrious hamster than a grown adult.

Christmas came and went, and the less said about this the better.

Tiny Mavis Sayer had been with us for almost nine weeks when one unseasonably sunny Tuesday morning she collapsed and died suddenly of a heart attack while out buying my aunt's prunes. Aunt Elizabeth had barely flickered an eyebrow at the news, merely holding out her withered claw and asking coldly for her dried fruit.

The wicked woman was clearly amused by this turn of events deep down in her blackened heart. I had needed to shut all the doors between my aunt's room and the box room on the morning that Mavis's dowdy sister came for her few belongings, for I did not trust my aunt to keep her jeers to herself.

Once more I was in crisis.

Enter Grace Kemp.

I was tired and irritable, having just returned from my preposterous and pointless meeting with young Mr Bilborough.

Payton Edgar writing Peggy's pointless Postbag! The man was insane!

Shaken and somewhat perturbed, I had followed this disastrous meeting with a similarly dissatisfactory jaunt along Savile Row. I had hoped to forget the ludicrous assignment offered to me that morning by purchasing a new hat, and yet was to find myself returning with fewer shopping bags than I had anticipated and no new headwear whatsoever; only a pair of brogues and a fine lime cravat with gold trim.

The purchase of a sparkling new pair of shoes would normally have been a delightful experience, however even this had been strangely displeasing owing to the tenacity of the irritating sales assistant, a slimy soul who I had been unable to placate or to shake off as he followed me about his shop, preening and fussing without end.

I had also been unable to shake off the very incredulity of Bilborough's offer. Payton Edgar writing a women's agony column? The very idea was preposterous in the extreme. When I arrived home at around four-thirty I was in desperate need of a warm mug of something, but was to receive a shock before I so much as put a key in the door.

My front door opened as I approached, and an unfamiliar young lady appeared. She blinked down at me as if I were the stranger in the wrong place, and not her.

Her lips were tightly pursed, her light-blue eyes wide in surprise. The stranger wore a beige knitted suit jacket with a calf length skirt revealing smooth tanned ankles, and I could see in an instant that the blonde young woman was what many people could call beautiful, despite the rimmed spectacles and rather conservative clothes. Her skin was clear without a wrinkle in sight, and her fair hair had been recently set in fashionable curls. Just what was a beautiful young woman doing coming out of my house?

'Can I help you?' she asked sharply. I was momentarily stupefied, but eventually found my tongue.

'And who, I might ask, are you?' I demanded as haughtily as I could muster, despite my malaise.

She inhaled sharply, pulling up her bust. 'I might ask you the same question, Sir!' echoed her reply.

These supercilious exchanges were all too Dickensian to my liking, and I toned down my manner just a little in my reply.

'I am Payton Edgar, and this is my house!'

She thinned her eyes.

'And how do I know that?'

'I beg your p-'

'How do I know you live here? You could be a complete stranger - an opportunistic house thief!'

How this young woman could have mistaken me for a common thief in my duck-egg tweed is beyond me. I stood rooted to the spot, incensed by her impertinence. After a deep breath I swallowed my fury.

'I am Payton Edgar, and this is my house. You, my dear, are the complete stranger!'

A soft hand was extended in my direction, which I found myself briefly shaking in some confusion.

'Mr Edgar, I would say it is a pleasure to meet with you, but I am not in the habit of telling lies.' She went on to introduce herself with the clipped precision than can only be brought about by good schooling.

'Miss Kemp. Grace Kemp. You have a very pleasant home. It must be lovely living in such comfort. Am I right, Mr Edgar? It's just a pity that you don't know how to share it, isn't it? I am quite sure that your own bed springs are most suitably set, unlike some others. Is it too much to ask for you to extend such luxury to an elderly member of your own family? I am sorry if I am speaking out of turn, but I have to be frank, Mr Edgar. People like you, selfish and inconsiderate people, make me nauseous!'

Her words had been delivered with a gentle grace and in such a matter-of-fact manner that they made me question my ears. Surely, I was being attacked! The young woman paused for a moment and studied a tiny wrist watch.

'Well, I have a bus to catch at five, so I must be going. Goodbye, Mr Edgar. Please behave. I will see you tomorrow!' With that, she stepped down from my threshold and made away down the street. I entered in something of a dream.

Once inside I posted my stick in the umbrella stand, plonked my tired old hat on the hat stand and pulled off my gloves, my scarf and my overcoat. I continued on my way to the kitchen in a daze, just stopping myself in the doorway, my hand frozen against the wall as it extended to the light switch. *Behave? See you tomorrow?* Just who was this girl? I turned back and stamped through the landing, reluctantly heading for the room I usually went out of my way to avoid.

The door was closed but I did not hesitate to issue a sharp knock.

'Go away!' Aunt Elizabeth shouted from inside the room in her familiar throaty bellow. Not to be deterred, I entered swiftly.

As usual I was briefly assaulted by the united stench of infirmity and carbolic soap. My aunt was sitting up in bed as one would to read a newspaper, her grey claws clasped together on her lap. As usual, the only light in the room was her bedside lamp, which cast eerie shadows across the walls and illuminated her face from below. Her aged phizog resembled some horrific tribal mask one might find hanging in a museum.

Her long white hair was swept back, erupting around her pillow, the two dark pools above her crooked nose giving the impression of deep empty sockets rather than functional eyes. Her teeth sat loose on the bedside table top, grinning in my direction.

Aunt Elizabeth's claw was moving slowly in her lap, and for the first time I noticed that there was a second stranger under my roof; a scrawny ginger cat curled up on the bedcovers. Unfortunately, this unexpected development wrong-footed me considerably.

'What is that?' I found myself saying with pointed hand.

'My darling nephew, you can see what it is,' Aunt Elizabeth replied wearily.

'Well, where did you get it? It's not ours!'

She smiled a thin smile.

'He is now. He came to me. He has no collar. I've called him Titty.'

'Titty?'

'Titty.'

'How did he get in?' I asked, a sour heat bubbling up in my throat.

'You have a cat flap, you know.'

'But your door is closed! Your door is always closed. How-' I stumbled over my words, rather vexed by her cool smile. It took a second or two for me to gather myself.

'Well he can go straight back out!'

'When he is ready I'm sure that he will.'

I fought back a deep sigh.

'Titty?'

'Heavens, Payton, did you never read Swallows and Amazons? I forget, your nose was glued to your mother's cookbooks!'

I caught my breath. The woman was intolerable! Aunt Elizabeth loathed my dear cat Lucille, who was transparently petrified of her and avoided the room at all costs. And understandably so. My planned confrontation had been ruined by the presence of the interloping moggy and I took a moment to compose myself.

'Aunt Elizabeth, I have just been accosted by a strange young girl. Did you let her in?'

She coughed for a minute, her chest crackling and rattling in a most unsettling manner, sounding not unlike buttons clattering in a Quality Street tin.

'Oh yes, I did let her in, my dear. Just after I had been for my morning run and before I climbed onto the roof to fix the chimney pots. Are you going to stand there all morning, huffing and puffing and asking me stupid bloody questions?'

She cleared her throat and raised her voice.

'My bag! I need my bag. Pass me my bag.'

A long finger pointed out to the chair behind me where her over-stuffed handbag sat. It seemed to me that everything my aunt needed was always just out of reach, giving her every opportunity to issue curt orders such as this. Always, without fail, as if she planned it.

I retrieved her tatty leather handbag, which was strangely sticky to the touch, and dropped it onto the bed. After shakily unclasping the fastening she began a familiar practice, pulling out a number of screwed up dirty handkerchiefs and dropping them onto the bedcovers around her, in search of some treasure deep within. As she did, the grandfather clock on the far wall gave a brief chime of a quarter to the hour, before resuming the grave clanging of its pendulum. The poor cat sniffed at a hanky before turning its nose away sharply.

'How can you stand that noise?' I said, despite myself.

'What noise?'

'The clock! Clacking away like that every second.'

'I like it, Payton. Like the beat of my heart, it reminds me that I am alive. Until I had dear Titty it was the only company I could hope for.' She paused in her fumblings to fuss over the cats ears for a moment. It thinned its eyes to a line and mewed gently, as if laughing at me.

'How long has that mangy thing been coming in here?' I asked.

'None of your business.'

'And how does it get in? I try and keep that door closed.'

'I know you do,' said my aunt gravely, 'to shut me away like an old coat in a wardrobe. And that hairy fat thing of yours is no comfort. Spoilt, that cat is. Horribly prissy. Not like my Titty.' She continued to fawn over her new pet before speaking again.

'My visitor was a nice girl, wasn't she?'

This statement caused me some surprise. To the best of my memory I had never heard her issue a compliment about another human being in my life. She returned to her bag and proceeded to rummage once more.

'Needs to learn a thing or two, I think. But she will. Aha!'

Aunt Elizabeth lifted out a final handkerchief and began to unwrap it, her dry eyes gleaming. Pulling back the last corner of cloth revealed one half of a fruit scone, once lavishly covered in butter which had now seeped through into the cake leaving a dry yellow hue. Its crumbly edges were a greenish-white. She picked off a small piece and popped it into her mouth to suck on. There was always something undiscovered in the depths of her handbag, some unlikely treasure she had grasped while on her secret wheelchair adventures.

I had become used to the woman's curious desire to hoard and had stopped questioning where she managed to get her finds. Indeed, as far as I knew there had not been a scone in my house since I had moved in many, many years ago. Perhaps Mavis Sayer had been busy baking before her untimely demise.

'Who is she?' I demanded, not really expecting a compliant response. Instead, my aunt chose to answer my previous question.

'She came in through the window.'

It took a moment for this to sink in.

'Through the what? Through the window?'

Aunt Elizabeth pulled a stubborn raisin from her gums and flicked it away to the corner of the room where it hit the wall with a tap and dropped silently to the carpet. The scrawny cat leapt up after it.

'I heard the doorbell when you were out gallivanting, and I called out. She must have gone right around to the back, because a minute later a face appeared at my window. I used this to unlatch it.' She raised her crooked stick by her side and jabbed it in the direction of her window.

'She came in through the window?'

'Yes. Must have been a bit of a climb. And with the window open, just now, dear Titty came in.' My aunt smiled slowly. 'She saw off that vile vase of yours!'

It was then that I noticed the broken remains of my Daulton Vase on the floor beneath the window sill, and my heart broke. I stood, stupefied, and muttered a little to myself.

'She came in...through the window?'

'I like it!' Aunt Elizabeth announced. 'It shows initiative. Miss Kemp can stay.'

'Stay?'

'I've hired her, Payton, she starts tomorrow, so clear up the box room ready.'

I should have been pleased, overjoyed even, that we had found another fool willing to take on my aunt. Not to mention one of whom she approved. But imagining the impertinent young stranger nosing through my private rooms and having her berate me in my own house had understandably turned me against the girl more than just a little.

Why had she said those harsh words? I stood for a moment in silence and studied my aunt's deathly-grey wrinkled face

'What did you say to her?' I asked.

Aunt Elizabeth laughed.

'Pah! Well I told her about this rotten mattress for a start! And how you keep me locked away day and night. And the food rations you allow me, not enough to keep a church mouse fat! Yes, I told her. She had a few choice words to say about people like you, and quite right! She's got your number, Payton.'

My aunt had clearly had a thing or two to say to the girl about her only nephew. The nephew who had taken her in without question and tried so hard to make her welcome. The nephew who had provided for her care and every need from his own pocket with little complaint.

'And what about her references?' I said, attempting to summon some calm to my chest where a now-familiar warmth of frustration was brewing. Ever since my aunt's arrival I had developed a problem with the acids of the stomach.

'What of them? I didn't care to ask. Mavis had references, didn't she? Didn't stop her from being bloody awful at her job and then dying on us, did it? I want this girl, and that is that.'

And, indeed, that was that.

It was not long before I was sat in my kitchen over a steaming cup of tea. I did not have the patience to wait for it to cool, feeling piqued at my aunt's brazen behaviour. I had felt a strong distrust for the girl on first sight, and my instincts are rarely incorrect even if I do say so myself. Even if I chose to ignore the girl's rudeness, it was clear that there was something wrong. This newcomer was just too perfect looking, too well kept for the arduous and unpleasant task of nursing my relative.

Yes, something just wasn't quite right.

In something of a frenzy I abandoned my steaming cup, took up my stick and jacket and fled down the street to Irving.

CHAPTER 3

In which Payton Edgar finds himself under analysis

Dear Peggy's postbag,
I am at the end of my tether, please help me. I only have a small collection of hats, but it is a collection that I adore. The problem is that my husband won't allow me to wear any of them except on a Sunday for Church. I really want to go to town in one of my hats, but Albert says I'm not to. What can I do?
Housewife, Ealing

Dear Housewife,
I should be very wary of displeasing your husband, for I am sure that he will have his reasons for limiting your fashion choices. It is very important for a wife to look good for her husband, and nobody else. I am sure you are quick to point out a tie he wears that you dislike, or a shirt that is torn, and you must allow him to do the same. The key to a happy marriage is compromise.
Love from Peggy

Picture, if you will, a happy artist.

You would see a man content to pick up easel and brush and waste precious hours splatting various paints about without a care in the world. Mealtimes would fly by, forgotten, and the world could grind to a halt outside the window and yet the artist would remain oblivious. This was my friend, Irving Spence.

As is the want of any true artist, Irving could be irritatingly fuzzy-headed and distracted at times, but at least he had been happy. To look at the man one would never believe that he had been born with a silver spoon in his mouth, and yet he had spent his formative years in a chateau in the south of Germany. Irving could have made a second fortune from his work, but his paintings rarely left the rooms of his townhouse.

And then, in the Spring of the previous year he had agreed to be the subject of an exhibition at the Holly Hill Gallery in Hampstead. He had spent the days and nights leading up to the exhibition in a frenzy of creativity.

The exhibition was, by all accounts, a success.

One would have thought that such a success would serve to fuel Irving's creative fire, giving recognition to his name as a talented artist on the London scene, so to speak. However this was not to be. Soon after the exhibition had closed Irving entered a period of depression and insecurity, and I lost my fuzzy-headed, carefree bohemian friend. I endured endless conversations about the nature of talent and creativity with the poor man.

Irving would rest his head in his hands and groan, tripping over his metaphors left, right and centre.

"I shouldn't have done it, Payton,' he would say, 'I've sold my soul to the highest bidder. I shouldn't have shared myself, I wasn't ready. Pieces of my once fruitful body have been taken from me and devoured by the strangers in shadows, strangers who play with their monies like I am nothing but a pawn in their game. It has stunted me. I am like a spent battery. A bicycle without wheels! I am empty. I have lost my outlet. I have lost myself."

He might as well have been speaking Portuguese for all the sense that this self-indulgent hogwash made to me. Had my friend broken a leg or some such thing then his needs would have been clear and I would know how I could help, fetching and carrying without excessive complaint. However, Irving was suffering nothing more than an acute attack of creative despondency.

Thankfully, Payton Edgar has never struggled in his art.

In the kitchen, the assimilation of harmonious flavours in my food preparation has always come as a natural gift. In my writing, words flow onto my page like water from a tap. Yet I did my very best to remain supportive, forcing myself to listen to his moaning and groaning without comment.

His easels lay abandoned, his paints sealed in their tin, and I was becoming almost desperate for him to shake off this very trying phase and to return to the man that I knew and respected. The things that had once irritated me such as the missed appointments, the unanswered telephone calls and the distracted vacancy on his face when one strove for a reaction, had now became endearing qualities that were greatly missed. I had long been used to the feeling of talking to myself while enjoying Irving's company. He would stand covered in drying flecks of paint, only half-listening to whatever I had to say as his thoughts danced around swirls of colour on some canvas in his mind.

The new Irving Spence was a different beast altogether.

As he opened the door that morning I could see by his clothing that there had been no change in his spirit. His old outfit of paint-spattered shirt and cotton trousers had been replaced by baggy cords and shapeless cardigans.

However, the first thing that struck me as I entered was not my friend's clothing but a new smell, a thick stench that hung in the air of the lounge. It was a heady, smoky smell, and, having to raise my voice over the noise of the confounded gramophone, I quizzed him immediately. Irving retrieved a pipe from the coffee table, where I was aghast to see that he had been using a saucer as a makeshift ashtray, and waved the thing at me by way of a reply.

'A pipe!' I coughed, half in surprise and half because of the smoke itself. 'Since when have you smoked a pipe, Irving?'

He was a little armoured in his reply, insisting that it was something he did from time to time. I have never seen it, and if I had then this particular malodorous weakness would have been quashed immediately. I said as much.

'It calms my nerves,' he stated coldly.

'Irving, dear, you don't have any nerves!'

He extinguished the leaf with a frown.

A pipe indeed!

My visit was pleasurable enough despite this unwelcome new development. As is customary, he attended to the gramophone to put a stop to the dreadful trumpeting wailing that was being produced before attending to our drinks. Irving liked his jazz. I most certainly did not.

'If I wanted to hear that kind of noise I would hang around the Monkey House at London Zoo!' I would tell him again and again.

My friend was never any good at making tea, always managing to create an over-milky beverage with a strangely grey hue about the edges, but combined with his company, sipping this inadequate concoction was a much preferable option to sitting alone in my kitchen and stewing. At times I had to discreetly spit into my handkerchief, for he had been rather cack-handed with the strainer as usual.

I told him all about the voguish young upstart in my lounge, being careful to voice my concern that she was a most unsuitable nurse for my aunt and an even more inappropriate house guest.

Irving, unfortunately, did not seem particularly interested in my domestic developments that afternoon. This was the third nurse that I had complained about in the past few months so one cannot blame the man. He was soon moving the conversation down other avenues. We talked through to late afternoon, entirely missing lunch, about politics and food (me), and then jazz music and the design of the Royal Mail's latest stamps (most very definitely him).

He was unusually keen to know when my next review would be.

Over the past few years Irving had become my official dining companion on each gastronomic quest, becoming something of a minor celebrity in print as '*Mr Spence*', Payton Edgar's faithful dining companion. This had only added to the success of my column. I am sure he would not mind if I described him as the perfect 'average Mr Bloggs' customer when it comes to a feast.

In contrast with my heightened expectations, I saw Irving as representing the man-on-the-street's opinion. At the start of our ventures to find culinary perfection a year or two back he could only be described as a reluctant companion, but in time, and with some gentle encouragement, his reluctance had eased. Irving enjoyed food enough, although nowhere near as much as I. But what he did appreciate was my company. He always showed a fascinated delight at my superior knowledge of all matters gastronomic and an honest appreciation towards my fervour for fine cuisine.

Our review meals were partially subsidised by the Clarion and happily topped up by my wallet, and so he received a free meal into the bargain, not to mention my exquisite company.

Despite all of this, I have never known him push for the next feast. This sudden enthusiasm over dining was most irregular, and a little unsettling. I gave him an imprecise reply that seemed to pacify him for the time being.

Unfortunately, and much to my silent horror, he then slid his little round spectacles onto the bridge of his nose and proceeded to pull out a crossword puzzle.

This was yet another new development for Irving, the daily puzzle in the Clarion. He did not know, for I had never had reason to tell him, that I abhor brain teasers, in particular the crossword. His sensitivities being as delicate as they were at present, and having just reprimanded the man over his stinking pipe, I was to keep this particular disapproval to myself. For the time being.

It is difficult to explain my dislike for the crossword. One may incorrectly conclude that I avoid such things due to a lack of intelligence. This is far from the truth. I have an advanced mind when to comes to matters of trivia, often surprising even myself with unexpected gems of knowledge that must have been lodged away within the wondrous labyrinth of my mind until required.

No, my reason for avoiding the crossword puzzle is a straightforward one; I simply have better things to do. To waste valuable time and thought puzzling over a particular type of soft cheese in four letters or the name of some Northern cathedral in seven, seems entirely pointless to me. The particularly galling thing about Irving's obsession was that he produced the puzzles as they were nearing completion and proceeded to present me with the clues to answers that he did not have, pushing the more troublesome questions on to my side of the fence.

Not fair-play at all.

'Four down, to drive out or dismiss, five letters,' read Irving.

Really, the quality of the Clarions crosswords left much to be desired. I had never met the man at the Clarion responsible for the daily puzzle, but was convinced he was not half as clever as he thought he was. I tried to overlook the riddle as best I could, and we sat in silence for some time before I told him some more of my news.

'I have been asked to write for Peggy's Postbag.' I said.

Irving finished up his tea before dropping the cup to snap his fingers.

'Expel!'

I ignored his outburst, dismissing it with a flick of my hand.

'Can you believe the cheek of it? Peggy's Postbag!' I persevered.

There was a moments silence as he joyously pencilled in his answer before he looked up at me with a vacant stare.

'Who's what-bag?'

There was nothing for it but to snatch the newspaper from his lap, and I did so with remarkably little argument on his part. After checking that it was indeed Friday's edition, I only had to flick back two pages to find what I was after.

'This! Peggy's Postbag, that dreadful problem page. The one that appeared opposite my piece last year. I made you read it, I'm sure. Well, Mr Bilborough called me into his office and asked me if I could take over while fractious old Honoria Betts has something removed, or some such procedure one can barely dare imagine. The piece really is the most dreadful old tosh. Listen,' and I read out the first of two letters on the page that day.

'Dear Peggy, I am at the end of my tether, please help me. I only have a small collection of hats, but it is a collection that I adore. The problem is that my husband won't allow me to wear them except on a Sunday for Church. I really want to go to town in my hat, but Albert says I'm not to. What can I do?'

I gave Irving a meaningful glare, which was returned with an infuriating blankness.

'Well?' he asked.

'Well, I ask you! Having to plough through such trite rubbish as that each week? I certainly have far better things to be doing. If I were writing for Peggy I would tell the poor unfortunate to get a brand new hat for every day of the week, and a new husband to boot! Either that or simply to stop moaning over nothing. There might be an epidemic of crime and pestilence sweeping all around the world but the only thing these people can worry about is the wearing, or not wearing, of hats? Unbelievable!'

Irving's face had gone frustratingly blank. Had he even been listening?

'Well? What do you think?'

After a fairly lengthy pause, he spoke.

'I think you should give the new nurse a chance.'

I bit my lip to contain myself before speaking, slowly and clearly as if to a child.

'Alright then, Irving, your opinion is noted. I have moved on from that singularly unsavoury subject. What do you think of my being asked to act as Peggy, Agony Aunt to London's more foolish residents?'

Taking the newspaper back from me and studying the page for a minute, Irving nodded his head.

'Yes, you are quite right, don't take it on. Is it a daily? Be quite a lot of work.'

'No, weekly, I believe.'

'Well, either way, it's not your style, is it? I don't think you could do it either.'

I bit my lip and examined his innocent face for a minute before replying.

'I am not saying that I cannot do it!'

'-should,' Irving was quick to correct himself, '-I meant that you should not do it.'

'And why not?'

'Well, it's just not you, helping people, now is it? Working with the public isn't very, well, not very Payton Edgar, is it? You have a very definite style which is more-'

'What? More what?'

'Well,' he looked up to the ceiling searchingly, and found the word he was looking for.

'Mercenary.'

'Mercenary?'

'What I mean is your work is much more, well, self-serving...'

'Self what?'

'Well, more disapproving, more negative. More in your own style.'

'Negative?'

Irving issued a sigh.

'Payton, it can hardly be news to you that you are...well-'

'I am... what?'

Carefully placing the crossword to one side, Irving moved to the edge of his seat, pushed his spectacles up the bridge of his nose and then raised a finger.

'Let's try an exercise, shall we? Word association…'

'Irving, I don't have time for this,' I said firmly. 'You clearly don't know what you are talking about. Have you been peeking at my psychology books again?'

'I'm serious, Payton, please humour me. Now, I will say a random word, and you say just whatever comes to mind. You may be surprised how much this can reveal about yourself. Okay? I will say seven words in total. Are you ready?'

I nodded jadedly.

'Sun' said Irving.

'Burn.' I replied swiftly.

'Countryside.'

'Bleak.'

'Field.'

'Boggy.'

'Hospital.'

'Pain.'

'Baby.'

'Noise.'

'Child.'

'Smack'

'Jazz.'

'Beetroot.'

'How on earth do you get beetroot from Jazz music?' Irving spluttered.

'Simple,' I replied, 'I loathe Jazz and I loathe beetroot.'

My companion sat back in his chair and bit his lip for a minute, shaking his head slowly.

'You are a textbook case of the disinclined, Payton, you really are.'

'Well I am terribly sorry to upset you, Irving, but you are talking a lot of rot. I really don't see how your reading a page or two of Jung when overcome by tedium can possibly make you an overnight psychologist. This has nothing to do with my ability to write this column. If you think so little of me-'

'Oh, for goodness sake, Payton! You know I admire your talents, of course I do. It's just that you have a very particular take on life, one that I'm not sure is compatible with answering people's trivial problems positively.'

'You think this would be too hard for me? Too much of a challenge? You think that I can't do it? Because I can!'

'I'm sure that you can, Payton, but-'

'And I will prove that I can!' I declared, banging my hand on the arm of my chair. 'I will do it! Yes, I feel inclined to take it on, Irving, if for no other reason than to show you just how versatile a scribe I can be. I will need to make adaptions! I must mould Peggy into a voice worth hearing; first I must create a biography, a history upon which to work. Who is this Peggy, and what drives the woman? Now, if you don't mind, Irving, may I use your telephone?'

Within a minute I was on the line to young Bilborough.

'Yes, yes, Mr Bilborough, I have decided to accept your offer,' I said, much to his delight, '-but with a condition. I wish to make one or two changes, if I may?'

CHAPTER 4
In which Payton Edgar creates a literary legend

Dr. Margaret Blythe, for years the anonymous voice behind 'Peggy's Postbag', is a most remarkable woman. Peppy and yet professional in manner, she is a towering presence, owing to her six-foot-something frame, and also a commanding presence, due to her astringent manner. At fifty-five years of age, Dr. Blythe carries herself with a certain mature dignity wherever she goes. Dr. Blythe received her doctorate with honours, and worked as a psychologist for some years before her marriage. A true leader of her sex, she had been playing down descriptive terms such as "pioneering" and "ground-breaking" ever since graduation.

As well as having many of her celebrated works published in renowned journals of science, she has also enjoyed some creative literary acclaim, having rattled off a successful romantic novel or two during the quieter times in her life. Her favourite words are ubiquitous and equivocate. A respectable mother of two, she now divides her time between voluntary work at a local hospital for the blind, her private practice in psychology and her role as counsellor to thousands in the pages of The London Clarion.

Should I give her an O.B.E? I asked myself, resting my pen to one side.

It had taken me some time to produce her surname, but I was content with the result. To me the word "Blythe" conjures up an image of warmth and comfort. It was the name of an old lady on my street as I was growing up. "Old Mrs Blythe" in her lace gloves and floppy knitted hat, who offered piano lessons in the Post Office window. She had always been kind to me, and I had always liked the sound of the name.

And now, the new, improved, peppy and professional Dr. Margret Blythe was about to make her debut.

I held that morning's Friday Clarion in my hands for a minute and took a deep breath. I had raced out first thing and bought it fresh off the delivery cart practically as soon as the strings were cut. I have to admit my hands were shaking just a little as I opened it and flicked through to the page I needed. The layout was just what I had wanted, the font of the heading perfectly imitating the hand of a sophisticate,

'Dear Margaret' it read, and then in smaller letters below 'Dr. Margaret Blythe helps you with your personal dramas.'

'Dr. Margaret Blythe helps you with your personal dramas' I said aloud to myself. It was impossible not to admire this fresh new approach.

In the corner by the title was a small picture depicting a smooth hand holding a rather lavish quill, a stylish inkwell was positioned just to the right. It was exactly as I had imagined. A very satisfactory embellishment indeed. Gone were the common block letters and poorly hand-drawn cartoon postbags that had once littered the page. Peggy's Postbag had been exalted, and was all the better for it.

After reading over my piece, I folded it under my arm and walked down the street to Number Six. I need not have worried about my timing as Irving remained creatively stunted, and was once again pleased to see me at the door. The poor man stood before me with rapt attention not unlike a doting puppy. Thankfully, there was no pipe smoke to contend with this time, and once the Jazz was silenced he perched on his dog-eared sofa and inspected the page.

His first question, however, was less than encouraging.

'Who is this Margaret woman? What happened to Peggy's Postbag?'

I snatched back the paper and was about to enter into a tirade when I caught myself. Mild confusion was bound to be the initial response, and I should prepare for the fact that change is never easy for people, even when it is obviously a change for the better.

'I have merely enhanced the good character of Peggy and called her by her true Christian name. The cheap tone of the old piece was grating, and well overdue for an overhaul. No more pedestrian scribblings about choosing accessories! I intend to encourage a rather more urbane clientele to write in, with their considerably more cultured issues. I have brought sophistication and class to what was once known as Peggy's silly, shabby Postbag. Mr Bilborough was quite happy for me to give the piece my own slant.'

'I'm sure he was,' Irving gently retrieved the paper from my grasp, 'let's have a butchers, then.'

I waited expectantly.

'Just the two letters?'

I nodded.

'I only received three, one of which was unprintable. I am happy to edit and correct silly grammatical mistakes in my letters, but that one took the biscuit. And I was appalled at the childishness of the poor woman's handwriting. Grown adults producing what can only be described as incomprehensible scrawl, can you imagine? I have written back to her, correcting her errors and advising her to stop fretting pointlessly about her weight and get some lessons on basic syntax. No, Irving, I am hoping that once my revamp is gladly received, the quantity and the quality of my correspondence will increase considerably. Looking back over past issues, though, the slot only allows for two or three letters, depending on length.'

'Indeed.' Irving proceeded to read out the first letter.

'*Dear Margaret, please help me. I think my husband of four years may be having an affair.* Ooh, Payton,' he chuckled, 'a juicy one!'

'Start with a bang, I say. No more letters about hats, if you please. Read on!'

Irving read on.

'*None of the usual signs of an affair are there. He is always right on time coming home from work and he is as kind to me as ever. I have just had a feeling, a suspicion, a hunch, over the past few months. Last week I found an unfamiliar bobby pin in his briefcase and there is something in his ardour that is different. I want to know the truth, but daren't ask him outright in case I am wrong. What should I do? Concerned, Clapham.*'

Irving lowered the newspaper to his lap.

'Well, Payton, how do you go about answering that one?' he gasped. I suspended myself on the edge of his tatty armchair, feeling a thrill at his rapt attention.

'Do you really want to know how? Before you read my reply?' I enquired cautiously, at which Irving nodded sweetly.

'Well,' I began, 'it seems that although they are keen to keep their names from being published in print, good letter writers still include an address in the top right hand corner of the page. This young lady did, and I was able to take myself down to her place in Clapham at the start of the week-'

'Payton! You can't do that!' Irving exclaimed.

'And why not? I only went for a little walk in her neck of the woods. A public byway! Is there a law against it? Besides, the writer clearly wanted to know what her husband was up to. Had she not asked for my help? So I was there from seven in the morning, in time to see him leave for work as usual at a half past. I saw the poor young woman saying goodbye to her husband. He was a handsome young man and I immediately took a disliking to him, I can tell you. Untrustworthy in the extreme. With a briefcase in his hand and an umbrella under his arm he set off down the street and I duly followed.'

'Payton!'

'And with good cause, I might remind you! Not to mention the fact that I was instantly rewarded. The young man did not go in to work that day, Irving! He took tea at a café near Wandsworth Road Station and then doubled back towards home. The rat checked first to see if the coast was clear and then set off back down his own road. What on earth is he doing? I thought to myself.

'For a minute it looked as if he were heading back home, only he went down the side of the house just next door to his! A clandestine rendezvous with the neighbour, can you believe? Through the nets I could just make out a female form leading him upstairs. Well as you can imagine, I was livid on the poor wife's behalf. I took myself out around the Common for the day, stopping for lunch at a rather grim little place with filthy saucers. I was careful to be back on the street before five, and would you know it, bang on half-past there he was! He sneaked out from the house next door, grasping his umbrella and case looking for all the world like a businessman returned from the daily grind. He simply straightened his tie and arrived home to be greeted by his poor wife once more. And that, Irving, is what helped me to write this!'

I tapped the newspaper on Irving's lap and he read on.

'*Margaret replies: Concerned? I should be livid! The man is clearly playing away and you must terminate this marriage immediately. I always say "never ignore a hunch", and this is one you ignore at your peril. Any man who returns from work bang on time each day without fail is undoubtedly up to something. If you want answers, I suggest that you look very close to home. Whether you challenge the man on this is up to you, however this is not time to equivocate. My advice is to throw his bags out onto the street, change the locks and hire an excellent solicitor. Good luck.*

'I say! That's really rather close to the knuckle, isn't it, Payton?'

'The truth hurts sometimes, Irving my dear, the truth hurts. And Dr. Margret Blythe is always one to tell the truth.'

'And what detective work did you do around this next letter?' asked Irving with an animated scowl.

'Oh, none whatsoever. Don't get me wrong, Irving, I am not intending on spying on all correspondents, you know. That would be far too much work. No, just those which, every now and then, might require it.'

Irving proceeded to read Margret's second letter, biting on his lip. At one point he stopped briefly and cast me a thin eyed glare before reading on.

Once he had finished he frowned up at me.

'Payton!'

'What?'

'You can't treat people who take time to write in like this. It's just, well, it's just rude! The woman says she is lonely, she needs some comfort, not a telling off.'

'Well she annoyed me, the miserable article! And Margaret tells it like it is.'

'She certainly does. You should call it *"Truth Hurts, with Margaret Blythe"*.

'Doctor Margaret Blythe!' I was quick to add. My friend swallowed.

'But really, Payton, is that what the readers want to read?'

I stood and reached for my jacket.

'Who cares if it is or it isn't? Hardly anybody reads the damn thing, anyway. That piece is shoved at the back with the adverts for second hand rabbit hutches, it's hardly going to set the Capital alight. Now before you start up, I am off. I will pop by on Sunday as usual. I'm sure I will need to get out of the house by then.'

'How is it going with Miss...?'

'Kemp, Irving, Grace Kemp. And to be honest I have been avoiding both her and Aunt Elizabeth quite successfully of late.'

That, unfortunately, could never last.

CHAPTER 5

In which Payton Edgar hits his stride

Dear Margaret,
I am lonely. I have been a widow now for just over a year. I have no children and very few friends except for those at church, and I don't get out much. I do enjoy my embroidery, but always used to find it easier in company. I am almost 70, and cannot bear the thought of living alone like this for the rest of my life. What can I do?
Lonely of Brent.

Margaret replies: *Good heavens! Not one to count your blessings, are you, dear? I should jolly well put up and shut up. A ubiquitous sensation of loneliness is to be expected at your time of life. However, you have a roof over your head and cotton with which to embroider and this is much more than some people have in the world, so just get on with it. You can't really expect any excitement at your stage of life, so don't waste your time. And most certainly don't waste mine.*

I did not realise it at the start of all this, but my life was about to beat to a very specific rhythm.

This pattern was entirely not of my choosing, indeed for the first time in my life I found myself working practically Monday to Friday just like any menial commoner. On a Monday I would pick up the package of letters gathered for Margaret, plus my own of course, and I then had until noon on the Thursday to deliver the goods, as Margaret Blythe made her grand appearance in print in every Friday early edition.

This gave me the weekend to myself, bar the odd monthly dining experience for my own column. I planned to pen the pieces as soon as I received the post on a Monday, nicely freeing me up for the rest of the week. How long could it take to jot down the obvious in response to the pleas of the public?

Not that long, I soon found out. Margaret's voice flowed naturally from my pen, when I wasn't interrupted, that is. The presence of my new houseguest had a strange effect on me. Where previous nurses had been oblivious to my need for silence, fussing about the house with clattering pots and heavy footfalls, Miss Kemp was an entirely different creature. She had been sure to treat my home as if it were her own, and whenever free of my aunt's grip was inclined to lounge in my living room, her shiny legs crossed over the chez-lounge as she flicked through some shining picture magazine.

In her work, however, she was entirely soundless. She appeared to do her job proficiently and entirely devoid of any fuss whatsoever, giving me no avenue of complaint. It was extremely frustrating, more so than any noisy hustle and bustle could ever have been. The second weekend after taking on my new job as Margaret Blythe I could take no more.

I had entered my living room to find Grace Kemp in position, lounging with an air of quiet satisfaction.

For a minute or two I stood appraising the nurse before she had spotted me. She was a pretty, confident and smart woman in the prime of her life. Even I could see that she had a certain fashionable style about her. What on earth, I thought to myself, was she doing here, scrubbing my aunt's back and the like?

I had fixed myself a whisky, pointedly omitting to offer the nurse a drink, and sat in my favourite chair with Lucille plump and warm on my lap. The evening paper lay untouched as I continued to watch the girl for a while and she pretended not to notice. After a time I broke the silence.

'You know, live-in nurses usually spend most of their time in their own quarters.'

'Which, I suppose, makes me unusual,' she retorted sharply and without missing a beat. 'And that tiny little box room could barely be called servants quarters, could it? I feel like a spider in a matchbox in there.' She licked her finger and turned a page lazily, careful not to lift her eyes from the periodical in her lap. The girl did have a point, the room was on the small side.

'Now, I meant to tell you, Miss Kemp,' I continued, undeterred, 'that the upper floor is my own personal study and is out of bounds to others, alright? Even Mrs Montgomery has restricted access. It is my own personal private space.'

Mrs Montgomery was my weekly cleaner. A most efficient and unobtrusive soul.

'Whatever you say.' The magazine was closed with a slap.

'I prefer, however, to work here in the living room at times, and need absolute silence.'

'Absolutely,' came the reply. I sipped my whiskey, which was pleasingly smoky.

'Good. Then we have an understanding?'

She inhaled deeply, as if tolerating the bleating of a small child.

'I said so, did I not? And now you have completely disturbed me, you have reminded me of something I meant to say to you. There is some shepherd's pie left over from supper. It's down in the kitchen if you want it.' This last comment was uttered casually, but I detected a hint of malice in her tone.

Yes, the offer was perhaps intended as a kindly gesture, but at that particular moment I saw it as nothing more than an indolent comment far from kindly in its intent. What on earth did she think that I, Payton Edgar, celebrated restaurateur and distinguished food critic, would possibly want with leftover shepherd's pie? Leftovers! I had done my share of rationing and making-do during the war and most certainly wasn't about to go back to that again.

I almost said as much, but instead balled my left fist discreetly and allowed a few minutes of calm silence during which I pondered just how to proceed.

What would Margaret Blythe do?

It seems I had a choice; fuss and complain, making an enemy of the young woman and possibly ostracising myself from my own home, or attempt to offer an olive branch and come to some sort of agreement.

Although the fussing and complaining sounded much more fun, my home needed to be a place of tranquility and comfort, even if it was infested by a twisted aunt and her spiky nurse.

Be nice, Payton, be nice.

'So how have you found working for Aunt Elizabeth?' I asked.

'Different,' came the reply. One word, no explanation.

'I suppose that different is one word one could use to describe my darling aunt, but it wouldn't be my first pick. Anyhow, you seem to be doing a good job so far.'

'I know.'

'It must get easier as you get to know-'

'Probably.'

Her short sharp replies were fired back to me like bullets. Miss Kemp had raised the magazine and turned another page.

'She does tell some untruths, however,' I persevered, 'I am good to my aunt, despite what she may tell you to the contrary. I try and try to please her, always have. And now I give her a roof over her head and feed her, all for nothing. You have to remember that I did not ask her to live here...'

Finally I received some eye contact, and the eyes were cold.

'You got the baby grand, didn't you?'

A rather strange thing to say.

'Well, yes, I inherited-'

'Then you should be happy. Never heard you play it, yet.'

'I don't play.'

Grace Kemp laughed. I studied her for a minute. What was this about? And then it hit me.

'Did Aunt Elizabeth tell you that I only let her live here if I got the piano?'

'That was a part of it.'

'That was none of it!' My dander was up now, the cool and calm Payton flittered away as rage descended over me. 'I had no choice about my aunt or the piano – they both had nowhere else to go. She just turned up and moved on in, no discussion. And I tried to make her welcome. No, I had a lovely life before she came-'

'Oh, I'll bet you did!'

'-but I wouldn't wish ill of the old thing, really. If she tried to get along with me then I wouldn't mind, but she does her best to make my life a misery, and-'

'Your life? She does her best to make your life a misery?'

And now she had raised her voice to match mine.

'Yes!' I snapped back, 'I am good person, Miss Kemp, whatever you think. I pay my taxes. I smile at passers-by on the street. I once found a little bird with a broken wing and-'

'Rubbish!'

She waved a dismissive hand and stood before rolling up her magazine and pointing it in my direction.

'I won't sit here and listen to such rot! I will retire to my tiny little match box - pardon me – the servants quarters, if only to get away from this pointless conversation. Nobody likes a bully, Mr Edgar. I have experienced my fair share of people like you, so don't pretend to be what you are clearly not. Pah! A good person!'

I saw red as I sat shuffling in my seat. Lucille shot away to the corner of the room. I could not let Miss Kemp have the last word, and found myself raising my voice even more.

'I'll have you know that last year I helped out with the Pimlico Scout's summer sale!'

I had, in truth, only taken a moment to donate a pair of old wing tips I had intended on leaving out for the rag and bone man, but the girl wasn't to know that.

'You help out? In between your lavish restaurant dinners-'

'I tip generously!' I found myself wailing, my voice wobbling just a little, for this was not entirely true. I went to correct myself.

'If the occasion demands it-'

'Ha!'

She had interrupted so loudly and so rudely, and I was silenced. And with that 'ha!' she was gone, clearly thinking that I was a bigger fool than she had first believed. Across the room Lucille watched me from her corner, unblinking.

'I am a good person...' I said to myself and the cat.

Lucille thinned her eyes and arched her back before padding slowly out of the room.

'I am....a good person...' I repeated slowly, my words faltering in my throat.

Cockney Guy was at the side desk as usual.

The East entrance is the one usually used by the workers of Thistle House not only because of the post collection, but also because it is nearer the pavement and one always gets a cheery greeting from the genial Londoner. That Monday morning was no different.

'Now, Mr Edgar, there's only a little one for you this morning, and it looks right dull.' Guy had perused his pigeon holes and passed over a flimsy letter that did indeed present little interest. I lifted a finger.

'And not to forget, I am writing for Miss Betts at the moment,' I said.

He smiled, revealing a spattering of teeth crying out for some considerable dental work. Cockney Guy was an unappealing, balding gent with a natural squint and an irritatingly cheery approach. But he was a good man who even I found it hard to dislike.

'Ah! You the Peggy's Postbag thingy now, I forgot,' he replied.

'The 'Dear Margaret' piece, yes. Don't forget that letters will be addressed to Margaret or even Dr Blythe from now on.'

He emptied another pigeon hole and flicked through a small bundle.

'Well's two for Peggy right here. And one for this Dr Blythe.'

'Thank you. Just the three again?'

'Oh, that's not so bad. Often Peggy's Postbag is lucky to get two a week, she is. Hole's empty some weeks, y'know. I reckon most of them problems come from up here, like.' He tapped his skull. It had never occurred to me that Honoria Betts could have been forging letters, but there was the evidence. I was determined that I would never, ever sink to those depths.

As I took the bundle I could not help but notice he was looking at me with some consideration.

'Is everything alright today, Guy?' I asked, to which the man nodded quickly and gave his parting smile.

One perk of the whole Postbag enterprise was that Honoria Betts was one of the few lucky employees with her own office, albeit a rather small one. One imagines that nobody would wish to share a space with her, so I suppose that there is something to be said for being unpopular. Bilborough had invited me to use this space, and use it I would.

The room was just big enough not to feel cramped, and the door closed behind you sturdily, giving one a pleasant feeling of detachment from the bustle outside. Here the rumble of the printers was barely audible.

A fair size desk looked out over the courtyard behind the building. Directly ahead, crumbling brickwork was dotted with sprawling ivy, and far below were some dustbins and bicycles. Hardly a beautiful view, but with the clear blue February sky above it was not an unpleasant place to work. I took a few minutes to make the desk as I would want it, squaring up papers and separating pencils from pens and moving items around to my satisfaction.

I moved the typewriter to the corner of the desk, for I would be writing by hand at first. I also watered the crisp pot plant on the window sill and moved away a cheap little ceramic ornament of a young boy in dungarees shyly clutching a bunch of flowers which was considerably tasteless in sentiment. This I dropped into the bottom drawer of the desk, out of sight. Why some people enjoyed such vulgar ornaments is beyond me. Such a vile trinket would have only distracted me from my work.

I have to confess, I had become less enthusiastic about what I was about to do. I placed the letters carefully aside and watched them as if they would open themselves. What on earth could I write? The first few letters had been fun, but that was all. It was hardly a sophisticated job.

The scuffling and scratching of a pigeon on the windowsill caught my attention. A clean looking pigeon. He froze for a second, blinking, and then continued to strut up and down the ledge. I watched him for a while in boredom, with a growing respect for his unusually smooth plumage. I named him Fitzherbert. He looked like a Fitzherbert.

Fitzherbert the pigeon. He had a strutting nobility about him.

Soon, tired of Fitzherbert, I turned my attention to the letters.

Three letters.

The first two were ideal candidates to pass on to Margaret Blythe for her page that week. One concerned finances, the other workplace relations. Both required the 'Dear Peggy' at the start to be updated and both were poorly written, ill-conceived and clearly penned by people with little else to do but write letters to a fictional gasbag.

I felt my blood boil as I read and re-read them, despairing at the inadequacies of the grammar within, and was to channel this reaction into Margaret's concise responses. I had picked apart each letter, editing fiercely, and written my replies within the hour. This job was really rather satisfying, I thought to myself.

All too easy, but satisfying nevertheless.

The third letter, however, was more disconcerting. I read it twice, unsure what exactly to do with it. As on all the other letters, an address was scrawled in the upper right corner, but the letter had been signed only 'Bothered from Bloomsbury'. It read;

> *Dear Margaret,*
>
> *Please help me. I have been married to my husband John now for almost sixteen years. He is a good man, and we were very happy together. We have one boy, Frank, who is growing up quickly. But now I have fallen in love, even though I daren't admit it to myself. I have been going to an amateur dramatic group now for a year, where I met Richard. He is unmarried and works at our local hospital, portering. I have been able to keep our affair a secret so far as we had many auditions throughout the week in the run up to our shows. Richard comes across as gentle and friendly, and he is at heart. He is clearly in love with me, but as we have gotten closer he has become more and more jealous of my family I have told him in the past that I won't leave my family, but now I'm thinking that perhaps I should. I think it may be best if I leave, as sometimes Richard has been so angry he has threatened to beat me, or even to hurt my family. I am sure he is capable of it. I think that he could be dangerous if I don't follow my heart and run away with him. I am frightened of Richard, but he is a fixture in my life now. We have our production of 'The Merry Widow' starting in a few weeks. What can I do?*
>
> *Bothered from Bloomsbury.*

I read over the letter once more. It was a miserable piece, even ignoring the grammatical errors. The woman had got herself into this bother, and I struggled to find an ounce of sympathy for her. One thing I was certain, however; I wouldn't want this on the pages of the Clarion, for the suggestion of violence was unappetising to say the least.

For while I looked up out the window at the cold blue sky, before turning back to my desk where I jotted down a private reply to '*bothered from Bloomsbury*'. I advised the woman to come clean to her spouse and stop attending the amateur dramatics immediately. I was extremely pleased with my reply, and typed it up with confidence. After handing it to Cockney Guy for the postbag on my way out I buttoned up my overcoat and took a deep breath of the crisp cold air. So sure I had done the right thing, I looked up at the clear sky and smiled to myself.

Perhaps my words would save a marriage, and possibly even a life.

Unfortunately, I was to be proved wrong on both counts.

CHAPTER 6
In which Payton Edgar takes up amateur dramatics

Dear 'bothered'.

What a difficult situation you are in. I can see only one thing you can do. Get help. The police must be able to protect you over this sort of thing. In your letter your husband, John, sounds like a pleasant sort of chap, so perhaps it is best to tell him the truth. Richard is clearly an unstable, even dangerous sort of man and one that you need to be very wary of. Drop out of the play as well, if that is where you see the man. 'The Merry Widow' is a screeching, messy piece of bunkum anyhow, even when a professional production takes it on. You have to think of yourself and your family, nobody else.

Yours sincerely,

Margaret Blythe.

(P.S, I will not be printing your letter, but accept your thanks in advance for this private reply).

The weekdays trundled on and Saturday evening came along once more. Irving and I were to dine that night at my dear favourite restaurant, Harvey's, which sat resplendent just a stone's throw from Covent Garden. But that morning, I received rather a shock from the pages of the weekend Clarion, a shock that would prove to be more than just a little fly in my ointment.

'*Suicide death of Bloomsbury mother*' the headline declared. It caught my eye from towards the foot of page four. This poor young woman, a Mrs Helen Capstick, had thrown herself from a building in the week, for reasons unknown. She had lived an apparently happy life, married to John and with one son, Frank.

John and Frank. In Bloomsbury.

Surely not..?

Could this really be *'bothered from Bloomsbury'*? I shuffled through my papers and retrieved the letter, and an icy fear gripped my heart. Surely this woman had received my letter before her death? I had sent it on the Monday; she had died on the Wednesday. If her death occurred later in the day, chances are that she had indeed read my reply. But if she had then why hadn't she acted? The advice was clear – come clean and get help.

And yet she had apparently jumped to her death. How could this happen?

My eyes settled on the address at the top of the page. I folded it and slipped it into my pocket.

That afternoon, I took my hat and stick and headed for Bloomsbury.

The London Underground is not a service I should ever casually choose to use. Mankind was not created in order to clamber through underground tunnels like rats in a sewer. However, I had begrudgingly taken the underground to Russell Square and walked through. This was in an attempt to restrict the amount of pressure on my feet as the brogues I had recently purchased were inevitably rubbing at my ankles and making themselves known.

Despite the grim start to my journey it was nice to amble along the streets of Bloomsbury. There is a rich peace about the place that is unlike any other part of town, and I took my time, so much so that it was well into the afternoon that I finally arrived at my destination.

It was not an unpleasant abode which stood before me on the corner of the street, largely hidden by trees. Like many of the houses in the vicinity it dated from the early 19th century, but was so well kept as to deny its age. There was an air of bold respectability about this particular house. It was certainly one of the few houses in the area to have its own garden laid out before it, and I deduced that the Capstick family were by no means a humble one.

I stood in the gateway and appraised the building for a minute, unsure of exactly how to proceed. All I wanted to find out was if I was right; if this was the home of my letter writer, and whether or not in the time before her death she had indeed read my letter. Deep in the depths of my mind there was that niggle, and only just a niggle, that I could in some way have been instrumental in what the young woman went and did. An unsavoury thought indeed.

I had not noticed a young lady perched aground to my right, foraging in the soil, but she had certainly spotted me.

'Can I help you?'

The bobbed-haired young woman was squatting in wellingtons and waterproofs, a muddy trowel in her hand. Although her words had sounded harsh she forged a smile, which I was careful to return.

'Yes, my dear.' I cleared my throat. 'I was looking for...well, I was wondering if this was where Mrs Capstick...'

I was letting myself down with this stammering and cursed inwardly for not having prepared myself better.

'Are you from the group?' asked the young woman sharply.

'The Group?' I replied. And now it was her turn to stammer.

'The, oh, erm, what is it? The am-drammers. The theatre-wotsit-workshop-thingy.'

I felt that I had no option but to lie, for this opportunity came with some relief on my part.

'Yes, yes I am.' I offered a hand as she straightened up and headed over to me at the gate. 'Payton Edgar.' I announced, wondering as I said it whether I should have chosen a false name to accompany my false identity.

Too late now.

'Good morning, Mr Edgar. I'm Jenny French, Helen's sister.' She spoke with the perfect diction of the privileged and well-schooled. Her skin was fine and clear, her features neat and proportionate to her delicate head and frame. However, despite her fresh appearance, there were tell-tell signs of disorganisation about the woman too. Her coat had been hastily buttoned and tied, and her rouge applied with a heavy hand.

'It's so nice of you to come around.'

'I felt I must pay my respects,' I replied, a little too easily.

'I'm sure the theatre group will miss her,' Jenny French said with a nod. She did not wait for an answer but began to pull off her gardening gloves.

'I could tell you were from the group the minute I saw you. You look the sort.'

Whatever she meant by this I could not figure, but let it pass.

'She loved it there, I know. The only one in our family interested in theatre and all that, but you know how she liked to shout and stomp about! Wish I'd gotten a bit more involved, now. Although I went to see that one last year...what was it? I'm not good with literature and plays. It was all about love and stuff, a bit soppy for me. There was a lot of crying and wailing. What was it?'

The woman was looking to me for answers, and I had to be quick to divert the fire. What to say? Think, Payton, think!

'Oh, last year, you say? Well, I wouldn't know it because I only joined the group following that particular production. I am a new addition to the team, I am sorry.'

'Which explains why I don't recall you from it!' she ventured, to my pleasure. 'You have a memorable face.'

'Quite. I only joined recently. *Very* recently.'

I was being led towards the house down a gravel pathway.

'You will come in for a cup of tea? It's so nice to talk to one of Helen's friends. Do you know you are the only one from the group to come so far? Perhaps they haven't all heard about it-' She stopped in her tracks. 'Wuthering Heights! That was the play, and a very odd production it was too. You might be glad that you missed that one. Anyway, do come inside.'

I followed the neat young lady through to the back of the house and into a substantial kitchen. Greenery that sprouted all around the building peered in through every window, and one would be forgiven for mistaking this for a countryside cottage kitchen and not one in the very heart of our capital. Seated at a chunky oak table in the middle of the room was a shrivelled old man, his hands clasped together on the table top before him rather officially.

'Dad!' my host exclaimed, 'when did you get in?'

The man was strangely familiar. Surely in his early eighth decade at least, his skin was dry and heavily creased, his scalp dotted by fine wisps of hair. Two jug ears stood out proudly at the sides, giving the man an eerie look of a primate. He did not smile.

'Came in the back way, Jen,' he sang, 'brought you back that casserole dish.'

When he spoke with his distinctive high, scratchy voice I immediately placed where I had seen him before. The man had become a familiar sight over the past few years. He could often be found standing smartly dressed in suit and tie preaching on street corners or accosting passers-by in the park. Without his 'Jesus saves' sandwich board I had not placed him at first, but it was most definitely the pest I had many times crossed the road to avoid.

Miss French took up the casserole dish with thanks, placed it aside and set the gas to boil the kettle.

The old man looked me squarely in the eye. 'Don't know you,' he grunted in my direction, demonstrating a complete lack of social grace.

'Payton Edgar,' I replied, finding a smile from somewhere, 'I am – was, well, an acquaintance of your other daughter. I came to offer my condolences.'

'Not needed, Sir, not here,' the man raised his voice again. I caught Miss French watching him nervously, biting her lip as he went on.

'Jesus said I am the resurrection and the life. He who believes in me will live, even though he dies...'

'Dad!'

'Jenny, you know it, and this young man must know it too. The sufferings of this time are not worthy to be compared with the glory to come that shall be revealed in us.'

I was rather flattered at being referred to as a young man, but nonetheless relieved when Miss French moved decisively over to her father and took him up by the shoulders and led him to the back door.

'Time to go now, Dad, I need to speak to this gentleman alone. Thanks for the dish. I'll pop by and see you later!'

In the doorway he turned to me, showing no resentment at having been hustled out of the room.

'Good day to you, Sir. Remember, God is our refuge and our strength-'

'Bye Dad!' And with the door closed the young lady turned to me and issued a faintly embarrassed smile.

'I am so sorry if I seem rude. My father can be wonderful company, sometimes. And at others, he just gets this kind of...I don't know what to call it.'

'I understand. Something of a bee in his bonnet?' I ventured.

'A bit like that, yes. Ever since Mum died. He was actually a very well respected high flyer in The City before all that - a canny investor. We've a lot to thank him for. But he's been like this for years, and there's no doubt that he's getting worse. You had a lucky escape there, really.' She spoke frankly but with a softness that showed she was clearly fond of her father despite all his nonsense.

A china teacup was placed before me. My host had placed a small plate of ginger biscuits in the middle of the table and I felt a sudden pang of hunger. Breakfast suddenly seemed to have happened a long while ago.

After watching Miss French remove her gardening waterproofs to reveal a plain, comfortable navy dress, I sat pondering on the niceness of mankind as she poured her tea. Sometimes, death can bring out the best in human nature. It seems to make people so much more accepting and trusting. Here I was, essentially a complete stranger, a mere acquaintance of her sister, being treated to tea and biscuits in their house without question.

I took one of the ginger biscuits discreetly as Miss French positioned herself across the table.

'The place seems so much quieter without Helen.'

'It's a beautiful house. Is it all yours?' I ventured.

'Oh no, it is all Helen and John's. I live on the next street back, just by Dad, but I've spent most of the last few days here, to be with Frank and things.'

At the mention of the boy her eyes dropped to the table top.

'Is Frank here?' I asked, my curiosity getting the better of me.

'No, no. He is out with John. Should be back soon, though. John is teaching Frank to drive, of all things.'

The image I had in my mind of a small apple-cheeked urchin popped; the child was older than I had envisaged.

'I'm a little nervous, actually,' Miss French continued. 'Frank is learning to drive the Vol-u-vent van and it's hardly reliable with its sticky clutch.'

'Learning to drive a vol-u-vent?' I repeated, perplexed. She gave a light laugh.

'Yes, sorry, we call it that, the vol-u-vent van. Just a silly name we use. We run a family catering business, did Helen never say?'

'No.'

'Well the van's a godsend, we couldn't do without it, which is a bit of a worry as it's something of a banger these days. I don't drive myself, do you? Why drive when we have the wonderful tube system, eh?'

I did not reply, and not because my mouth was full of biscuit. My thoughts on London Underground would never be swayed. Instead, I forced another smile.

'A catering business? That sounds interesting.'

'Capstick's Catering. It was Helen's hobbyhorse, actually, until a few years ago. Community cooking, she liked to call it. Been doing pretty well, really. Helen got a bit bored of it in the end, and now we all muck in together. It's grown and grown in the past year or two. We've got two cooks and over twenty call-up waitresses on our books now. Frank helps nowadays too, with the loading and preparation, so it's a real family affair. He does it for a bit of spare cash,' she gave a weighty sigh. 'John and I will carry it on, though. We must. We have our biggest annual booking coming up, which John thinks we should cancel, but, well, life has to go on, doesn't it?'

I took this as a rhetorical question and sipped my tea, my eyes drifting to the biscuits once more.

'Mind you, we've agreed not to do the spread for the funeral, doesn't seem right really. I don't know. Such a difficult time.'

This bleak observation was followed by a considerable silence. I felt that I should say something.

'It will, I imagine, take some time for them to adjust' I said, at which her eyes looked back questioningly. 'To just being the two of them, I mean.'

'Well, yes. That's why I am here. They need me around at the moment. Mind you, there is the lodger in the house too.'

'The lodger?' I ventured. Chatting to this pleasant young woman was very easy. She grinned a little and gave a shrug.

'Yes, this place is big enough, and has a large en-suite spare room at the back that has always been used for someone or another. I used to live here myself a few years back, just for a while before I got my place down the road. And there was a time just after that when Helen took on a young foreign student, Patience. Nice name, isn't it? Patience. She was a terribly flighty thing, though, despite the name. Always on the go, couldn't stick to anything. Left her course and went back to South Africa in the end. Now we have Mr Limestone.'

This name she said with some exaggerated gravity.

'He is the deputy at St Peters, the school where Helen worked. Frank hates having one of his teachers here, but the poor man had nowhere else to go and I think Helen took pity.' She continued in a faux whisper. 'I shouldn't say, but his wife chucked him out, not that I can blame her. Been a bit messy it has, if you take my meaning. You know how divorces can be? He's been here a month or two now. Stewing.'

'Helen worked at a school?' I asked with some surprise. This was not the image I had of the dead woman at all.

'Yes, although I'm not surprised she never told you. It was nothing fancy, and very part time. That was a while ago now. Supervising the dinner hall, food standards and all that. She loved bossing the children about, I think. Yes, she loved to boss people around, did my sister. I'm sure you saw it in rehearsals or whatever it is you call it. Yes, she liked the school. Done it for years, she has...had. And she liked being able to keep tabs on Frank, too, back when he was a nipper.'

'How is he dealing with it?' I asked, adding, by way of explanation, 'the young can be so vulnerable when it comes to matters of bereavement.' I said this without a clue as to its accuracy, but it had sounded good. Margaret Blythe was in there somewhere.

'Oh, he's holding up fine from what I can tell. Frank's a quiet one. He's at that age, you know? If only his father were that timid. No, it's good that they've got the driving thing on at the moment, to keep them together and keep their minds off of everything that's going on. I don't think it'll feel real for either of them until the funeral, really. Or even after...' She took up her tea and appeared to snap out of her reverie.

'The funeral will be sooner rather than later, we hope. The police are holding things up a bit. But do come. We'll be putting a notice in a local paper. Which do you think is best?'

'I'm sorry?'

'Which local paper is the best?'

I had not expected to be asked for advice, but duly promoted The Clarion as the best option for messages of such solemnity. There was no element of loyalty in my recommendation, for what I said was true. The Clarion was indeed a superior read. Miss French took this in and felt a need to explain her query.

'It's the thing to do, isn't it? To put a piece in the newspaper? We grew up without papers. Dad has always believed that they lie and corrupt the mind, as he puts it. You'll not find a single newspaper in any of our houses, nor a television either. Don't get Dad started on television!'

There was nothing to say to this but to nod. A thought flittered through my mind, how strange it was that Helen Capstick should chose to write to the Clarion when newspapers had never been her thing. I shifted in my seat. In truth, the deceased's sister's easy conversation and trust was making me a little uncomfortable. I had no intention of going to this stranger's funeral. Coming to Bloomsbury that afternoon had been a mistake, and I planned a swift exit once the tea was finished.

Unfortunately, a swift exit was not going to prove possible.

John Capstick and his son returned from their drive just as I finished my third biscuit. In the time immediately before their arrival, Miss French had spent a moment toying over something to herself before speaking to me with a certain careful directness over the kitchen table.

'Mr Edgar, when John comes, please take anything he says with a pinch of salt. It has been a terrible shock for him and he is very upset. He is-'

It was at this point that John Capstick and his son burst through the backdoor to the house. Frank looked much older than I had expected, although I would have put him at around the fourteen or fifteen mark. He was a tall, lanky young man, who carried a grim expression. His first gaze at the stranger sitting around his breakfast table was not a welcoming one.

John Capstick, however, gave me a hearty greeting as Miss French explained my presence with some warmth. She enquired about the driving lesson and Capstick answered with a bark.

'Yeah, the lad did well. Better driver than I am, I should say. We'll have him out on the open road on his own before long.'

The young lad said nothing, but kicked off his shoes at the back door. I found myself smiling welcomingly at the young man and, as was my way with youngsters, holding out my hand and offering him a lemon sherbet. He glanced down at the paper bag, shook his head sharply and moved out of the room without a word. At the door he cast one last shadowy look in my direction as his father pumped my hand.

'So nice to meet you, Mr Edgar. Do you know what? I don't like to moan but you are the only member of the theatre group to contact us? You'd think the amount of time she spent there that there'd be an outpouring of some sort. But no, nothing!'

His initial smile had quickly faded. John Capstick was a large man, thick-set with a barrel chest and taut-looking shoulders. He wore what resembled farmer's casuals and spoke in a rather sprawling manner. His hair was overlong and his cheeks flushed despite a clean complexion. There was something rough-at-the-edges about the man, and he held himself with the gait and approach of a commoner that told me it was the dead woman's heritage alone which had provided the evident wealth of a Bloomsbury address.

Despite all this, I took an instant liking to him. He had an interesting and handsome face.

'Poor Helen's not had half the people here I would expect,' Capstick continued rather sadly, 'Still, you're here, Mr Edgar, and it is very much appreciated.'

In a dutiful silence, Miss French had stood and was preparing tea for her brother-in-law. He took her place in front of me at the table, and I said the most appropriate words for such an occasion.

'I am so sorry for your loss.'

'Don't bother,' came the gruff reply. 'Do you know what really happened, Mr Edgar?' he asked sharply.

Answering meekly, I took my time to speak.

'Only what I read in the papers,'

'They don't know anything, the newspapers! And neither do the police. Well, shall I tell you the truth, Mr Edgar?'

'John!' Miss French growled a warning over the kettle.

'My wife was murdered, Mr Edgar. *Murdered.*'

CHAPTER 7

In which Payton Edgar fears the crack of the cane

Dear Margaret.

My husband is more interested in trees than he is in me. He has worked as a tree surgeon all of his life, and sometimes it feels as if he is married to his precious Silver Birches and not to me. The only holidays we go on together are planned according to the local woods and forests on offer. I yearn for intimate company and a good beach holiday. What can I do to change this?

Beatrice, Islington

Margaret replies; Trees are indeed beautiful things. Unlike us mere mortals, they are sturdy and reliable, and often outlive us generation after generation. One can understand why your husband has this particular passion. In your overlong letter of complaint, which was not difficult to edit for these pages, you sound like the most badgering of fishwives. I suggest that you give him some leave of his own and go on that beach holiday alone. It may be good for you both. One cannot blame the man for attempting to get lost in the woods.

It was difficult to know exactly how to respond to such a curious declaration.

The word *murder* hung in the air like a potent smell. John Capstick jabbed a pointed finger down onto the table top, his eyes wide. What he expected me to say, how to reply to such an announcement, I do not know. Finally, he sat back in the chair with his dark eyes fixed on mine and folded his arms.

'Goodness!' I was eventually able to reply, although I kept this barely audible.

'John, don't start this with Mr Edgar, please,' said Miss French with practiced patience. 'Have some tea.'

She placed a steaming mug before him. I noticed with some appreciation that his was a chipped mug whereas I had deserved the best china. Miss French drew out a chair and joined us at the table, drinkless. She placed her hands clasped together on the table top before her in a rather official manner, just as her father had earlier. What her brother-in-law had said was hanging in the air, I felt it and I'm sure that she felt it too.

Murder.

'There is absolutely no reason for us to think that she was murdered, John. She took her own life, hard as it is for us to understand it. We know this.'

'We know nothing!'

'We know that she was terribly troubled, John. She wasn't herself. There is no evidence to suggest that there was foul play.'

'-and no evidence to suggest that there wasn't, Jenny!' Mr Capstick put in sharply. 'And what about where she died? The same damn building where she met with her little theatre group? Why was that? Do you know Mr Edgar?'

I was understandably startled at his directness and wished once more I hadn't posed as an acquaintance of the dead woman. I sat speechless.

'John!' shrieked Miss French, 'Mr Edgar is our guest!'

'I just need to know the truth,' he said, softening somewhat. 'Come on, Jen, you know Helen as well as I do. She was made of bloody tough stuff. She wouldn't have done something so stupid.'

'She was dreadfully dispirited, John. She wasn't herself at the end, we've said so before.'

'But not that bloody dispirited, surely,' John replied, his voice cracking just a little.

'Mind your language, please, John. It was very difficult-'

'What was going on with her? She just wasn't the type to do it, you know that. Was she, Jen? Was she?'

A cold silence fell. I had felt like a spectator at Wimbledon, watching as words were volleyed to and fro across the table. But now this particular pause was growing positively frosty.

'Go on then, Jen, answer me. What was your sister like? Bossy, yes. Stony, maybe, at times. But not a woman to take her own life like that, surely?'

John Capstick fixed his sister-in-law in an icy stare.

His approach was uncomfortably harsh, and I did not blame the young woman from squirming under his glare. She gave up the argument with a deep sigh. It was at that moment it dawned on me just how much I knew from the letter I had received for the agony column. I knew about the other man. I knew all about her affair with the young man at her club. I knew just how he treated her. It appeared that I knew more than both her own husband and her own sister did.

I clenched my teeth together.

Just at that moment, the doorbell chimed. While Jenny French got up and made her way to the front door I took the opportunity to stand and make my excuses. I was keen to escape to a quiet place where I could mull over what I had seen and what I had learned. Part of me knew that I would have to go to the police with the letter for Margaret, as embarrassing as that might be. The last thing I wanted was to reveal myself to be Dr. Margaret Blythe.

I had just pulled on my coat when a stranger entered the room. The man was short and stern-faced with a mottled complexion, a ridiculously bushy moustache and thick rimmed glasses. The hair on his head was patchy and coarse. He nodded a greeting to Mr Capstick and then gave me a swift appraisal.

'Oh, Inspector, this is Mr Edgar, a member of Jenny's drama group. He just popped by to offer his condolences.'

The man puffed out his cheeks and widened his eyes as if there were a bad smell in the room.

'Did he indeed?' he blustered.

I smiled weakly, picked up my hat and retrieved my stick.

'I was just leaving.'

The newcomer gave a gruff cough.

''fraid not, Mr Edgar. I shall need to have a few words with you before you go anywhere. Would you mind waiting in the hallway just for a minute? Thank you.'

And so I was banished to the hallway, curiosity burning inside of me like the boiler of a steam train. Making sure that I did not close the door tightly behind me, I took a few noisy steps away from it before turning and moving steadily back. There was nothing of interest to see through the crack in the doorway and I could barely hear a word of what was being said, but I heard enough to know that this man, the Inspector, was delivering some very important news.

I heard that word once more, this time uttered by the inspector.

Murder.

'I knew it!' I heard John Capstick cry out, followed by a plea from Miss French.

'Where was she? What did she see?'

The Inspector's tone was infuriatingly low and barely audible. I caught enough words to gather that an unnamed witness had seen a second person on the roof with poor Helen Capstick some minutes before her fall from the building. After a good five minutes of eavesdropping I gathered that the conversation was reaching a climax and, with considerable stealth for a man wearing barely-broken-in brogues, crept back down the hallway.

So the husband had been right. It was murder. The enormity of what I knew sunk in. I had concrete evidence that could solve this poor Inspector's mystery instantly! I inhaled deeply, stood erect for a minute and revelled in my glory.

Suddenly and without warning the front door opened behind me and a lofty gentleman with a gleaming bald head entered, his cheeks flushed pink in tight spots. He gave me a steely glare through tiny glasses, lifted a bag from his shoulder and set it down with a thud. I saw that the bag was full of exercise books.

'Good morning, I take it you are the lodger?' I said with confidence.

The man did not immediately reply. There was no proffering of hands nor exchanges of pleasantries. Instead he took a long deep breath in through his nose and widened his eyes in my direction.

'And you are?'

He may as well have added "boy?" after these words, and I immediately found myself propelled back into the draughty corridors of St Augustine's, those cold and lonely corridors. He was awaiting my introduction.

'Payton Edgar,' I announced, squaring up somewhat and reaching out for his hand. I did get a hand, but it was dry and reluctant. 'I am a member of Helen's theatre group, paying my respects.'

This lie was now coming alarmingly easy, despite my natural dislike for all things theatrical. At my words his face dropped to a pained expression.

'I see.'

He clearly was not one for the arts. An ill-humoured history or geography Master, I should imagine.

'Well, I suppose it is nice of you to drop by.'

He made no direct reference to the dead woman, and offered no words of sympathy. He removed his coat and retrieved his bag. I noticed a waft of chalk dust reaching up over his jacket shoulder and gave an involuntary shudder.

'Poor Helen,' I said, goading the man somewhat. His lips remained sealed as he returned his eyes to mine for a searching glare.

'Mmm, indeed. Name?'

It was a second before I realised he was asking for my details once more, no doubt marking me down in his memory as a troublemaker.

'Edgar,' I repeated, 'Payton Edgar.' He raised a grey eyebrow before turning on his heel. 'So very nice to meet you, too,' I muttered to his back. As he made down the corridor I watched him go with a cold dread in my heart. The very worst kind of dusty Master indeed. I heard voices from within the room as he slipped out of sight, leaving me alone once more.

For a moment I stood inert, running my fingers over the brass owl which perched happily on top of my stick.

Then something in a pile of post on the console table caught my eye. A familiar style of handwriting on an envelope. Perfect, educated, stylish handwriting. It was my handwriting; my letter, addressed to 'Bothered of Bloomsbury'.

I picked it up, seeing instantly that it had been sliced neatly with an opener. I clutched it to my chest. The poor woman must have read it before her death. But then why had she not acted on my advice? Surely if she had read my reply then she wouldn't have gone on to do the terrible thing she did? Perhaps in her mental anguish she had opened it and then pushed her post aside, leaving it here, untouched, on the morning of her death. What a dreadful error! To think that the words of Margaret Blythe could have saved a life! But fate clearly had other ideas.

I inspected the envelope thoughtfully for a minute, turning it several times, before deftly sliding it into my inside pocket. 'Bothered of Bloomsbury' had no need for this anymore. I would keep the letter as a reminder of the power of Margret Blythe.

Besides, if discovered, my involvement in this appalling tale would only cause confusion.

The Inspector was standing in the doorway to the kitchen.

'So, Mr Edgar, was it? If I can have your address, please Sir?'

I issued details of my residence with practiced bravado and watched as these details were jotted down in the Inspector's pocket book. As he wrote he was scowling, and I realised that I had taken a fervent dislike to the man.

'Can I give you a lift home, Mr Edgar?' He continued as Miss French moved to show him out.

'No, no. Thank you very much, but I enjoy the walk.' A lie, of course, as the brogues were at the very worst stage of the breaking-in process.

'Oh, I insist, Mr Edgar! I absolutely insist!' the coarse man boomed, and before I knew it I was seated beside him in his car out front. Once the doors were closed and Jenny French had disappeared from seeing us off at the gate, he turned to me with refreshed gusto.

'Now then Mr Edgar, I shall not be taking you home, I am afraid,' he stated. 'You are coming with me down to the station. There, you can explain to me exactly why you surreptitiously took a document from the Capstick residence just now, and why, when I was with James Claremont of the Claremont Amateur Dramatic society just an hour ago, he failed to give me your name as a member!'

CHAPTER 8
In which Payton Edgar tolerates an interrogation

Dear Margaret,
My seven year-old boy has a musical gift that I am keen to nurture. However this has led to a disagreement with our neighbour, who cannot tolerate his practice sessions on the piano and clarinet. I have tried to explain his talent, but all my neighbour cares about is the noise. He has even threatened to break the clarinet in two! I do not want to upset my neighbour, but my son must practice if he is to succeed. What can I do?
Concerned mother, Ealing.

__Margaret replies;__ Queen Victoria had it right when she said that children should be seen and not heard. I am siding with your neighbour on this particular issue. The clarinet is a ghastly instrument, all screeching and spittle. And what of the lad's schooling? Maths and Geography homework make no sound and will surely stand the lad in better stead for a prosperous future than puffing pointlessly into a pipe.

I was to be very late in getting home that day, thus missing a highly anticipated dining experience.

Poor Irving would sit patiently at home in one of the suits I had picked out for him, expecting to be collected at any minute. He would be left waiting. I have never been known to stand anyone up before, but that night we would both be missing out on a treat. Harvey's restaurant would have to wait.

However, if one has to be inconveniently dragged to a draughty interrogation chamber then it might as well be down at Scotland Yard. I had imagined the place to be far cleaner and more efficient than it turned out to be. The building had clearly outlived its purpose, and with its crumbling brickwork and shoddy papering, it showed all too well.

It transpired that I had done a number of things to arouse the fool Inspector's suspicion, and I have to say that he did little to encourage co-operation on my part. In fact, the more time spent in the vile man's company the less I was inclined to tell him.

Igniting this reaction in the general public is surely a significant impediment for someone in his position.

'You haven't even had the decency to tell me your name and title!' I had been careful to emphasise in my most outraged tone once the car had started and I had been officially abducted.

And so it was in the spirit of mistrust and suspicion that I was interrogated by the rather unimpressive Detective Inspector Albert Standing in that sparse and draughty room, and even then only after a good hour-or-so in which I was left sitting alone waiting for the blustering idiot to make a re-appearance.

My only solace was that my interrogation chamber had a rather fine view of the glistening Thames, and I spent some time watching over it, deep in thought.

So what was my position?

I was an innocent member of London's elite. A writer and valued member of the Forth Estate, with good standing in city society and a broad outlook on life. I had stumbled across the late Mrs Capstick after she had written a pleading letter to my column, and partook in some mild investigation out of idle curiosity. That was all, and nothing more. The Inspector could choose to believe in my testimony or not, but it would surely be obvious to the man that every action made by Payton Edgar was one of honesty and integrity?

I turned from the water and eyed up the cool sparse room, hoping that the interrogation I was about to suffer would be of a gentle nature.

When the Inspector finally made a re-appearance it was with no pleasantries whatsoever that the man plonked himself before me. He had no instinct for ceremony, that much was clear.

I rummaged in my jacket pocket and pulled out a paper bag. I couldn't help myself, something about the man just willed me to goad him further.

'Lemon sherbet, Inspector?' I asked.

'No,' came the reply, 'and I'd rather you didn't either.'

I carefully replaced the sweets in my pocket.

'Have I been arrested, Inspector? Because if so, I wish to call my solicitor immediately.'

In truth, I was less than inclined to do so. My solicitor, one Mr Crack of Hammond, Hammond, Hammond and Crack Solicitors, ironically situated at Cheapside, was an exceedingly dubious gentleman. The last remaining Hammond had passed on some years back, and now Crack ran the business with a son I had yet to meet.

It was an understatement to say that Mr Crack had not overly impressed me on our few previous encounters, the last being when I had used him in an advisory capacity over some trifle regarding a privet hedge and Irving's neighbour. He appeared to be one part genius, two parts imbecile, and I was relieved when Inspector Standing dismissed my query and uttered through his moustache something about routine enquiries.

After registering my distaste at being so shoddily treated, I went on to inform the Inspector of what little I knew; that the deceased had been having an affair with a rather unsavoury sort, and had met her death at that hands of this beast. Rather disappointingly, the Inspector had not registered any surprise at this revelation.

'It appears that you know a lot about this case, Mr Edgar,' he sneered. 'Well then perhaps you can tell me just where Clay is, then?'

'Clay?' I enquired, sweetly. Surely the man was not asking me about geological points of wet earthen deposits?

'Now don't go all coy on me, Mr Edgar, not when you clearly know plenty about what has been going on. Well, I know plenty too. Since the girl's death I have had my suspicions, and today I have been proved correct. I am going to clear this all up, and clear it up right away. I know all about Clay, you see. So, if you can tell me something of your relationship with the young man it would be a start. What is your true connection to the Claremont Society? Did you meet Clay through the theatre group? If not, what is your association with our offender? Mmm?'

I merely raised an eyebrow, despite my confusion. The man's technique of interrogation was most inefficient. How could one possibly answer this barrage of foolish questions, even if one knew the answers? He carried on, bullishly.

'Mr Edgar, are you aware that Helen Capstick died by falling, or I should perhaps say being pushed, from the roof of Onslow Hall, the building where you and your kind have your little drama meetings? And now with Clay gone, it doesn't take a genius to see the connection here, does it?'

My heart racing, I gave my stick a sharp crack against the floor.

'Do you know who I am, Inspector? I am Payton Edgar, ex-restaurateur and serviceman, presently employed as scribe and restaurant critic for the London Clarion, not to mention a dear friend of this force if you'd care to do your homework. Indeed, it was only last year that I was garlanded with praise from this very station for reporting a vulgar young man who I had seen loitering suspiciously around the tea shop in St. James Park. The bobby was just in time, and a handbag snatch was thwarted! All thanks to me! It will be in your records somewhere, if you care to look. Kindly cease from speaking to me as though I were an imbecile, or worse, a common-or-garden member of the public. Now I do not know this "Clay" of which you speak, so I cannot help you there, without further information. I am sorry.'

The Inspector apparently thought I were playing some game, for he informed me rather rudely that such tactics would not work with him and went on to demand to know the whereabouts of Richard Clay.

The penny dropped.

'Ah, *Richard* Clay, you say?' I exclaimed, singing somewhat in the reverie of sudden realisation. I continued, more to myself than to anyone else. 'Her letter did say his name was Richard now I come to think of it. Yes, Richard from the drama group. I take it he is the swine who attacked poor Mrs Capstick? So he has done a runner, has he? A clear indicator of guilt, I'm sure you agree? Well, I am afraid I cannot tell you where the man is, I'm sorry. I have never met him.'

'And yet you are a member of their dramatics society, are you not?' the Inspector was quick to reply.

I cleared my throat.

'Well, yes, I may have told a modest white lie about that, Inspector, but all in a good cause I assure you.' There followed an uncomfortable silence.

'Any chance of a cup of tea?'

The man reacted as though I had cursed his mother. He screwed up his face, each cheek turning a flaming deep purple as he issued an alarming low gurgling groan.

'I don't know quite what you think you are playing at, Mr Edgar, but I must tell you that this is an extremely serious situation you find yourself in. I suggest you cooperate and tell me everything right now. We will have it out of you, one way or another.'

'Is that a threat, inspector?' I replied coolly.

A heavy silence descended on the room, during which I took in a breath and straightened my jacket around my shoulders. Be careful, Payton, I told myself, you are a good person and the truth will out, but you need to help this poor man who is struggling in the darkness of his own mental limitations.

'Alright then,' I began, and proceeded to tell him all about my new contract with Bilborough and the letter received from 'Bothered from Bloomsbury'. As I spoke I could see the Inspector was struggling to keep up, his brow descending ever further South to cover his bloodshot eyes. Once I had finished my story and produced the letter I had retrieved from the Capstick household, I sat back in triumph. It was a sweet tale of a literary success, demonstrating with crystal clarity exactly what an astute and solicitous gentleman Payton Edgar truly is.

The Inspector sat back in his chair, slowly folded his arms and spoke very slowly and with an alarming acerbity.

'And so you,' he said slowly, 'are telling me that you…are…Dr. Margaret Blythe?'

Put like that, it sounded rather silly.

'I am,' I replied guardedly.

'You are..?'

'I am,' I said, slowly and with caution, 'Dr. Margaret Blythe.'

The Inspector opposite appraised me for a good half-a-minute in silence.

'Well, if that is all there is to it, I no longer need you, Edgar. I can see that I was barking up a wrong, not to mention particularly odd, tree. You may go home then. I shan't need to see you again.'

He stood abruptly and gathered his papers, taking my letter that had obviously become evidence of some sort. He did not ask for the original letter to Margaret Blythe and I did not give it to him, even though it sat neatly in my inside pocket. My heart sank. He clearly considered me to be of no importance whatsoever.

'Inspector, I can be of help to you in this,' I found myself saying.

'In what way can you possibly be of help? Do you have more to tell me?' This question was fired without hope of an answer.

'Well then the answer is "no", I think I have learned all I need from you, that is to say nothing that I didn't know already. You are lucky I am not going to charge you with wasting police time. Goodbye, Mr Edgar.'

Standing held open the door and gestured me out impatiently.

'You know the way out,' he stated, before trumping away in the opposite direction. I watched him go with a shiver of revulsion. I pulled out my sweets and sucked on a lemon sherbet rebelliously.

At the desk I requested a taxi call from the clerk and seated myself unhappily in the far corner of the miserable lobby. After a minute-or-so a mature grey-haired lady was ushered through the back doors by a smooth faced young officer.

'Are you sure you won't let us call you a taxi, Mrs Clay?' he was asking, to which she shook her head firmly and gave a wave of a gloved hand.

Mrs Clay?

'Well, thank you for your cooperation anyway. We'll be in touch.'

She turned a sad face to his.

'I'm sure you will be.'

With that, she was out of the doors. I sat for a short moment in indecision before ordering the clerk to cancel my taxi. I followed the old woman outside. Mrs Clay had stopped a few metres from the building and was fumbling in her handbag. I approached her noisily, and as I did caught sight of her red, tearful eyes cast downwards.

'Would you like a handkerchief?' I ventured, only to be waved away rather curtly. The woman found her tissue and dabbed her eyes before forcing a dentured smile.

'I'm sorry. I didn't mean to be rude. I just, well, I just am a little-'

'I understand, Mrs Clay.'

'You know my name?' she asked with some alarm.

'I heard the young officer address you. Not very nice inside the building, is it? You'd have thought it a bit more plush, being Scotland Yard, wouldn't you? I have been in a similar position as you in there, I think. You are Richard's mother?'

I saw hope and trepidation flicker across her face simultaneously.

'You know where he is?' she croaked. At my shake of the head I saw all anticipation drain away from her.

'I'm sorry. I have never met your son, Mrs Clay. But I know that they are keen to know where he is, too.'

She nodded faintly and turned to go.

'I must get home, it's already getting dark.'

'May I walk you home? Do you have far?' I said, bravely disregarding my sore feet.

'No, please, I-'

She was about to get away when a loud shout from across the forecourt gave us both a start.

'Edgar! Hie! Mr Edgar!'

It took me a minute to identify just who it was that had shouted and was heading in our direction through the darkness. Approaching us was young Constable Jones, the very bobby I had joined forces with in thwarting the tea shop theft the previous autumn. His beat usually took him through St. James Park and we had met and exchanged niceties on a number of occasions since. Jones was an agreeable lad, but perhaps a little on the dim side when it came to doing anything that required thought and discretion.

His attire was most unsuitable for a cool winter evening. He wore a bright red and green checked shirt underneath a garish blue knitted pullover that resembled an unwanted Christmas gift from a distant relative. He was carrying a coat despite the cold evening air. Jones must have seen my look of horror at his apparel because he glanced down and gave a laugh.

'Oh, sorry about how I look. I'm on night shifts, see. You don't care what you wear on the way to work after sleeping all day, so long as it's cosy.'

I fingered the knitwear gingerly, unable to keep the look of distaste from my face. It was surprisingly coarse.

'I don't know how my old Mum does it, but her knits turn out a bit tough.'

'Tough?' I retorted. 'It's akin to chainmail!'

They chuckled.

'You could grate cheese on your chest!' I continued, at which they both laughed. Still laughing, Jones reached out and pumped my hand.

'Good to see you, Mr Edgar, it really is. And who is your lady friend?'

This was said without a hint of sensitivity and must have caused some blushes for both of us standing there. I was quick to maintain formality.

'Ah, Jones, this is an acquaintance of mine, Mrs Clay. Mrs Clay, this is Constable Jones, the bright and shining future of our police force.' Now it should have been his turn to redden at my faux flattery, but he mistook the sarcasm for fact and nodded like a puppy.

'If you say so, Mr Edgar, if you say so.'

I saw an opportunity.

'Now, Jones, a quick question before you go in to work - I was just offering to walk this dear lady home but she is understandably unsure. Can you vouch for my character?'

'Not half!' the youth chimed, moving in closer to the poor woman at my side. 'Mr Edgar is a true gent. You'll be in good hands. In fact, I insist you let him accompany you, it'll be dark soon. Have you been in there?' He gestured to the department behind us and Mrs Clay nodded. 'Hope they was good to you, tea and biscuits and all. Oh, there was something before you go, Mr Edgar! I'm glad to have seen you now. I have some advice for you.'

'Advice?'

'Well, a recommendation, so to speak. I thought of you just the other day. I ate at a lovely place last week over in the West End. Went there for my Uncle's birthday, we did. Place called Humpty's. I don't eat out much, but it was really nice, very old fashioned. Portions were big enough, like. I think you should do one of your pieces on it. See if you can find anything bad to say like, 'cos I didn't. Lovely grub.'

'Indeed.'

The young man hesitated.

'In all honesty, it's our old Chief's place. He retired last year and has opened up Humpty's with his wife. They could do with promoting a bit.'

'Well then, I may take you up on that. I am currently recruiting for my next conquest. Humpty's it is.'

'Well, whatever you think. You'd be doing me a favour. Better get on, late already. Pleasure to meet you, ma'am. Mr Edgar!' And with a cheerful departure, Jones made his way into work.

'A nice young man,' I said, 'not to mention a very good judge of character. May I assist you home then, Mrs Clay?'

And now she smiled.

'Of course, thank you.'

. . .

It turned out that Mrs Clay lived right over near Farringdon Station, and this was a distance I was not prepared to walk, despite my companion's intentions. The poor woman would surely end up spending on shoe leather what she hoped to save on transport, but there was no talking to the elderly. Her generation see a bus or tram as luxury, never mind the back of a taxi cab.

We had talked our way right up and along the Strand before she told me of her exact residence, at which I had stopped and insisted we take a black cab, that I would still see her safely to her door and that I would foot the bill. I am unsure exactly what had possessed me to make a move closer to Mrs Clay, although a desire to locate the fugitive Richard Clay was not far from my mind.

It would have been a sweet victory over that cretin of an Inspector.

However I was to obtain no clues, for this woman was his mother. Richard Clay could do no wrong in her eyes. A gentle soul, she had informed me as we passed Charing Cross, never one to do so much as raise a hand to others. And never one to run from his troubles usually, the poor dear thing. I sympathised with this most devoted of mothers so far as I could, never losing sight of the facts that had been laid before me; that Clay was a bully and a cad who must suffer for his crimes.

I kept this opinion to myself in front of his mother, naturally.

I learned that Richard Clay's father had been lost at Dunkirk, but we passed over this gloomy detail rather quickly. Momentarily forgetting the concern she felt for her son's whereabouts, we had a nice chat as we walked, revisiting the conversation that would never die; how things have changed since the war.

How many times had I had this discussion? I could not bear to imagine. And yet I didn't mind as it gave me some opportunity to voice my delight at the slow but sure rise of the British restaurant scene. Mrs Clay turned out to be a very good listener, and I dare say I impressed her with my rhetoric.

'Don't you ever get old, Mr Edgar,' said Mrs Clay as we crossed the road. This non-sequeteur was no doubt the result of some ache or pain she had felt as we bustled along. 'Mine's a thankless existence. All these years of graft and pain and nothing to show for it. No legacy, no wise teachings to pass on...'

'You have your son,' I replied, only find to myself on the receiving end of a stony silence. When Mrs Clay did speak, it was with some hesitancy.

'I may have been a little-' she began, before clearing her throat. 'It is the duty of a mother to see the best in her child, is it not? Despite their...nature.'

A bully and a cad, I thought to myself.

It was around this point that I finally managed to flag down a passing cab.

The Clay residence was drab, squeezed into the centre of a row of fairly modern terraces that were already crumbling. Mrs Clay halted at the blue door and expressed her gratitude while fumbling for her keys. As a last gasp of investigative desire surged through me, I asked my first frank question.

'Do you have any idea where your son might be, Mrs Clay? Any idea at all?'

I was not surprised at her reply.

'Mr Edgar, I wish I did, I really do. If I could say where my boy had fled to then I would have said, I really would. He is innocent, Mr Edgar. I know. I just wish I could convince the Inspector. Now, good night and thank you again. It has been a pleasure.'

Standing alone on the street one thing niggled at my mind. She had said her son had fled. *Fled.* She identified that he had ran away, and therefore she perhaps knew why. Yes, I decided, Mrs Clay was not as uninformed as she was letting on; her boy had ran away from something, and she knew it.

What I didn't know at the time was that Mrs Clay was just as proficient at amateur dramatics as her son, and that she was all too aware at that precise time exactly where the man was hiding.

CHAPTER 9

In which Payton Edgar exposes a cuckoo in his nest

Dear Margaret,

I am the only pretty female in an office full of males. I am writing because I sometimes find it difficult to maintain professional relations with my colleagues. I am constantly attended to, with offers of tea at teatime or lunch at lunchtime, and rarely have time to get my own work done. I fear that I cause too much of a distraction for the men in my office and wonder if I am in the right job, however I cannot afford to be choosy about where I work. Can you help?

Ruth of Tooting

Margaret replies; *you really are something of a strumpet, are you not, Ruth of Tooting? It seems to me that you wrote to me with pride rather than concern, and I was in two minds whether to condemn your boasting to the wastepaper basket. However, I feel that I must use you as an example to women and employers everywhere. Your story is a perfect illustration of how such loose and sluttish behaviour in the workplace can serve as a distraction to our workers and can so very badly affect our already fragile British industries.*

It took some time for Irving to forgive me over our aborted date at Harvey's restaurant.

He sat stony faced and with folded arms, pointedly neglecting to switch off the gramophone which was blaring out some awful brass-heavy ditty as I attempted to make my excuses on the morning after my unscheduled trip to Scotland yard.

I was very keen to get the man back on my side, principally because I sought refuge in his house from my aunt and her spiky nursemaid. If Irving closed his door to me, where would I have to escape to? He must hear my excuses, I thought. And very good excuses they were.

I told Irving everything; about Margret's letter of distress, the missed reply and the murder. I had integrated myself successfully into the Capstick's household as efficiently as the deftest Secret Service agent could ever wish to, and then I had been held at the constabulary like some common criminal! Admittedly, I embellished some facts as to my treatment at the hands of Inspector Standing, but this helped nudge Irving towards forgiveness.

He even turned off the abhorrent jazz music.

By way of apology, I brought forward our next "Payton's Plate" meal, and took Irving to Humpty's restaurant on the following evening, taking my cue from the recommendation of young Constable Jones. When we set off Irving was in fine spirits, however the poor man was under the false impression that he had brought another ghastly crossword book with him.

His recent habit for whipping out a puzzle after every meal was most irksome and this time I had made sure that it had fallen from his jacket pocket into the umbrella stand as I passed the garment over to him just before we left the house. Thankfully, he had accompanied me out of the house none the wiser to my sleight of hand. Once he caught on to my act Irving was only marginally peeved at my intervention. He could certainly never prove that it was anything more than a minor accident.

Why the man would feel he needed a crossword to muse over when he had my company to bask in, I do not know.

It was not the worse dining experience I have ever had, but it was far from the best and consequently supplied bountiful material for my piece. As I wrote with an easy flow I felt the first pinches of anger towards Honoria Betts and her problem page, which was granted a weekly appearance compared to my monthly restaurant reviews. I knew that I would never have wished to sustain a weekly piece, not only for reasons of expense but also to ensure the exclusive nature of the piece, however I was sure that my public hankered for more than was currently on offer. A fortnightly appearance would do very nicely.

I resolved to mention it to Bilborough at an opportune moment.

The following Monday as I collected my latest batch of problems, Cockney Guy at the desk astounded me with a problem of his own. I was in early to collect my post. Just the two for Payton Edgar, but thirteen for Dr. Blythe!

Thirteen!

Guy issued a broad smile as he handed them over, exposing that unmistakable set of teeth crying out for some urgent work by a brave dentist.

'That's three or four times more'n old Peggy's Postbag ever got before!' he said with some relish. 'You done well, Sir. Read your piece last week, cracking stuff it was. Right on the money. Never bothered to read it before but as you were doin' it thought I'd give it an eye.' Guy raised an ink-blackened finger, 'Now! I have a quandary for you, Mr Edgar. '

'Really, Guy?' I replied, not disinterested.

'Well, it's one for Dr. Margaret Blythe, if you like...'

I pointedly looked all around me before issuing my reply with a pointed eyebrow.

'She is listening. Pray, continue.'

'Well, okay, yeah. It's about my missus.'

Oh wonderful, I thought to myself, now I am being asked to sort out the marital problems of commoners in my spare time. The man failed to notice my disappointment and proceeded to tell me a tale.

'Now I like to have a Sunday afternoon down at 'The Dragon' at the end of the road each week with Alan, a good friend I got from school, like. He's a butcher, and a bloody good laugh. We do like a drink, yes, but not so much that I can't manage my roast later y'see. Well, my missus went and put a stop to it. Say's she's sick of my being out, not seeing me all week and then me slinking away at weekend, like. But I see her every night, and I don't want to let Alan down, do I? S'all right for her to have her knitting group in my house all of a Sat'day afternoon, clacking and clucking all over the place. It is...what is the phrase?'

'Double standards?' I put in, wearily.

'Yeah! Double standards, int'it? Now then, what can I do?'

He looked to me as if I were a healer or prophet of some sort. I gather that this kind of domestic irritation is not uncommon, but I found it unquestionably tedious in the extreme. However something about Cockney Guys' wide-eyed appeal to me softened my response.

'Okay Guy. That is a tough one. Have you considered divorce?'

His face fell.

'Ah, no – she's my girl! I couldn't-'

'Alright, Guy, alright. If you insist on persisting in your less than perfect relationship...' I pondered for a matter of seconds. 'Now, you need to fight fire with fire, and you have to do what I tell you to do. In the short term it will be a bit tricky, as all good plans take time and patience, but it will come good and I guarantee she'll be only too glad to push you out the house of a Sunday to drink with your friend.'

'Really? How?' the poor man gasped.

'It'll take a few weeks, and mean a sacrifice in the short term.'

'Fine, good, just tell me how?'

I rested my elbows on his counter and leaned in a little.

'This weekend, do as she asks and don't go out. Have Alan the butcher around to your house on the Sunday afternoon instead. If it's alright for her have her friends over then it should be alright for you too. She can't complain at that. And get on with your drinking, roaring and bawling - or whatever it is you do at the pub - at home instead. Act like the two of you are having the time of your life. Make sure you get in her way a bit, make a lot of noise, that kind of thing, and I assure you she will wish for the days when you used to go out and give her some peace to prepare the dinner. You watch!'

'Genius!' Guy whispered to himself.

'Indeed,' I replied and waved my bundle of letters at him by way of a parting.

Immediately as I entered Miss Bett's office my eyes fell onto the ceramic lad in dungarees which sat in the centre of the desk, his unnaturally wide eyes gazing up at me. The vile trinket had made its way out of the bottom drawer of the desk, surely at the hands of the office cleaner. The thing was both unattractive and strangely unsettling, and I snatched it up and went to return it to the drawer before deciding on a more permanent action.

I took the figure to the back window and placed it on the window ledge outside. With a sharp "goodbye!" I inched the lad to the edge and then over it with the back of my hand. Without waiting to listen for the smash I returned to my desk and surveyed my post.

The one true letter for Payton Edgar was a corking rant from Honoria Betts that I merely scanned the first sentence of before setting aside for perusal later on in the day. There was also a note in folded paper that gave me a chill – a summons form Bilborough. In the few years in which I had been working for the Clarion I had been in his office only twice now and yet here I was again, called to the Head like a guilty schoolboy. One sentence in particular stumped me. He wrote;

'I have been entertained each week by your recreation of the agony column, and believe it gives our traditional rag something of a contemporary boost – well done. I like it, such as it is.'

Such as it is? *Such as it is?* What on earth did that mean?

Fitzherbert, my well-groomed pigeon friend, fluttered down to the window sill and peered at me suspiciously. I waggled Bilborough's note in his direction as if to say "*look at this rubbish!*"

I decided I would put this unwanted summons to the back of my mind and pass by the boss's office on my way out when he had hopefully skipped off for golf. If I missed the man, it would not be my fault.

I moved on, and studied the letters for Dr. Blythe with relish.

A number of dull moans from people living in undesirable areas of London, one letter clearly feigned by some childish mind, and three or four with considerable potential. I spent a pleasant morning as Dr. Margaret Blythe worked her magic, sound advice flowing freely from my pen. At a quarter past three, as I was just completing my typing up, there was a polite rapping on my door and Beryl Baxter put her colourful face around the side and bellowed unnecessarily loudly into the room. Fitzherbert took sudden flight.

'Payton Edgar! Working hard I see?'

She had a woven basket hooked over her forearm, and fumbled within it with a chuckle.

'Guess what happened to me as I was coming into the building this morning?'

I didn't trouble myself to guess, but waited for her to continue. She pulled out a ceramic figure.

'This fell into my basket! I do believe it belongs up here? Poor little mite!' She rested the little boy in dungarees on my desk and I gave it a sour look. Was I cursed to be plagued by the thing for evermore?

'Now that I've done a good deed for you and rescued your little friend, you can do something for me! I insist that you come all the way along to my office and share a little something with me, I am bored to tears, darling! And it's only Monday!"

There was no way I could have got out of this invitation, and so I didn't even try. Even when on her best behaviour Beryl was still officious and forthright. I swiftly deposited the ugly figurine back into the bottom drawer of the desk and followed Beryl out. This Monday tipple was to become more or less a tradition of sorts over the coming weeks.

Beryl Baxter, principal of the gossip column, was always curiously good company and was surely the only Clarion worker whom I could call a true friend. Her offices were three doors down from where I had sat, and although shared with two other ladies they reflected the glamorous dysfunction of the columnist perfectly. The far wall was spattered with hundreds of snapshots, a collage of the rich and notorious, the talented and the auspicious. The majority were candid shots, black and whites from some launch, ball or party, but there were some fashion shots dotted about which stood out with their bright colours. A desk sat against each of the other three walls. One desk nearer to the door, clearly Beryl's, was littered with flowers, gifts, bottles and cards.

Thankfully, we were alone in her office that afternoon.

Beryl slid open her top drawer and grabbed the neck of a bottle in one hand and pinched two short tumblers up with the other.

'Tipple?' she squeaked without waiting for a reply and I had a generous scotch whisky in my grip before I knew it. I do like a good whisky, but usually after sunset and always with a generous splash of water to even out the balance. In normal circumstances I would have requested the mixer, but there was no water in Beryl's office, as her dried old cyclamen in the tiny office window was testament to. She chinked her glass against mine.

'Gosh, Beryl, it's only Monday afternoon-'

'How do you think I get through the week, Darling?' my colleague screeched, pecking at her wig with the fingertips of her free hand. Beryl was a notorious wig-wearer, and today she sported a standard chestnut affair, pulled upwards into a tight bun.

'Mondays, Wednesdays and Fridays, towards the end of the day, I treat myself to a little jolly. Nothing wrong with that. Today it is my pick-me-up jolly. To say "it may only be Monday, but we can still have fun"!'

'Indeed.'

'Now then, Payton,' she pulled a faux serious face and chinked my glass once more, 'to new ventures!' Beryl drank.

'New ventures.' I echoed, took a sip and then stopped myself. It was not the best whisky in the world, but it was passable.

'New ventures?'

'Yes, the re-creation of our dear paper's problem page. Payton you have really set it off! I have loved the last few Fridays, and it's all been thanks to your hilarious interpretation of Peg's Postbag. It's common knowledge that Honoria was way beyond stale, and good riddance say I! Long live Payton's Postbag!"

'It is a temporary project of mine,' I was quick to contradict her, 'to cover Miss Betts while she is ill, and that is all. And I would far rather it be considered innovative and stimulating than hilarious, as you put it. I am not a humourist. Besides, I will be handing it over as soon as-'

'I wouldn't bet on it, Buster! You watch.' She drained her glass and replaced the deficit before offering me the bottle. As I took it and deposited it discreetly behind me, Beryl wobbled her head a little, tauntingly, speaking in a childish sing-song manner. Her very animated conduct caused me to wonder to myself if this were truly only her first drink of the day.

'Modest Mr Edgar! I think that your weekly word to the wise is a winner!' she continued.

'My dear, it is not the wise who require the advice, it is the other poor souls out there.'

'Well, you'll be called up to see Billy before long, I'd wager my best wig on it. He'll want to keep you on.'

'And if he asks I will tell him a firm "no". I am a restaurant critic and that is all. I took this on as a favour. A *temporary* favour.'

Beryl Baxter grimaced as I took what was only my second sip.

'Mmm. Pity,' she sighed, leaning back. 'It is handy, you being a problem solver. I have a particular problem I could do with solving myself.'

'Oh?' I enquired with some regret. I was already starting to get a little tired of unscrambling problems, no matter how naturally the skill appeared to come to me.

'There's nothing you can do about this one, though, Payton darling.'

'Oh well, never mind.'

Beryl stretched and then tossed a copy of that morning's London Messenger carelessly onto my lap, causing me to almost spill my drink.

'It's that damn Germaine Proxy in the Messenger. If I read another of her jibes I don't know what I'll do. Did you know that she calls me the Purple Peril, now?'

'Well, you do wear a fair amount of the colour,' I said, perusing the paper.

Beryl sat mindlessly fiddling with the buttons on her purple cashmere cardigan as I read. The Messenger was our rival, to all intents and purposes, although I have long been convinced of the Clarion's superior quality in print. Germaine Proxy was their version of our Beryl Baxter, spilling good and bad gossip all over the society pages with scant regard for reputation. If I have to be honest, I would say that the two ladies were each as bad as each other, although I do not think I am speaking with bias when I say that Beryl certainly issued a more stylish turn of phrase.

'She's had a number of scoops over me these past few months. Am I losing it, Payton? Am I losing my intuition? My style?'

I know a cue when I hear one.

'Never!' I replied with aplomb, much to Beryl's approval. She continued.

'I just need to get one over on her. I need more-'

She was interrupted by a sharp rap at the door and a tiny bird like thing with a pinched nose and dry mousey curls appeared in the doorway.

'Afternoon tea, Mrs Baxter?' she trilled.

Beryl slapped her hand to her glistening wristwatch.

'Oh, gosh, Jane, I almost forgot we had arranged to meet. Can I meet you there? Be down in ten..?'

The newcomer's eyes were on me, and she was smiling like a child with a lollypop. Beryl made the introductions.

'Payton this is Jane Burden, a friend. Jane, this is Payton Edgar, a much respected colleague of mine…'

'Good day,' I chimed.

'Pleasure!' the lady squeaked childishly. She had an odd way about her, as she were surely about my age if not older, but dressed as if she were a twenty-year-old flapper.

'Downstairs, Jane. Be there in a jiffy.'

Dismissed, Jane Burden vanished, and it was only as she was gone that Beryl turned to me with a sneer.

'Jane's a dear friend of mine, but watch out, Payton! You would be pushed to find a more timid and retiring person from the look of her, but believe me she is a man-eater! I've seen it with my own eyes! She clocked you, all right! You really wouldn't believe it to look at her but my goodness, there's always some poor fool on the go. She gets through men like I get through scalp adhesive. She-'

I had stopped listening. Suddenly something had caught my eye. A face on the wall. Just over Beryl's shoulder a face looked out at me from one of the photographs taped across the board. A face I recognised.

Before I knew it, I was on my feet following my finger in its direction. The finger found the face and I stared for a while in confusion. Beryl had appeared to take this interruption with good grace.

'It's her!' I gasped to myself. 'You have a photograph of Grace!'

The picture had been taken at some sort of glittering function. Two well-groomed men stood to her right, beaming at the photographer, whereas Grace Kemp, my aunt's nurse, stood stony faced in a flowing cocktail dress, clutching a tiny shiny handbag at her front. She must have been a good few years younger, but it was most certainly my aunt's latest skivvy.

Beryl had joined me at my side.

'There's no Grace there, darling' she said, 'that's little Pim!'

I jabbed my finger at the image with much certainty.

'That is most definitely Grace Kemp, my Aunt Elizabeth's new nursemaid, Beryl. I should know! I live with the woman now.'

After a short pause in which she stood and appraised me brazenly, Beryl reached over to a drawer and pulled out a pile of magazines. She rifled through them for a minute before removing what she had been looking for. It was some sort of society rag, and the front cover of this one had rather unusual couple in the foreground; an uppity-looking gentleman who looked a little as if his face was melting as skin slid down over his eyes and collar, and besides him a tall, thin and somewhat opulent-looking lady in a sequinned gown, who wore her age well despite the whitening locks of hair. I had not seen at first, but to her side and in the darkness stood a figure.

Beryl placed her finger beneath it.

'Is this her? Is this your skivvy?' she asked.

It was indeed. Grace's smooth features were apparent through the shadows despite not having been the focus of the piece. Beryl huffed a little and dropped the article onto her desktop.

'My dear Mr Edgar, that girl there is Marianne De Groot, daughter of Olga De Groot, one of London's pre-eminent fashion designers, and Lars

De Groot, one of the world's greatest entrepreneurs and member of one of Europe's greatest dynasties. We are talking Swedish Royal family connections, my darling. The man's a stuffed old goat who'd barely matter were it not for the heritage, but as for Olga - well! You would be hard pushed to find a more splendidly glamorous figure in my column of a week, I can tell you. You must be mixing up your faces-'

What Beryl was saying was absurd in the extreme.

'But I am telling you the truth, Beryl. This young woman here is living with me at this very minute. She could be pulmicestoning my Aunt Elizabeth's dry heels as we speak. You can't be telling me she is actually Swedish Royal family?'

'Connections to the Royal family, my dear, connections. And yes I can. So she attends to menial tasks, does she? Well, that is most definitely little Pim, in the picture, and, therefore quite possibly, in your house. True to form, I suppose.'

'Pim?'

Beryl waved a hand. 'It's a nickname they use for her, what she has become known as, over the years. Poor Pim De Groot. Her real name is Marianne.'

'But you can't think that she would possibly want to-'

'Oho! I most certainly can, Payton, my dear!' Beryl was enjoying this news I could see. She sat at her desk with a sparkle in her eye and told me a story.

'Marianne De Groot has long been, shall we say, the dark sheep of the De Groot family. The dear thing is their only child, and it must have been a struggle for the poor love brought up as she was; as a showcase for her mother. Olga's quite insane, you see, as befits her position. I have followed little Pim right from the gold-tapered nappy days. Always pushed into shot, she was, forever besides her mother having been squeezed into some pencil thin tubular skirt or some such article. Never a smile, never! Poor Pim De Groot. Aren't some families dreadful? Makes me almost glad my Ma and Pa popped off when they did. Now there's just me and my sister, and she went and married a Bavarian of all people, so there's not much to do there. Where was I?'

'Poor Pim De Groot,' I put in, keen to keep Beryl on track.

'Yes, poor Pim. Never a smile. And then bang! Must have been two or three years ago, suddenly the child Pim was out of it. Something obviously snapped in the young thing, and she was no longer in her mother's shadow. Reports of her whereabouts became sketchy at best.

'She was spotted travelling Germany with some youth on a bike, and there were rumours of an arrest in Paris fairly soon after her disappearance. Olga De Groot must have been distraught, but she hid it well. After a while it became clear why the girl was doing these things. She would do absolutely anything to hurt or shame her parents, I'm sure of it. Suddenly one day Marianne De Groot turned up working on a dig near Cairo, getting muddy in the name of archaeology with some long-haired lad, or something along those lines. A De Groot, getting their hands dirty, if you please! That was, until her parents found her there. Turns out her father was one of the financiers of the dig, which he promptly pulled in outrage. That man has his cash in some very odd pots, I'm sure. The last thing I'd heard, rumour had it that little Pim was washing up in kitchens in Scotland. And then there was the inevitable ding-dong, I'm pretty sure her father bought out the restaurant or something, and the girl vanished again. Until now, it seems.'

'This makes no sense,' I spat

'It makes perfect sense,' Beryl continued, 'where better to work than a private residence that her father surely cannot interfere with? And what better menial task to do but nursing an old dear? You wouldn't catch me giving a bed bath and I'm sure Pim's mother would say the same. She'd probably faint right then and there on the spot! I'm not even sure the woman blows her own nose. It's the prefect rebellion, Payton. Now, tell me about the girl. What is she like?'

Beryl had gathered a pen and paper and sat expectantly.

'Oh no, my dear Mrs Baxter, none of this goes in print,' I waved a finger, 'this is extremely sensitive. Yes, extremely sensitive. If I so much as read a word of this you can consider our association well and truly-'

'Alright, Payton, alright! Goodness! Are you sure you couldn't do with a second drink?'

I realised that I had emptied my glass. During the last part of our conversation I had easily drained the last of my whisky, gathering that I would have to have words with the young fraudster in my house.

Ripe for a confrontation, I decided that I would indeed go and see Bilborough as requested. And after that, I would head home and have it out with the cuckoo in my nest.

Grace Kemp, indeed!

CHAPTER 10

In which Payton Edgar dines at Harvey's Restaurant

Mrs H Betts
Preston Ward,
South London Hospital for Women,
Clapham Common,
London
20th February

Dear Mr Edgar,

Can you imagine my surprise as I sat wracked with pain in my hospital bed and read over your version of my 'Peggy's Postbag' column? Over the past four years I have worked hard to achieve a column that is friendly and open for all, with good old fashioned motherly advice. And what have you done but gone and ruined all my hard work?

This ogre you have employed into your imagination is no better equipped to advise the public than those chimpanzees from the television advertisement. Please can you see the error of your ways and revert back to my template immediately.

I shall be returning to work in mid-March as planned, and expect my problem page to remain a going concern, and not an embarrassing joke.

Yours sincerely,
Honoria Betts

Payton Edgar
21 Clarendon St
Pimlico
London (SW)
February 22nd

    Dear Mrs Betts,
    It is clear that you do not understand my intention in the restoration of the Clarion's problem page. I'm sure you cannot deny that the piece I inherited was rather stale and sedate and what it lacked in challenge and vigour it made up for in monotony and cliché. I have merely added a touch of class and invention to this piece. By creating Dr. Margaret Blythe I have increased the input of letters received by over four times the original amount each week.
    In addition to this obvious statement of approval from the public, on opening your Clarion this Friday you will observe the 'Dear Margaret' column to now be situated on page 8, and no longer in the very bowels of the newspaper as it had festered under your leadership. This decision has been made independently by Mr Bilborough, who is extremely pleased with its sudden success. I have also negotiated the inclusion of up to five letters a week, print space permitting.
    I have just come from meeting with Mr Bilborough, where I informed him that you will be taking on this page in the format now seen with enthusiasm upon your return to work. I am sending you a short biography of Dr. Blythe, including her likes and dislikes. This will give you time to get acquainted with her before your return.
    Yours sincerely,
    Payton Edgar

When I got home that evening my ardour had cooled somewhat and I was in no mood for a confrontation with the cuckoo in my nest. Bilborough's words of support that afternoon had dampened the fire in my belly, and I was pleased to find the living room empty.

I was to be prevented from challenging the fraudulent care-worker for some days. Almost as if in conspiracy the two women, my aunt and Grace 'Marianne De Groot' Kemp, were either hidden away in my aunt's chamber doing whatever stomach-churning cleaning rituals they do together, or else the nurse was nowhere to be seen. By the Thursday evening I took the bull by the horns and knocked sharply on my box room door.

'Miss Kemp, may I have a word?'

No reply.

'A word, please, Miss Kemp,' I stated, unfortunately raising my voice enough for my crumbly old aunt to hear from her room down the stairway.

'Don't let him in, Gracie!' she hollered from her room, sending a shiver of fury through my bones.

'Miss Kemp, I know you are in there-'

'Alright! Alright! Alright!'

The door was flung open to reveal Grace Kemp, curlers firmly in place, adorned in her long white robe. For the first time I noticed that the dressing gown she had trudged around the house in since her arrival was not the usual towelling affair one would expect, but was well cut and rather chic, clearly having cost a number of pounds. How had I failed to notice this? I blinked at her, preparing myself for a showdown. She stared at me lazily. Although it was barely eight o'clock she appeared to be ready for bed.

'May I have a word, Miss Kemp,' I began before hearing the involuntary reluctance in my voice. I toughened up.

'In the living room - at once!'

My fat black cat Lucille appeared indifferent to the fire in my belly as I stormed into the room. She remained firmly in her favourite spot on the arm of my much-loved antique Chesterfield armchair and opened one eye languidly for just a few seconds. The young nurse followed me into the room and stood glaring in my direction from over by the piano. She was keeping her distance.

'Please take a seat, Miss De Groot,' I instructed, and she reluctantly perched in a temporary fashion on the edge of the Chesterfield aside Lucille, who didn't move a muscle. Now Miss Kemp had opted to feign a look of boredom. Our talk was not a long one, just long enough for me to reveal that I knew the truth about her double life and to demand an explanation for such behaviour. I regret that this may not have been the best approach, for it seemed to rile my houseguest, and I was treated to a barrage of 'mind your own businesses' and 'how dare you's'.

'Surely all that matters is that I am a good nurse to your aunt, and a satisfactory lodger, and is that not the case? Am I not a good nurse?'

I could not disagree. The girl spoke with a forceful confidence that rendered me wordless. As she went on I studied her face, realising that her features, once taken as youthful and plain, were in fact those of a beautiful young woman.

'Then that is the end of it. I want to hear no more about my family, is that understood? That is all ancient history now, and it is most certainly no business of yours! Please address me as Grace Kemp and nothing else. Goodnight, Mr Edgar.'

For a while I stood, alone and speechless. And then a curious thing happened - I found myself agreeing, just a little, with what she had said. Where I should normally have felt ignited by being spoken to in such a way, I could not help thinking that perhaps the girl was right, that perhaps this was indeed none of my business. One could not deny that she had proved her worth over the past few weeks. And there was something kind behind those fierce eyes. With some hesitancy I let my anger dwindle.

However, she had not won! I was merely reconsidering my position.

The following evening, I took Irving on our belated trip out to Harvey's restaurant.

It was the only thing I could think of to cheer myself up after an afternoon of moping around St James Park in the drizzle. I had sat for some time with the majority of the Clarion on my lap, having deposited the sports pages between the damp wood of the bench and my houndstooth suit. Under the umbrella of trees I watched as people went about their business. Every single person around me seemed even more drab and lacklustre than usual. Perhaps it was the rain, perhaps the time of year. There was certainly very little excitement to be found in the park that day.

There had also been little of interest in the paper, except for the notice for the funeral of Helen Capstick that was to be held on the following Wednesday.

There had been no pieces about her death in the paper since the news first broke and even on that occasion there had been only a surprisingly muted report about the suspected murder on page four, followed by an appeal for the whereabouts of Richard Clay the following day. Again, this had been tucked away a few pages into the newspaper, and I wondered if more had been reported and that I had missed it, or if Inspector Standing was playing his cards close to his chest on this one.

He could have stirred up a frenzied national manhunt had he chosen to.

It was as I was sitting there, a touch damp but well wrapped in my thermals and sheepskin that I decided to get out that evening, if only to sooth my grumbling angst over the whole sorry Capstick affair.

Irving took my invitation with unimpeded gratitude and, surprisingly, I received no snide comment alluding to our aborted trip to Harvey's only a matter of days ago. It seemed that I had indeed been forgiven.

I made our usual reservation for seven.

Harvey's restaurant has been a favourite of ours for some time, and it had been a conscious decision on my part to avoid using it as the subject of one of my columns thus far. There would come a time when it felt necessary, however in those early days of the establishment I feared jinxing our run of pleasurable dining experiences, not to mention the fact that a number of their staff had become agreeable acquaintances of mine whom I would not wish to offend in any way.

The head chef, Arnold Prosper, always made a point of joining us at our table when he could to recommend any specials he was featuring, a move that I had found quite irritating at first, but one that I had soon become accustomed to nevertheless. Prosper was a rather unsavoury character and something of an oaf. The man was noticeably inebriated each and every evening I had attended the place. However one could not deny the man his talent.

Reynolds, the head waiter, was, as befitted his position, reserved and distinctly chilly in his approach. Despite numerous visits to the establishment he had made no move to acquaint himself with either of us, nor should I have wished him to.

My third and final regular acquaintance was nowhere to be seen at first. Mandisa was a chef-de-partie working under Prosper. The immigrant girl had no friends or family in England to speak of, and she seemed to enjoy talking to Irving and I when she could escape the steam of the kitchen. I dare say she saw me as something of a father figure.

Of the proprietor himself, I have never met Mr Harvey Blake and know very little about him, only that he chooses to remain very much in the shadows both with regards to the business and to any press coverage, of which Harvey's had received its share if one knew where to look. It had been such a discreet success on London's restaurant scene that it was considered to be a leader in the capital's new love affair with food by those in the know. And yet Harvey's remained inconspicuous.

Even the naturally curious Mandisa had been unable to garner any information on her employers, much to my chagrin.

Over the past year, head chef Prosper had become the face of Harvey's, to his great delight. It would not be that long before I would learn more about both the restaurant's proprietor and the head chef but that - to coin a phrase and running the risk of being slightly irksome - is another story.

Our favourite table besides the pleasant corner fountain had been saved for us upon my request. I needn't have bothered, as on that cold wet February evening there would only be a handful of diners through the restaurant doors. Indeed, we were the first to arrive and I graciously let Irving have the seat that looked out on the restaurant.

This seemingly small gesture took a fair amount of effort on my part, and had I not had a pleasing view of the foliage around the fountain and access to a view of the restaurant in a mirror beside Irving's head then my sacrifice would have been even more trying.

Reynolds showed us to our table with a tight thin smile and offered us our usual bottle which we received with some gratitude. He did not need to be asked to turn off the fountain, as its pools already sat stagnant. They knew that I enjoyed sitting by the showpiece, but disliked the constant, bladder-twinging tinkling of water during my meal. The Bordeaux, when it came, was smooth and plummy and just what I had needed to settle my jangling nerves.

In silence, we studied the handwritten menu for a while.

I could tell that the evening menu had been hand-written by Mandisa as the scrawl was extravagant but the grammar was once again a little haphazard. I had discreetly mentioned this to her on a number of occasions, at which she had insisted that she were always careful to look up any English words that she was uncertain about. That said, the mention of a cut of beef to be served with "running beans" had forced me to offer up one or two lessons in basic culinary English over the Christmas period. An offer that had been unfortunately declined.

As we seated ourselves Mandisa had appeared momentarily from the kitchens and gesticulated her welcome, just to show her dark face from under a white cap and to let us know that she would try and join us for a minute at some point in the evening. Why she insisted on doing this I could never fathom. A chef's place is in the kitchen. It may be customary in Africa for a chef to fraternise with diners but it sat most uncomfortably with me. Irving was fascinated by the girl, however, and only encouraged her.

Soon Arnold Prosper made his customary appearance and was barely sober enough to stand still at the table-side. As he stood swaying like seaweed in the pull of the tide, Prosper sweated horribly and pushed the liver stew suspiciously strongly before vanishing again through his kitchen doors in a puff of steam. Thankfully the man was steering clear of the current rising fashion for Eastern cuisine, plumping for honest seasonal English food, and I could see that his countryside contacts had been busy hunting despite the weather.

I opted for the beef terrine to start, a comfortable favourite, and Irving had the pea soup as usual. I attempted to get him to widen his experiences, but to no avail. Irving insisted that I was just as safe in my choices, having had the terrine the last four out of five visits. As if he had been counting!

After considerable discussion we agreed not to agree. Following this I did my best not to fuss or judge for this was not a meal destined for print. For our main course we both branched out a little further than usual, with Irving weakening under Prosper's influence and ordering the heavily promoted liver stew while I opted for the pheasant, to catch the bird before the season ended.

Once again I reminded myself why I had chosen not to rate the restaurant's food in print. It would certainly have been refreshing for me, (and I dare say for my readers too) to pen a glowing review, however given the choice between a bland but favourable account of an establishment or a damning, scathing slaughtering piece, I know which I'd prefer to read. Also one enjoyed the exclusivity of the place and did not wish to threaten this by advertising the restaurant's merits to the entire city.

Many a worthy business has been ruined by the curse of popularity.

My terrine was typically exquisite, although I confess to feeling slightly bored by the now-familiar crusty bread that accompanied the dish. Irving was pleased with his soup, as always. His tastes are without a doubt simpler and less demanding than my own, although I have to admit that it did smell good. I did not taste it as I would not be writing about it.

As for the main course, all I can say about his stew is that it was interesting and yet far too chunky for my liking. I was, however, most pleased with my perfect pheasant, not too dry and without shot, and its accompanying sweet vegetables sat unadulterated by fanciful ideas. The surprisingly complex wine lasted nicely throughout the meal.

I rarely have a dessert unless reviewing, but Irving had a fancy for the custard tart and so I ordered a cognac. It was at this late point in our meal that Mandisa made her appearance during a momentary lull in her work.

The dear young thing had pulled off her cap, leaving the impression of a bowl rim around her crown. The wide smile she greeted me with was enchanting and she proceeded to watch with delighted eyes as Irving polished off the last of his tart with considerable gusto. His appreciation of the tart clearly pleased her deeply, for it was Mandisa who was usually responsible for the pastries.

We chatted a little about our meal, before she enquired after my aunt, as she always did. In normal circumstances one would look down upon such personal banter with service staff, but something about her simple honesty made me overlook this yet again. Mandisa is perhaps one of the few people I feel I can talk to on matters of domesticity. The girl had never met my Aunt Elizabeth, but thought it wonderful that I was so charitable as to invite an elderly relative into my home, and always asked after her out of the goodness of her heart.

'Here we go!' said Irving, accompanying his comment with exaggerated eye rolling. He reached into his jacket pocket and, much to my horror and disapproval, produced his crossword puzzle which, once he had moved aside his empty plate, he slapped down on the tablecloth before him.

I cursed myself for not anticipating this.

'Irving!'

I was treated to a firm glare before he whipped out a pencil and took to his task.

'Twelve down, Impersonating, nine letters.'

I drew in a tolerant breath. The man might as well have pulled out his stinking pipe too. I began our conversation with a pointed dig at my companion.

'Thank you for asking about my Aunt Elizabeth, Mandisa. It is so very nice to know that some people still respect the art of polite conversation. We have a new nurse for her.' I emphasised this last point with a dark poignant tone.

'That is good.' Mandisa replied in her sweet simple way. Irving, tapping his pencil to his chin, spoke out mindlessly without moving his gaze from the page.

'Payton does not approve.'

'Oh, really?'

Her eyes were wide with enquiry. I drained my glass.

'Let's just say that if you ever want to leave the catering business and are looking for work as a nurse, there will be a job open for you at my house.' I said this only half in jest, and not for the first time. I had always seen Mandisa as the perfect person for this impossible job, although I'll admit that it is a job that I would never wish on even my worst enemy.

Irving sucked in air through his teeth rather irritatingly.

'I don't know about that, Payton. It sounds like this Grace is there for good. From what even you say about her she sounds very adept at what she does, and your aunt likes her which must surely be-'

'Whose side are you on?' I asked curtly. 'Stick to your puzzle, if you must.'

From the corner of my eye I could see Mandisa bite on her bottom lip, her eyes darting from Irving to myself as I sat glaring at him. She soon broke the silence, but unfortunately chose to persist with the conversation at hand.

'Have you met this Grace?' she asked Irving.

'The mysterious Grace Kemp!' he replied whimsically, 'Not yet I haven't, but I can't wait. If she is everything that Payton says she is...'

His tone gave me cause to pause. The picture I had painted of my young house guest, that of the devious opportunist cuckoo, was possibly a little harsh on the girl. However, I was quick to remind myself that recent events had exposed her as a liar and a fraud. I looked about the place to ensure no eavesdroppers were circling, and then leaned in closer to my friends. In hushed tones I told them the curious tale of poor little Pim, the affluent Marianne De Groot, daughter of a family of great repute, and of her notorious rebellious streak. It was no surprise that Irving looked perplexed.

He even lay down his pencil.

'Well it seems most odd to me, coming to live with you to sponge down your aunt every day in order to get back at Ma and Pa.'

Mandisa grunted. 'Seems strange to you? Not to me, it doesn't, no, no. People will do anything for a parent's love, I am sure. Mr Edgar, this girl is playing a game with you, and I don't like it.' Her bluntness was refreshing, and yet Irving was waving a hand as if fanning a flame.

'Oh, no, I don't think it pays to be like that, my dear' he stated in his usual irritatingly fair-minded way, 'Payton, you need to give the girl a chance, to hear her out.'

'I have tried that, of course,' I replied with some swagger, 'she won't talk to me. Says she is doing a damn fine job and that I should lump it.'

Irving cocked his head.

'Well then, there you are. She does do a good job, you said so yourself. I think you should leave the girl alone and focus more on your other pet project of the hour, that poor dead woman who sent you that letter.'

I was exasperated to see him retrieve his blunt pencil and return to his puzzle.

'Twelve down, Impersonating,' he said slowly, 'nine letters.'

'Dead woman?' asked Mandisa with renewed interest when suddenly a movement in the kitchen doorway took her attention. Prosper was circling pointedly, his red eyes fixed firmly on our table.

'Oh, I have to go. Payton, we meet soon, and you tell me all about this dead woman, yes?'

And with a sweet smile, she was gone.

I sat for a minute in silence, with only the cheerful chatter of other diners and the tap-tap-tap of Irving's pencil against the table top to listen to. Finally, I broke, snatching the implement from his grasp.

'Put that down!' I boomed, slamming the pencil to the table top so hard it must have broken the lead in several places. Irving was far too gentle-natured to appear cross. He merely lifted his gaze to mine and spoke lazily.

'Impersonating, nine letters.'

'Mimicking!' I announced triumphantly, as if the answer had just come to mind when, in fact, I had been musing this over in the back of my mind since he had first issued this poser out loud. Such was the galling contagiousness of the crossword puzzle.

Irving grabbed back his pencil but then paused.

'Nope, doesn't fit with four across, fungoid,' he said. 'How many letters in performing?'

'As in acting? Impersonating isn't acting my dear Irving. No, impersonating is pretending to be someone that you aren't. Mimicking them. Mimicking! Are you sure it doesn't fit? Perhaps the puzzler got it wrong. Now this is why I hate you doing this, Irving. You've got me all jittery now.' I patted my chest. 'I've got that horrible knotted feeling again.'

'You really should see a doctor about that, Payton,' said my friend plainly.

'Just a bit of indigestion!' I replied sharply.

'Even so, the doctor-'

'I will, I will!' I snapped, then sat back, folded my arms and tried to think of anything to forget the burning in my chest.

Mimicking. Impersonating. They were the same thing. Just as I was doing with Margaret Blythe in some way or another. And then a thought came to me. What if it worked the other way too, if any of my published letters had been fraudulent in such a way. Yes, I had received one that was clearly a rather rude and childish prank, but others must surely write from the heart. Surely?

I pondered to myself if, during my stint as Margaret Blythe, I would unwittingly fall for a fraud at any point.

And then it hit me.

'The letter, Irving!' I exclaimed, more to myself than to my friend, 'the letter could have been a fake.'

'I beg your pardon?'

I reached out and grasped the air between us, clenching my fists in the air. 'What would you do if you planned to murder someone, Irving?'

An unwelcome smirk flittered across his face as he eyed my drink.

'Poison in the cognac?'

'Not what with, Irving...but how. We know that Mrs Capstick's death was a premeditated murder. If I were planning to murder someone, and to get away with it, I would be sure to fix the blame elsewhere...wouldn't you? And the missing Richard Clay is getting the brunt of it! What better way to frame somebody for murder than to create a cry for help from the victim, practically accusing an innocent man from beyond the grave? Perhaps somebody had found out about their affair and put poor Clay in the frame-'

'Sounds a bit far-fetched to me!'

'But it is possible, nevertheless! Life can be far-fetched sometimes, Irving.'

'It is ridiculous!' Irving went on.

'It is murder!' I swiftly replied, knotting my fingers together. 'Yes, it fits in with everything. I am becoming more and more convinced that Clay is innocent.'

'But you have never met the man!' said Irving.

'No, but I have met his mother. And she was so certain of her boy's innocence. A mother knows, Irving, dear.'

'Anyhow,' my friend went on, 'you said you didn't print the letter in the end-'

'No, but the intention was there. I was merely a spanner in the works.'

'Well, I'm sorry, Payton, but what you're saying is all a bit over-blown, isn't it? Bet the woman just saw the Dear Margaret column one day and thought "why not?"'

'But she can't have, Irving, for they don't take a newspaper. I thought it was odd, but it fits my theory.'

'Beg your pardon?'

'At the Capstick's house, his sister told me they don't get newspapers. Reduces the chances of her writing to the problem pages, right?'

'Payton, I still-'

'Good grief!' I exclaimed, now rubbing my hands together with something akin to glee, 'we could be dealing with a very clever murderer indeed. Imitating Helen Capstick to pass the blame on to Clay? What an ingenious idea.'

Irving jolted up in his seat and waved his pencil.

'Imitating!' he shrieked, seizing the crossword.

I sat back in my chair, resigned to my fate.

'I have a funeral to attend,' I said grimly, to the top of Irving's head.

CHAPTER 11

In which Payton Edgar acts the firebrand

Dear Margaret,
I suffer terribly with loud, nervous laughter. In even the most serious of situations, a shrill titter is out of my mouth before I can stop it. It can be terribly embarrassing, but I really don't know how to stop it. Any advice?
Giggler, High Barnet

Margaret replies; how annoying you must be, Giggler. There is nothing worse than that shrill twitter that pierces the air and sets one's teeth on edge. I am glad you have written to me, however, as I think I can be of help. Remember that the noise is coming out of your mouth, of which you are in charge. Simply stop doing it, you silly, irritating girl.

It was perfect funeral weather.

The sky was a clear blue, and yet rain had moistened the place earlier in the morning leaving the trees a crisp green and the stones of the graveyard dark and soggy. The ceremony had been advertised as starting at eleven on the Wednesday and I was sure to get there early. If I was correct in my suspicions and the letter supposedly sent by the dead woman had indeed been a fake, this meant that it had come from somebody close to her, somebody who knew enough to be so bold.

A person who would undoubtedly attend her funeral.

My intention was to behave like an inquisitive hound, sniffing around for the merest hint of insincerity or guilt. Perhaps I should have visited Inspector Standing with my suspicions, but following his discourteous and insolent display at Scotland Yard I had no intention of giving the man aid of any kind. He clearly saw me as a fool and a time-waster, and I had no desire to stoke that particular fire.

On the Monday morning before the funeral I had collected the latest batch of letters for Dr. Blythe, and was thrilled as Cockney Guy handed over a substantial bundle, requiring a large elastic band to hold them all together. I counted sixteen in all, thumbing through them with considerable glee. Guy informed me that he had acted upon my advice and had had his butcher friend to dinner on the Sunday, with much drinking and celebration by the side of the wireless. He also reported that his wife had grumbled endlessly, to which I shot him a knowing smile.

'My motto is to never give advice unless asked, Guy. You asked, and I merely gave it. Keep it up and you'll get your way in no time, you'll see,'

With this, I had swept up to Mrs Bett's office to work my wonder for the needy public.

Much to my delight Fitzherbert the pigeon, my feathered friend, was there. He looked no dirtier than before, and just as wise. A smooth, clean pigeon; a rarity. We watched each other for a while.

It was as I was seated at that desk, watching Fitzherbert on the window ledge blinking innocently through the glass at me that I thought some more about attending Helen Capstick's funeral. I would have given anything to be a pigeon in that graveyard, innocently pecking and flapping about while keeping a spy's eye on my suspects. But I was not a pigeon. What strategies did I have to blend in to the background like one of our feathered friends? How could I pick up seeds of gossip without being noticed?

I was fully prepared to lie or to bluff in order to get to the truth.

As it happens, I would indeed gain a few seeds of insight amongst the sizeable crowd that gathered that day, and yet I would also gain considerably larger dollops of humiliation and discomfort into the bargain.

The discomfort started almost immediately, as I ran headlong into Jenny French on the corner of the churchyard, the lower half of my stick striking against her long black dress with some force. She had been bounding along, distracted, and almost cursed aloud at our collision before smoothing down the front of her frock and squeezing out a smile for me.

'Oh, Mr Edgar! So glad you could come,' she rattled out the phrase that she would no doubt be using a hundred times that morning. At this early stage in the day it was said without a hint of insincerity.

'I am so sorry about that, Miss French, it's most unlike me to be so maladroit. Did I hurt you?'

'No, no,' she patted her leg gently, 'that's the beauty of a black dress, not a mark to be seen. Are you heading to the church? It's this way.'

In truth, I had been circling the graveyard in a kind of surveillance operation, and was a little disgruntled to be turned around on the spot and practically marched up to the churchyard gate. As we walked, I felt a sudden pang of guilt for deceiving the nice young lady; for lying about having known her sister, and about being a member of the undoubtedly dreadful amateur dramatics group. It was, thankfully, only a passing pang.

All necessary, I reminded myself, to get to the truth.

At the gates John Capstick paced a little, looking much smarter in his mourning suit than in the casuals I had seen him wearing on our previous encounter. He scrubbed up well, to coin a phrase, and with sunken shoulders and eyes cast downwards he looked the very picture of a man about to bury his wife. A flash of something like alarm moved across his face as he caught sight of Miss French and I approaching, but it was quickly replaced by a placid smile.

We shook hands.

And so I ambled down the pathway accompanied by the immediate family of the deceased. Quite a feat for any curious investigator.

We exchanged some rather dull pleasantries before reaching the periphery of the black huddle that gathered outside of the church. The vicar, an ancient creature with bushy white hair, appeared as if from nowhere and clasped Capstick's hands, muttering something or other through a wiry beard. As he did this, Miss French exclaimed, clutching my arm with one hand and raising a pointed finger with the other.

'Look, Mr Edgar, it's your drama group!'

The place was littered with pockets of people in black.

'Where?' I enquired fearfully.

'Just by the tree over there. Isn't that Mr Claremont up front?'

I really should have foreseen this complication.

'Of course,' I said with false delight, 'how good of them all to come.'

'Well, you must go and say hello,' said Jenny French with a friendly nudge. I bit my lip.

'No, no, my dear. I think I'll stay with you for now.'

'Oh, Mr Edgar, go on,' she continued,' look! They're waving!'

And indeed they were, to which Jenny French returned a polite signal. To my horror, the four expectant faces appeared to take this gesture as an invitation and began weaving through the throng to approach us. I could not let my deception be exposed, not here, not now.

'I will go and see them, Miss French. You'll have enough people to meet and greet - you stay here with the vicar.'

And with that I moved with some urgency from the young lady's side to block the approaching amateur actors and actresses. At my advance they stopped in their tracks. In the few seconds it took to move over I had prepared myself for the fact that I would need to do a fair amount of fibbing in order to maintain my relations with Helen Capstick's family.

Any ideas that I may have had brewing about a member of the theatre group being responsible for Helen's murder were quickly dispelled, for they were a motley crew. Up in front an uncomfortably tall skeletal gentleman with greying curls and piecing grey eyes presented himself as the leader of the pack. Behind him stood two short round ladies in black hats and a fresh-faced and handsome young man. They each watched me with questions in their eyes. The group, feeling they had been summoned by Miss French, clearly did not approve of my blockade.

'Good morning?' said the ringleader, more as a sharp enquiry than a greeting.

'Good morning to you, Sir,' I replied with a theatrical geniality that surprised even me. 'Miss French, Helen's sister, is so very glad that you could come, and she asked me to tell you this and to give you her thanks. Unfortunately, she has many people to see, as you can imagine. She is tied up with the vicar at the moment.'

At this, one of the ladies in the pack gave a snort of nervous laughter. I proffered my hand to the front-runner.

'I am Payton Edgar, friend of the family. And you are...?'

'James Claremont. Actor, orator and founder of The Claremont Society,' the man replied as he pumped my hand. 'We were so sorry about poor Helen. A terrible, terrible thing to happen.'

'Indeed,'

'And, of course, this leaves us without a Sylviane for our Merry Widow. And at such a late hour too. We have had to postpone our opening, can you believe? A most dissatisfactory state of affairs.'

The trio behind him had the good grace to cast down their eyes at this indiscretion. This man was clearly a buffoon, and yet I pretended not to have clocked his blatant tactlessness.

'Helen loved being a part of the, er, what do you call yourselves?'

'The Claremont Dramatic Society,' the man replied. I noted the glaring omission of the word amateur. It was time that I started fishing. I feigned obliviousness.

'Is Mr Clay not with you?'

At this innocent query all eyes grew wide in what could have been disbelief, the ladies turning their heads aside. I tried to read their reactions. Did they know of the affair between Helen and Clay? It must have been happening under their noses. I was, unfortunately, to be left wanting. Even Claremont was moved to silence by my innocent enquiry. I shifted the conversation onwards.

'You know, I have always envied Helen's passion for the theatre,' I continued, spitting out lies to all and sundry. 'I should love to be a part of your group, and I am local. I have always wanted to, well, you know...'

The correct phrase had escaped me.

'To tread the boards?' said Claremont with a sly hiss.

'Exactly the saying I was searching for, yes,' I replied.

'Such a vile idiom,' Claremont remarked, dragging his words out with unnecessary length, 'not to mention so very clichéd.'

I struggled within to overlook this rebuff. The truth of the matter is that I can imagine nothing worse that standing in front of a crowd of strangers like an idiot and shouting words over their heads, knowing that each and every one of them is just waiting for me to stumble or to slip up in some way for their entertainment. James Claremont sucked in his cheeks before he continued, stony faced.

'You must audition sometime, Mr Edgar,' he said.

'Audition? For an amateur society?' I replied with much gusto, thrilled to have the opportunity to pop in a discreet snub. 'Surely you'd be glad to have any Tom, Dick or Harry join up? Anyway, as you seem to have a place free now poor dear Helen has passed, perhaps I can just, well, slip into it? It seems that you need the numbers.'

The trio behind Claremont were grinning, unlike their leader.

'Everyone has to audition,' he stated. This lie was soon exposed by an uprising from behind him.

'We didn't audition, Jim!' cried the young man.

'Let him in!' squeaked the plumper of the two women.

'The more the merrier!' sang the other.

Clearly outnumbered, there was nothing the gangling idiot could do but issue a thin smile and nod in unhappy resignation.

'Very well. But I warn you right now, I expect a lot from my players, and I do not play it safe in my direction. Our art is all about experimentation. Last year we did Wuthering Heights on stilts - a great success indeed, although not without its challenges. Our production of The Merry Widow is again a bold leap into the dramatic unpredictability of the arts. I have set this particular production in our own East End of London. Plus, we are playing it straight, not for laughs. Having said that, I assure you there is a roaring can-can at the finale.'

How dreadful!

'How wonderful!' I chimed. He continued.

'We meet on Tuesday and Thursday evenings, Onslow Hall Community Centre, just off the Fulham road, around from the South Kensington tube station. Six o'clock sharp.'

'Twice a week?' I asked in surprise, although why I bothered to enquire I do not know, as I had no intention of ever attending.

'When we are within weeks of a show, yes.'

'Right-o,' I grinned, and one of the ladies behind Claremont gave a little clap, which was suddenly halted. Her podgy face dropped as if she remembered she were at a funeral, and it became clear that she had spotted John Capstick approaching our little union.

'Good morning, Mr Edgar, so glad you could make it,' he boomed, clasping my hand in his. His grasp was firm and dry. 'This is the am-drammers corner, eh? Pleased you could all make it.'

He was greeted by a twitter of humbled replies from the little gathering.

'I'll bet Mr Edgar is your biggest ham, what?' Capstick continued, and my whole physical being tensed. I had to intervene.

'I only joined recently, Mr Capstick-'

Very, very recently.

'They have yet to appreciate the full force of Payton Edgar in r-r-r-role.'

I had rolled my r's at the end to signify my magnificence, as I have seen actorly types do. Beside me, Claremont was openly scowling, but nobody appeared to take notice.

'I imagine you are quite a player, Mr Edgar,' smiled Capstick. 'You have the stance of a great actor. I will make sure to come to your next show.'

'See,' I declared to the others with a false delight, 'I am drawing them in already!'

This theatrical persona of mine was such an irritant that I was even irritating myself, and so I didn't mind too much to see Claremont rolling his eyes. Capstick gave a throaty chuckle which became a chesty cough and ended up being followed by a great sigh. He cast his red-rimmed eyes over the crowd.

'Quite a turnout,' I said, perhaps a little too predictably, to which he nodded sadly, and then bowed his head.

'How are you holding up?' I asked rather uselessly. Claremont had stepped away a few feet, either out of discretion or discomfort.

'Just about on it, Mr Edgar, thank you for asking,' answered Capstick, 'It's all such a mess. I can't believe she would do what she did.'

'No, indeed,' I parroted idly, before taking in what he had said. Capstick knew that his wife had not died by her own hand, so what was it she had done?

'You can't believe she would do what, exactly?' I asked, pointedly.

'Have, well, relations. An affair.'

'You didn't know?' the words were out of my mouth before I could think.

'Of course not, Mr Edgar,' said Capstick. 'Nobody knew. But it's all come out now, the Inspector told us everything. The husband is always the last to know. Broke my heart when I heard about it, it did. This Clay sounds like a rum character. Listen, you knew him, what was he like?'

I was about to reply that I had never met the man in my life, before recalling that so far as Capstick was aware I had been an associate from the drama group. I stammered over some words, and thankfully Capstick saved me.

'Not to worry, it's not the time to talk of it, is it?'

After a minute the widower made his excuses and departed to greet more mourners as the crowd grew larger. This left me forced to spend the next ten minutes in the company of my new theatre troop who had remained congregated nearby.

I was introduced to the three others, but theirs names were unremarkable and instantly forgettable. The young lad seemed bored and distracted, while the two women clucked away to themselves like a pair of bickering hens. Claremont seemed to prefer an austere silence and I was inclined, not to mention relieved, to join in it with him.

I rescued some leaves from a puddle with the end of my stick mindlessly for a few minutes, wondering why it was that wherever I went there were always brash and foppish actorly types to avoid.

Perhaps, I thought to myself, this is what comes from living in the capital.

It was not long, however, before I caught sight of a familiar face and a kind of relief washed over me; there was a chance of escape from the actors, albeit an undesirable one. Thomas Limestone, the Capstick's lodger, was loitering alone. In his pressed suit and woollen coat he looked every inch the grumbling headmaster. One could visualise the cloak and cane with ease.

Something incited me to report to the man, a twist of mischief which led me to his side. I knew he would be as displeased to see me as I was to see him. After issuing a few words of farewell to toady old Claremont I pushed gently through the throng to where Limestone stood, his hands clasped at his front.

I reminded myself that the man was not a headmaster. He was merely the deputy at young Frank's school. Thrown out of the family home and in the midst of a turbulent divorce, Miss French had told me. What a fool. He looked every inch the sufferer that morning, with a long pale face and an over-large grey hat hiding his shining bonce. Despite the fact that his mourning suit was cleaned and pressed, there was still the impression that clouds of chalk dust hung about the man.

He saw me coming, and was almost welcoming.

'Ah, Good morning, Mr…?'

The idiot had forgotten my name again. It was a good job that I had such a thick skin and an unnaturally superior memory.

'Edgar, Mr Limestone, Payton Edgar,' I clamped my stick underarm once more and shook the man's hand whether he liked it or not. 'Payton Edgar of the Claremont Dramatic Society?'

'Yes, yes, I remember. We met in the hallway,' he stated sharply, as if I did not know it. Although the man's words were pleasant enough his expression was one of troubled concern. A dark look indeed. The pink spots at his cheeks were the only dashes of colour about the man.

We exchanged a number of the usual pleasantries; the weather, the turnout, and then the tragedy of it all. It was as I grew weary of this that I decided that Payton Edgar of the Claremont Drama Society was a fairly brazen chap, the sort of chap a college Master should abhor. I spoke rather conspiratorially in Limestone's ear.

'Of course, you have heard that she was murdered?' I uttered in a half-whisper. His cheerless expression did not shift an inch.

'Evidently,' he groaned, 'but one elderly witness from across a fair-sized road is not the most reliable of sources.'

'One witness, is that all?' I replied with genuine interest. Limestone could turn out to be a good source of information, if I played my cards right.

'Please, tell me more?'

'Now is not the time or place!' Mr Limestone replied sharply.

I persevered, and with some success.

'Well, I suppose that you probably wouldn't be in the know anyhow, would you? Not being family.'

'Of course I know what's been going on! Something and nothing! Little old lady stood at her window watering a window box saw two people on the roof a minute or so before Helen jumped. Or was pushed, I suppose I should say. The poor dear can't say any more than that though, apparently, she didn't stay to watch what happened. Could've been anybody up there. May not even have been anybody, you know what the elderly can be like?'

'Well,' I replied, having some fun, 'they can be very well-placed, astute and watchful witnesses, I dare say.'

'Poppycock! My father thought he was a blacksmith near the end, and he'd never so much as sniffed a horseshoe in his life, so far as I know. All rubbish, if you ask me. Unlikely in the extreme, a murder. I know the family well.'

'Yes indeed, you have been lodging there for a while?'

It was a small question, gently asked, yet the man furrowed his brow and looked me in the eye for a good ten seconds.

'Have you ever been married, Mr Edgar?'

I paused. This was not information I was usually comfortable to give out.

'Once, yes' I replied truthfully, 'although I am divorced now, thankfully.'

He issued a short hoarse cackle and I realised that there was now something between us; a common understanding.

'There is nothing thankful about my divorce. One terrible mistake, and now I am paying the price for it. And the children have become some sort of bargaining tool, it seems. How about you? Did children get in your way too?'

I shook my head swiftly. He went on.

'It's like having a parasite fixed to one's side. I may be a leader in my field, but it is a far from prosperous one. She goes at me as if I don't need a penny to live on myself. Did that happen to you?'

'Can't say that it did, I'm afraid,' I replied, although my relationship with Rosemary post-divorce had been far from cordial. Much like our relationship pre-divorce, actually.

'Well, she's left me with nothing. Nothing!'

His simmering anger was threatening to bubble over, and once again I feared the crack of a cane or the snap of a belt. Limestone was glowering at me in a most unsettling manner.

'You said, Mr Limestone, that it doesn't seem likely to you, Mrs Capstick being pushed...'

He waved me off as if I were a flying pest.

'Oh, cease this silly talk immediately! Nobody would've wanted to kill Helen. You met the woman, you knew what she was like! Could be a bit bossy if she wanted, but she knew her own mind. Most unlike a woman, these days. It was impossible to say "no" to her. She did her fair share of manipulating, just like the others. Saw me as something of an unpaid taxi driver at times.'

'Really?'

'Indeed. The last time I saw her, on the morning of her death, she was flagging me down in my car and ordering me about. Who cares if I were busy – Helen needed a favour, and Helen got a favour. Still, she was never intolerably overbearing, like other women. Or rarely. Anyway, she had met her match in old Capstick. Tamed him well, she did!'

'You knew him before they were married?' I ventured.

'Oh yes, yes. Funnily enough, I knew them both, husband and sister, before I ever knew Helen. I am perhaps what you could call the common link. John's mother knew my mother, years back. She worked at my parents factory. Old John was a bit of a cad back then. And I knew Jenny French years before I really knew Helen, through teaching'.

'Miss French was a teacher?'

'Oh, yes, just for a while though. You know she works for the family business now? Much more suited to that, she is. Not cut out for the hard world of education, I think. Yes, I knew them both. But never as well as grew to know Helen. She livened up the kitchens, did Helen. She had spirit. Oh, she could be bothersome at times, but the woman had spirit. She was troubled, yes. She had her fair share of problems, and I of all people know how they can mount up and weigh you down...'

I wanted to ask what problems the dead woman had had, but could not word this easily enough without sounding too prying. Did Limestone know of the affair with Clay? Also, this was not the first time I had heard more about the dead woman's nature. Bossy and bothersome at times, was she? What could this mean?

I let the man continue.

'However, as little as I might really know about Jenny and John, neither of them are killers. No, all was happy in the house, more or less.'

This he said slowly and without conviction.

'A lot can happen behind closed doors,' I replied darkly.

'Maybe, but I still don't believe it. Any fool can see that this evidence of a second figure on the roof is not proof enough,' he stated, fingering the brim of his hat. 'But Scotland Yard have got a hold of it like a dog with a bone. They want it to be more than it really is.'

I watched the man for a moment in silence, and then took it on myself to reveal a little more tittle-tattle. I would get nowhere near the truth of this murder without a little risk.

'There is more evidence,' I said, returning to my half-whisper. If I could mention the Dear Margaret letter without revealing my involvement, it may spark something in the man. I looked all around me, as if fearful of eavesdroppers. This new man, the Payton Edgar of the Claremont drama society, was turning out to be quite the firebrand.

'More?' Limestone parroted with a raised eyebrow.

'Yes. An incriminating letter.'

'A letter?'

'That's right. A letter sent by her murderer!'

This gossiping, theatrical side to me was fun to play, I must say.

'And not only that,' I continued, 'Mrs Capstick was having an affair! An affair with a young man in her - our - theatre group.'

Limestone was watching me intently. He did not ask how I knew this information, but after some thought reacted in a most alarming manner. At first he gave a light laugh, a startlingly patronising laugh, and then fixed me with a stern gaze.

'Well I can give you one to strike off of the suspect list then. John couldn't possibly have had anything to do with any letter. The man's illiterate, literally cannot read or write! And quite proud of it, he is, when you challenge him, Lord knows why. A dying breed these days, of course. And Helen having an affair? Poppycock! I can't quite believe that, now, either. That just doesn't fit. Are you sure you've got the right sister? There's a lot about this that just isn't- '

'There is evidence,' I persevered, 'written evidence. A letter that lead to her death.'

His gaze was fixed on the chimneys of the houses opposite, his puckered mouth open. I found myself rambling just a little.

'A letter supposedly written by Helen. Queer really, isn't it? To think what could have driven her to do it.'

'What did you say?'

This was said sharply, as if I had stumbled during a recital. I repeated my words loosely.

'I thought that's what you said, yes. Mmm.' Limestone's brow was furrowed, and he looked more than a little rattled.

'A letter, you say?' he muttered. 'Are you quite sure?'

'Without a doubt!' I announced seriously. Limestone bit on his lip.

'But written by Helen, not her murderer. Dictated, perhaps? No. To get her up there! It can't be!'

And I had lost him to his thoughts. Something of importance had clearly occurred to the man. Suddenly he straightened and clasped my shoulder. The colour had drained from his face.

'Excuse me, Mr-?'

'Edgar!'

'Mr Edgar, yes. I suppose I should thank you for the, erm, the information. I need to take a stroll and...to think.'

And with that he turned and swept away between the gravestones of the churchyard. Had I said something of import? Would the man be rushing to the police with new information? I had too many questions, and not enough answers, I thought to myself with frustration.

And then something Limestone has said in passing registered a fresh curiosity within me, something he had asked when speaking of love affairs; "Are you sure you've got the right sister?"

Just what did the miserable old crony mean by that, I wonder?

CHAPTER 12

In which Payton Edgar comes to the rescue

Dear Margaret,

I am acting as my brother's best man at his wedding later this year, and I am petrified. I have been asked to make a speech to all the guests, and I suffer terribly from nerves. I break into a cold sweat just thinking about it, but it is so important to him that I do this. What can I do?

Stephen, Hammersmith

Margaret replies: this is a problem that I sympathise with, Stephen. Public speaking is indeed an unfavourable concept. All eyes on you, crowds of folk scrutinising your every word. Horrible! If you were to make a mistake you will never live it down, and you would be reminded of this for the rest of your life. I only have one piece of advice; boycott the event altogether and stay away until all the fuss has died down. It is only a wedding, after all.

It soon started spotting with rain and the funeral crowd took this as a cue to shuffle into the church. I moved along with the horde. On the way in I caught sight of Helen Capstick's father, standing grim-faced and austere in his suit, his face set not in an expression of mourning, but one of deep concentration.

He disappeared into the darkness of the church.

As I was nearing the doors I found myself being pulled back sharply and I came face to face with Jenny French once more. Her hair bobbed about her ears. The woman was clearly in a flap.

'Oh, Mr Edgar, I'm sorry to yank you about, but we have a crisis! I need your help!'

'Certainly,' I replied, perhaps a little prematurely.

'Poor Frank is beside himself, in bits he is. Poor lamb. He has written a piece, with a bit of help from me, for his mother. He was going to read it out today, but he can't stand up there in his state. He can barely speak! He gets these moods you see, and, well, you can't blame him for it today. And I thought of you!'

'I beg your pardon?'

'Well, you being part of the dramatic society, of course, and being used to public performance. And you've been so kind. We thought you might, well, get up there and read the eulogy for him. I know it is a big favour to ask, but it would be ever so much appreciated.'

I was trapped.

Public speaking? It was the worse idea I had ever heard. I have never ever been a public speaker, and can imagine very few things that I would like to do less. Crowds of strangers scrutinising my every word? Horrible! My mouth went dry at the very thought of it.

'I'm sure one of the other members of the group is happy to-' I began, at which point I was nudged in the ribs rather harshly by James Claremont's bony elbow. He was smirking openly.

'No, no, Mr Edgar, this one's for you. You go up and show us what you are made of,' he spoke into my ear with the air of a slithering snake, 'and consider it your audition piece.'

And so I found myself, not twenty minutes later, standing at the altar and delivering a eulogy for a complete stranger. It turns out that I am actually quite an impressive public speaker, although I suppose that one shouldn't really have been surprised at this. It was the document in my hands that I ended up having some difficulty over. I was well aware that this piece was the creation of a grieving child, and I am glad that I could be of help to the boy however reluctant I was, but it really was the most sickening and mawkish tripe I have ever had the misfortune to read. To read it aloud only made it even more cloying.

I could not help but stumble over some of the poorer grammatical errors as I ploughed on, my voice echoing from stone wall to stone wall above the sobs and sniffles.

At one point I lifted my head to catch sight of hairy old Inspector Standing at the back of the hall, his wide eyes fixed in my direction. I could not see his lips, but his moustache was certainly turned down into a bushy frown. I had recently confessed to the man that I was a mere stranger to the Capstick family, and yet here I stood, grieving before the congregation. The poor fool must have been wondering what on earth I was doing up there, and one couldn't blame him. If I had been given time I would have wondered what on earth I was doing, too.

And then another face in the congregation caught my eye; Thomas Limestone was also positioned near the back, his grey face as sombre as the expression it held. He was not looking my way, but up at the stained glass windows, his brow furrowed in thought. Once again I wondered just what I had said to put that look on his face.

Before long, figures were once again spilling out of the church, each person giving a little jolt or exclamation at the rain which had started up with considerable force. Umbrellas were thrust into the air all around me as I followed the throng. The Capstick family stood sheltered in one archway.

Despite my misgivings, the Capsticks seemed very pleased with my performance, yet the author of the piece, pale-faced young Frank, barely acknowledged my presence. The ungrateful tike! He kept his eyes out to the church yard and his lip curled in a grim sneer. Words were still beyond him. Catching sight of Inspector Standing edging through the crowd in my direction, I shrugged off John Capstick's thanks and made for a getaway.

Young Frank Capstick's stark lack of respect and gratitude had stoked a fire in my belly and I had come to a resolution. I would hot-foot it out of the churchyard leave the whole thing alone.

It was as I tromped down the wet and poorly paved pathway that I caught sight of a small dark figure in amongst the headstones at the far side of the graveyard. She had only cast her eyes once over her shoulder, but it was enough. I had spotted her, and I changed my direction accordingly. Using my stick to push aside the longer of the grasses in my way, I cursed myself for not bringing an umbrella.

Old Mrs Clay was not the fastest of movers, and so even I was able to catch up with her fairly speedily. She halted and turned around in the shelter of a chestnut tree.

'Oh, Mr Edgar!'

It was gratifying to see the relief on her face.

'I wondered who was coming after me for a minute!'

'Were you in the church, Mrs Clay?' I said, cutting to the chase somewhat.

She peered at me from under her transparent plastic head scarf, her eyes blinking.

'Only for a while, at the very back.'

Why had she come? Did she hope that her son would be stupid enough to attend the funeral? I did not dare to ask, and yet, she answered for me.

'I came for Richard. To represent him. Because he couldn't be here.'

So she hadn't come in hope that the boy would appear. She knew he wouldn't attend. I cleared my throat, and took the bull by the horns.

'Mrs Clay, I am sorry if I am speaking out of turn, but I think that you know where your son is,' I said gently and with false confidence. Her expression gave her away - she did indeed know where her son was. Yet she remained tight lipped.

I persevered.

'Mrs Clay, I believe that your son is innocent, but I do not have enough evidence to help him. Not yet. He may know some things that could help me. I must speak with him-'

'No.'

'-just for a few minutes, to see if I can help him. Please? I may be able to get him out of this. I may be able to help him. Please?'

I had reached out to her as I spoke and laid one hand against her arm in appeal, and now I let it drop. We stood for a minute in the shelter of the tree. The elderly woman looked up at me, and I dazzled her with my most sincere smile.

She nodded, slowly.

It was a fairly short taxi ride to the Clay residence and I didn't mind paying, given the circumstances. We set off in a calm, amiable silence.

We had no idea that we were being followed.

The house by Farringdon station was as drab in daylight as it had been on the night I had walked Mrs Clay home. I paid the cabby, who reeked of pear drops, and followed her inside. The décor in the hallway was dated and a little shabby, just as I had expected.

The house was surprisingly close to the railway line, and we had only been in there a matter of seconds before the thunder of a train rumbled through the tight space. To one unused to the sound like I, it was more than a little unnerving, as if a stampede of buffalo were careering around the building. The plates mounted on the wall shook alarmingly. Thankfully, the noise abated rapidly as the train disappeared. We removed our coats and shoes, after which Mrs Clay turned to me.

'Cup of tea?' she whispered automatically.

'I'd just like to see your son, thank you, Mrs Clay. Where is he?'

She didn't immediately answer my question, but stepped in a little closer to my side.

'He's been up there for days now. Almost two whole weeks! It's not good for him!'

For a fine-framed and elderly lady she managed the stairs considerably well. At the top, she gave a little call out to Richard, and after a few seconds a metal staircase clattered down from the loft. After raising her palm to me, indicating that I should wait, she rattled on up the steps. I waited as bid. There was a further minute or two before the murmuring of voices I had barely heard became more audible.

Finally a face appeared through the hatch. I gave my widest smile and a little wave.

Richard Clay was nothing like the man I had imagined. The stocky bully I had unwittingly planted in my mind following the fake letter from the dead woman was in fact a rather watery looking gentleman only a few years my junior. His hair was mousey and greying at the temples, his eyes wide and blue. Bookish would be the correct term, I believe.

Clay was not an unattractive man, though, as there was a certain intelligent studiousness about him that outshone his ordinary appearance. The contrast between this man and the stocky John Capstick was quite remarkable, and yet Helen Capstick had apparently loved them both.

Once his mother and I had convinced him of his safety, he allowed me up. Mrs Clay then scuttled away downstairs and we were able to talk openly. It was a sorry story.

He was a broken man, clearly devastated by the death of what he considered to be his one true love. The man had had no relations for over forty years of life before he had met Helen Capstick at the drama group, though he did not enlighten me any further as to why. He cried and cried as I sat like a lemon in my best funeral suit in amongst the dusty bits and pieces of his makeshift bedroom.

This wet specimen was clearly no murderer.

Clay lamented over his lost love in quite a theatrical manner, clutching a photograph to his chest. One could only assume this was a photo of Helen Capstick, for I didn't get to set eyes on it.

I was about to tell him about the letter to Margaret Blythe and to ask if he could spread any light on this when there was an almighty racket from below as fists were pounded upon the front door.

Richard Clay's jaw dropped, and within seconds we heard his mother pulling open the door and crying out in alarm. Heavy footsteps abounded as two officers bundled up the stairs and ordered us down in no uncertain terms.

Clay grabbed at my sleeve.

'You brought the police?' he spat.

'No - no, they must have followed me!' My sincerity was evident. Clay tugged once more at my sleeve.

'I didn't do it!' he gasped. A train rumbled by, practically shaking the cobwebs from their corners.

'I know,' I replied over the noise.

'I didn't!' he repeated rather unnecessarily.

He was pulling rather harshly at my cuff and for a moment I feared it would tear. Luckily for the fabric he pulled away as Inspector Standings hirsute visage poked through the hatchway, raindrops still dripping from his cap.

'Come down now, Clay,' he boomed, 'the game is up!'

Well! Who'd have thought that people really said such things in real life!

PART 2

CHAPTER 1
In which Payton lists his suspects

Dear Margaret,
My dog dislikes me. We have had him since he was a puppy, but
as he grows older he seems entirely indifferent to me and sometimes
snaps at me. He even tore a hole in my favourite raspberry trouser
suit. He is gentle and playful with my husband, but never with me.
What can I do?
Belly, Ealing

Margaret replies; what on earth do you think I am, a veterinary surgeon?
Judging by your irritating calligraphy, your foul scented notepaper and your penchant for
describing colours as fruit, I am not sure I like you either. One cannot blame the dog for
snapping.

The following morning found me complaining over tea with Irving at
Mario's cafe in town.

It was easily time for elevenses and so I treated myself to a macaroon
and cream, while Irving was happy just sipping his tea. Mario had
unenthusiastically turned the radio down after I had informed him that he
was playing it a tad on the loud side - yet again. The man had owned the
café for many years, and the bags under his eyes had slipped lower and
lower with time, as had his standards. Still, he knew exactly how I liked my
eggs.

It is an understatement to say that I was annoyed at the bullish way in
which Inspector Standing had hauled poor Clay away on the previous day.
He had had nothing to give but deaf ears towards my pleas and

100

explanations, and had merely turned to me at the door to his car and issued a stark rebuff, informing me in no uncertain terms to get away from his case. He had followed this with an unnecessary dig, rudely ordering me to get back to being "a lady of letters". A job which suited me well, he went on to cackle.

Needless to say, this latest act of discourtesy had only fuelled my fire. I was convinced that the police had arrested the wrong man, and I was going to prove it! Having remained with Clay's pale-faced mother for some time after they had left, I had promised to do all that I could to prove her son's innocence.

But what exactly could I do? What leads did I have?

Irving reluctantly agreed to go through with me what I knew so far, and the times in which he chipped in, though somewhat irritating, proved to be helpful all the same. There were a number of facts that I felt I could work with, and we listed them carefully.

Fact one; Helen Capstick had been <u>murdered</u>

I underlined this last word, to give some gravity to the detail.

Fact two; the murder took place in the same place as the drama society meetings
Fact three; Helen was having an affair with Richard Clay
Fact four; the murderer was probably somebody that Helen Capstick knew
Fact five; the letter to Margaret Blythe was most probably a fake

Irving and I had some disagreement over the final fact. I firmly believed that the letter to Margaret had been forged, yet my friend needed some convincing. Admittedly, I had scant evidence; much of my conviction was down to a hunch and nothing more. I have, however, never been one to ignore a hunch. That said, after talking with Clay I was even more certain that he was innocent of murder. The man had been distressed and desperate to clear his name.

I told Irving all about Clay's sad eyes, his sheltered life and of the first true love he had found, only for it to be shattered so cruelly. It was also, I informed him, the very first and very last time that I would ever enter such a dirty, grubby place as an attic. I sat for a moment and pondered on this out loud, and soon my thoughts swept to my glorious townhouse. Did I have an attic at home? I had never even thought about it! If I did, I vowed never to venture up there. Nasty, dirty, poky places!

Irving listened for a while, but soon tired of my story and requested that we talk in terms *"less flowery"*.

I was used to these odd, nonsensical requests of his.

Now that we had listed the facts to the bottom of our page, Irving then used his pencil to make a list of our suspects in a blank margin of the morning's Clarion.

"Richard Clay", he scribbled immediately at the top.

'I insist,' my friend said irritatingly, waggling his pencil at my furrowed brow.

"John Capstick".

'I really don't know about that,' I put in quickly, 'he seems terribly sure that his wife was murdered, and wanted to tell anyone and everyone about it. Why do that if he is the murderer?'

'A smoke screen?' said Irving with delight.

'A what?'

'It's always in mystery books, the murder always does the opposite of what you expect. Or is the least possible suspect. It's all there to confuse you.'

'Poppycock!'

Where had Irving gained this intimate knowledge of crime literature? The man had barely left his studio for years and so far as I knew the last book he had taken the time to read was probably one about Peter Rabbit, Squirrel Nutkin or some such vermin.

'So we're looking for the least possible suspect are we?' I caught sight of an elderly lady shuffling through the street outside in her rain mac and headscarf, a scruffy damp mutt following her obediently. I pointed her out. 'What about that old dear, then? Did she do it? Or her dog, perhaps?'

Irving just gazed at me, his stern expression unyielding.

'You know what I mean. So, it's not the husband, then?'

'I doubt it. I like John Capstick.'

'Oh, you like him, do you? So he couldn't possibly be the murderer, if you like the man!' muttered Irving rudely. 'I'm sure that Jack the Ripper was a pleasant, popular chap when he felt like it. Now, what reason could Capstick have had for killing his wife? Could he have known about Clay and his wife's affair? Jealousy? Money? People often murder for money. Could that be a motive?'

'Hear that one off of the wireless did you?' I said wryly, 'Anyhow, we are not here to list reasons, Irving-'

'Motives!'

'Reasons, motives - whatever. This is a list of suspects, and suspects only. On with it!'

"Jenny French", Irving wrote at my command.

'A nice lady, a bit scatty,' I said. 'Makes a good cup of tea.'

'But a suspect, nevertheless,' my companion reminded me. I nodded.

"Frank Capstick".

'The boy is a child!' I insisted. Irving was quick to reply.

'I thought that you said he was having driving lessons? Then if he's old enough to drive he's old enough to throttle his old Ma-'

'Nonsense!'

'Had he heard about his mother's affair with Richard Clay? Discoveries like that can do strange things to a child.'

'Well, perhaps, but-'

'He is a suspect and I'm putting him down,' said Irving in determination, and we moved on. The next name I was only too happy to have listed.

"Mr Limestone".

'Who?' Irving asked as he wrote.

'The lodger,' I said.

'What's he like?' my friend asked with genuine interest. I shrugged.

'A rancid scholar; the worst kind of educational bully. I'd put him at about our age, perhaps a smidgeon older. Bald, covered in chalk dust. Hah! Broken by divorce.'

'Money! See?' Irving exclaimed.

'How would murdering Helen Capstick get Limestone in the money?'

'Do you know the details of her Will? What will go to whom?'

I had to admit that I didn't. And I was not sure what I could do to find out. There can't have been that much money involved, could there? It was clear that Helen Capstick was comfortably off due to her upbringing but she was hardly an heiress.

'Is that all for the family?' asked Irving.

'Oh!' I exclaimed, remembering, 'if we are including everyone, then there is a father too. Helen's father is still alive, living nearby. You would probably recognise him actually, Irving. Funny fellow, stands around the corner of Leicester Square tube station usually, shouting the odds about the end of the world coming next Tuesday week and God living in your biscuit tin and all that twaddle'.

'Can't say I can place him,' said Irving.

'Mmm. You don't go in to town enough,' I replied, 'but still I think you'd know him if you saw him. Can't think of a motive for murder, though. Not sure about the man's sanity...'

'Could he have found out about the affair? Helen's affair? That's quite a sin in his book, I should imagine.'

'But enough of a sin to murder your daughter over? I think not.' I answered with a shake of the head. 'The man is not playing with a full deck that much is clear. Best put his name down anyway.'

'What is his name?'

'Just put Dad or Mr French or something,' I instructed, as Irving scribbled.

'So, outside of the family home?' Irving said with a sigh.

'Well, you've insisted on including Clay...'

'Yes,' Irving tapped his pencil lightly but irritatingly on the table top,

'And there must be others, persons known to Mrs Capstick. What about the theatre group?'

I shook my head in certainty.

'Too wet, too narcissistic and far too annoying, the lot of them.'

'That doesn't rule them out, Payton. I'm sure that wet and annoying people can be murderers as easily as the next person. And she fell from their rehearsal hall, didn't she? That must count for something.'

'Perhaps. However, it was a Wednesday and they don't meet on Wednesdays. But I suppose that you're right, there is a link.' I issued a sigh. 'They are a motley crew, altogether unremarkable. And yet, there's something fishy about the irksome director-'

'Right then, what's his name?' asked my friend.

'Claremont. James Claremont. Put him on the list then, because I don't like him. The worst kind of grumbling dandy, believe you-me!'

At this observation Irving smirked at some private thought that I chose to ignore. And so that was the end of our list that morning. I was convinced that somebody close to Mrs Capstick was the culprit, not one of the fair-weathered friends and distant relations who had attended the funeral. And it was most definitely not Richard Clay, whatever the constabulary thought. I was studying our list once more in satisfaction when Irving gave a grunt.

'Seems to me, though, that if you are really taking this seriously,' he began.

'I am. Yes.'

'Well,' he declared brazenly and with an exasperating finality, 'the husband did it.'

'I beg your pardon?'

'It seems pretty clear to me, the husband murdered his wife. It's always the husband. Say that he cottoned on to their affair, gets blinded by jealousy and then had it out with her on the rooftop and Bob's your uncle. Yes, that's what happened, all right. I'd bet my best palate on it!'

'And what drew you to this dazzling conclusion?' I dared to ask.

'It just seems the most obvious to me,' he shrugged. At this, I pounced.

'I thought you just said that it was always the least obvious suspect that did the murder?'

I had him there. He looked at me with barely concealed contempt.

'Whatever I may or may not have said I stick by this one. The husband did it.'

'Well, I'm sorry old chap but I disagree there. You haven't met Capstick. He is a big man, yes, but he has very soft eyes and a nice manner. If we are now into wild guesswork, as we seem to be, I would put my money on someone else entirely. What you just said about young Capstick, the boy. You were right, he is not a child. And he is sullen, that much is clear. Perhaps-'

'On what grounds?'

'Am I not allowed to plummet into amateurish conjecture too, Irving? I imagine that he was possibly the closest person to the dead woman, and the one set to suffer most on hearing of her affair. And he didn't thank me for reading his piece at the funeral, after all I had done! Most ungrateful.'

Now I had declared this particular theory out loud it actually sounded quite plausible, and I made a vow to focus my attentions on the shifty lad from then on.

'Does he have an alibi for the time of the murder?'

'An alibi?'

'Now, Payton, as well as considering the suspects and their motives, you should also be considering their opportunity; where were they when the murder occurred? This is the stuff of crime fiction! And it is text book detective work, Payton.'

The stuff of crime fiction? Irving was starting to annoy me a little and I felt heat rising inside of me.

'Since when have you known about the stuff of crime fiction, as you put it?'

Irving's eyes widened. 'I have been reading a few books recently. Getting my nose into whodunits a fair bit.'

Good lord! First the pipe, then the crosswords, and now my dear friend was even wasting his time on cheap suspense fiction. Nevertheless, as concerned over his malaise as I was, I was much more irritated by his newfound expertise on the subject. I fixed him with a glare.

'How am I to find out just where everyone was at the time of the murder, eh? I can barely go thrusting into each conversation rudely with a quick *"and where were you at the time of the death?"* can I? *"Oh, hello, so-and-so! Very nice funeral, and the flowers are lovely, but did you kill Helen Capstick?"* Is that what you want me to say? I am not ruddy Inspector Edgar of blinking Scotland Yard!'

Irving had done his best to ignore the entirety of my retort, and was packing his pencil and newspaper into his bag.

Involuntarily I clutched a fist to my burning chest.

'Been to the doctors yet, Payton?' asked my friend, archly.

'I have an appointment, thank you,' I lied. Irving zipped up his bag and sighed.

'I don't know why you are getting all hot under the collar about this dead woman anyway. You're going about it all wrong too. You haven't even examined the scene of crime, have you? For all you know there could be a bloody great wall around the roof meaning she could never have been pushed in the first place. Eh? Scene of crime is very important, Payton. They always return to the scene of the crime, murderers, did you know that? And the detective has to see the place to know what they are talking about. It's common sense. Anyhow, I still stick by my instinct, that the husband did it. Now I must go-'

'Where on earth are you off to? And why the big bag?' I asked. Aborting one of our meetings in this manner was all most irregular.

'I'm off to the swimming baths,' my friend replied. I drew back in shock. This was unheard of. Irving knew what I thought of the municipal baths. They were nothing more than a fetid soup of skin disease and spittle!

'The swimming baths? What the Dickens for?' I demanded.

I was treated to a sour look before Irving took off with a rather curt farewell, his bag slung over his back like a navvy, leaving me sitting alone and baffled. First crossword puzzles, that stinking pipe, rubbishy crime fiction and now the swimming baths? What next – the cinema? My mind boggled at the thought.

Where was the loveable, distracted bohemian friend I had once known?

And so I found myself bracing the bitter cold of a cloudy Thursday evening in late February standing on the flat roof of Onslow Hall, the grotty old construction where Claremont and his cronies met to dress up and pretend like infants for hours on end in the rooms below.

The building was Edwardian, unimaginative and extremely tired and neglected - where the plaster was not crumbling, the paint was peeling. The building may once have stood proud as sturdy chambers or a stately Council Offices but now it had been relegated to rot as a kind of village hall in the centre of London. The place stank of jumble sales and afternoon tea dances. Suffice to say, it was not my kind of place at all, and I felt sorry that it had been spared a bombing during the blitz while many other admirable structures around it had been completely obliterated.

I was not in the best of moods that evening.

Irving's suggestion that I should observe the scene of the crime, although not in itself a bad idea, had reaped little reward. The roof of the four-story building was square and clean with only one sizeable turret of chimneys rising from its hindmost quarters. There was no great wall to climb around the edges as my friend had suggested, in fact the ledge was shin-height and actually quite perilous. As I dared myself to peer downwards I could easily see how one might stumble and fall.

Looking around the square lit windows of the surrounding buildings I wondered in which building the witness had peered out of and seen that second figure on the roof. It would certainly be easy for a second person to burst from the stairwell, alarm an unsuspecting lone figure and push them to their deaths before retreating, all within practically a matter of seconds.

If they had indeed done the deed quickly, they had been unlucky that they had been spotted.

Most of the buildings around me were in darkness, but there were a small number of lights in those rooms which were not offices or storerooms. I could just see the turrets of the Victoria and Albert museum looming in the dark not far from where I stood. The traffic below was merely a light rumble, and there was very little wind.

I observed only one unexpected detail on the level of the roof. Someone had dragged an old wooden park bench up through the stairwell and placed it diagonally facing out over the south-facing ledge. I circled it thoughtfully. Around its feet were numerous cigarette butts and dead matches. Someone had made this their base.

Was that important?

It was too nippy to stay out and ponder on the roof for long, and I was soon heading down through stairway after stairway. I had taken the rusty caged lift upwards, but it had been a slow and uncomfortably juddery journey heavenwards and I did not wish to repeat the experience. I had just set my foot at the first floor when I encountered a familiar face.

'Mr Edgar!' James Claremont hissed, his expression one of wide-eyed surprise as he stood before me having climbed up the staircase from below. He was sporting a despicably loud green and yellow cravat.

'I have to admit,' he continued with some animation, 'that I didn't think you would come tonight. And yet here you are, large as life. The others are in the hall downstairs. There's only five of us today, but we do have some costumes to reveal so it should all be quite energetic. I'm just going to get the masking tape. Those devils from the Women's Institute have been peeling up our markings again.'

With horror I realised the time and the day. Thursday at six.

How I had missed this? This was the exact time I should be avoiding the place!

I had no intention of partaking in any kind of amateur dramatics, not that night, not ever. I bit my lip as Claremont twittered on.

'And do you know I thought for a minute that we were getting two new recruits here tonight! Helen's sister was here a while ago. You've not long missed her.'

'Jenny French was here?' I asked, distracted. 'Why?'

'Well I had her welcomed and cast - almost! Turns out she just wanted to see where-' he waved a limp hand in the air, 'to visit where it happened. Where Helen-'

'I see.' I put in, saving the man his words. So Jenny French had been sniffing around too. It seemed perhaps a little odd, and sent her a little higher on my list of suspects. What was it that Irving had said?

They always return to the scene of the crime.

It was just possible that I had been wrong about young Frank, and Miss French had offed her sibling. But why? I had no time to dwell any further on this. As Claremont made way to move around me I stepped in his path sharply.

'Listen, Claremont, I am not up for the drama group! What I mean to say is, that is not why I am here,' I blurted all this out while wondering myself what I would come out with next.

'No?' said Claremont archly.

'No. I won't be joining the group, unfortunately. I came to inform you that I have other arrangements. I have a sick aunt, whom I can't possibly leave in the evenings.'

'Indeed,' Claremont said without a hint of regret. 'And yet you're here now, aren't you?'

'I came to tell you in person,' I replied, 'I thought it only fair.'

Claremont gazed at me momentarily. His grey stare was not intended to be a pleasant one. I forced a smile against this evident frostiness, but the man did not break his stance.

'You had no intention of joining our society at all, did you, Mr Edgar?'

'I-'

'Well you didn't fool me! I could see the lack of commitment in your eyes from the very start. You, Mr Edgar, are the worst kind of thespian, you really are. What is it? Think you're too great for the likes of community theatre? Played in better places have you? Professionals like you make me sick. Best friends with Larry and John, are we? Well I can tell you the sweat and tears we put in to our work right here in community theatre fills more buckets than any professional theatre cast ever can. To be a true actor is to fight at the front line, to breathe the theatre in and out, as sure as the tide flows. To live it, with real people. We don't need your type, to be frank, Mr Edgar. Kindly leave!'

And with that he turned on his heel in the most melodramatic of ways and slithered away down the corridor. I was not perturbed. In fact, I had rather enjoyed the confrontation.

Smiling, I continued on my way down the stairs, content with my hunch that nobody in the ridiculous Claremont society had anything to do with the murder of Helen Capstick. Anybody mixed up in the theatre, community or otherwise, surely can't have the brains to carry out a complex crime such as this. The worst kind of thespian, was I? I cannot think of anyone less inclined to the theatre than I.

I like my literature printed on the page, not shouted at me by a man in silly trousers.

CHAPTER 2

In which Payton Edgar has a to-do in the middle of the night

Temple Bilborough
Proprietor, London Clarion,
Thistle House,
Fleet Street

Dear Mr Edgar,
Following our conversation last week I am delighted to confirm that we shall be keeping the 'Dear Margaret' page at around the page eight mark, and will have print space for 4-6 letters a week. Keep on doing what you're doing - top hole!
Yours sincerely,
Temple Bilborough

I have very rarely attended my General Practitioner for I am lucky enough to be in robust health, as a rule. Dr. Malik had only had the pleasure of seeing me once in his surgery within the past five years and that was to examine a protuberance of a personal nature which turned out to be nothing of concern and had soon dispersed of its own accord.

That said, the man greeted me on that Friday morning as if we were old friends as I entered the room and I felt at ease in explaining my symptoms. After a number of enquires on his part and a quick examination behind his screen, I sat awaiting the verdict.

His hands had mercifully been warm at the touch and yet this uncomfortable but necessary intimacy led me to nervously ask a few questions of him as he rinsed them at the sink.

Dr. Malik was of Indian origin but he had informed me without a hint of pride that he was able to speak over seven languages and dialects. Having lived for most of his adult life in London he has little difficulty in communicating in English, and certainly managed better with me that day than many Londoners that I can think of. He was a slight man who wore black rimmed glasses and a wide smile. The man was clearly a good clinician too.

He was, however, going to severely test my respect and liking for him over the next few minutes.

'Do you enjoy your food, Mr Edgar?' he asked.

I am a restaurant critic. Asking this question of me is like asking a fish if they like water or a bird if they like the clear blue sky. I told him as much, to which he nodded and jotted something or other in my notes.

'From the symptoms you describe, Mr Edgar, I believe you are certainly suffering from a case of pyrosis, or acid indigestion as it is more commonly known. This may be due to a more sinister underlying cause.'

Sinister? I hoped that his meaning had been lost in translation despite the man's professed multilingualism.

'Diet plays a big part in the irritation of the gastric lining, and I ask you to think about yours a little more carefully for the foreseeable future. Less citrus fruits and more vegetables. Reduce the amount of spicy food you eat - that kind of thing. However, it seems to me that the main cause of your symptoms is simply the stress of life. I would like you to avoid all stressful situations for the foreseeable future.'

Avoid all stressful situations?

Who on earth runs towards stressful situations with open arms? And how I was I to do this while living under the same roof as my Aunt Elizabeth? I shelved this advice on one of the dustier recesses in the back of my mind and asked if there was anything else I could do to stop the pain. He blathered on about gastric acids in unnecessary detail before declaring that what I probably had was a peptic ulcer. He then wrote out a prescription for some bicarbonate of sodium solution and asked to see me again in a few months to review my symptoms.

I left the surgery disliking the man considerably more than I had on entry, and did not make the requested appointment.

I had entered his practice with nothing but a nagging discomfort and what had I left with? A condition.

We had a to-do in the middle of the night on the following Sunday. I was awoken by the most dreadful caterwauling, high shrieks that pierced the still calm of the night. It sounded like the tortured souls of mutilated wraiths wailing at the gates of hell. I think that quite nicely sums it up.

I awoke, instantly petrified.

By the time I had slipped on my slippers and thrown on my dressing gown, the screaming had stopped, and I bustled out and down the corridor in a half-asleep panic. I failed to notice my aunt's door ajar as I moved on into my living room, where cushions and sheets of newspaper lay strewn around the floor. At my back door I heard a scuffle and turned just in time to see Lucille vanish through the cat flap in haste.

Leaving the mess on the floor I retraced my steps, beckoned on by whoops and cackles coming from my Aunt Elizabeth's room. As the door was open I did not knock and simply swung my head through the gap. Aunt Elizabeth was sitting up in bed, laughing in her rotten screeching throaty way.

'What..what?' was all I managed to stammer.

'Cat fight!' she cackled, 'Cat fight! Wasn't it something? A real cacophony of cats! Titty's under the bed. She had the upper hand, I'm sure, the little dynamo! You couldn't open up the window a crack, could you, Payton? Let the poor thing out. They can fight it out outside then. Where is your cowardly, fat hairy beast?'

I refused to reply, but did move over to slide up the window a little.

'A little more,' croaked Aunt Elizabeth, and I did as I was bid. Almost immediately the rancid skinny stray of hers leapt from under the bed, scrambled on the window sill for a moment and was gone into the darkness. Slamming down the window, I turned to my aunt.

'I don't want that cat in here again. Okay?'

It was her turn to ignore me, and instead she slid down her eye mask and shuffled lower in her bed.

'Close the door on your way out, Payton.'

Her grandfather clock struck twice as I did so. I stomped unhappily up my staircase only to encounter a fresh apparition at the top. Grace Kemp hovered over me like a pale-faced somnambulist, clutching a tissue to her chest, her hairnet firmly in place. The young woman looked like the wakened dead.

'What happened?' she asked quietly.

'Aunt Elizabeth's stupid moggy attacked my dear Lucille, that's all. It was just a cat fight, go back to bed.'

I trudged on past, all too aware that I would find it near impossible to get back to sleep after such a disturbance. It was only as I settled fussily in under my sheets that I stopped and appreciated what I had just seen. The dark rings around the girl's eyes and the sore redness within.

Grace Kemp had been crying in her room.

CHAPTER 3

In which Payton Edgar rails indignantly against the jigsaw

Dear Margaret,
I suffer with dreadful acne. I had it all the way through school and hoped that it would clear, but now I have been in a job for a few years and it only seems to be getting worse. I feel terrible and daren't go out with my friends to all the best places. What can I do?
Claire, Stoke Newington

Margaret replies; I am not a medical doctor, and if I were I would simply say *buck up your ideas and stop fretting over a couple of pimples. Some people have to suffer amputations and cancers of all kinds, and yet they don't all come moaning to me, so why should you?*

Monday morning and yet again it was time for me to collect the mail.

There were only nine letters this time, a slight reduction on previous weeks, but I reminded myself that this was far more than the one or two that used to dribble on in when the feature was ran by Peggy and her softly-softly rubbish.

Unusually, Cockney Guy was not at his desk that morning. I had hoped to garner the latest from the man about our plan to rail against his domineering spouse. Instead I was greeted huffily by a bored looking and somewhat grubby young man. The sorry specimen before me was surely a college student filling in time for some easy money. He didn't question why I asked for mail in a number of names and handed the letters over with little care. However, when I questioned him about Guy's absence, he awoke a little and issued a cheeky laugh.

'The bloke who's usually here, you mean? Turns out his wife has had a fling with a butcher apparently, some friend of his he kept bringing over to the house. Goes to show, you can't trust women, eh? Or your friends, for that matter. One of the porters was telling me she's kicked him out. Poor bloke was in a right state, apparently. Came in here half-cut, he did, and Billy sent him on his way. There was a bit of a kerfuffle, apparently. Poor bloke's lost his wife, his friend, his house and his job now. Some people have all the luck, eh?'

'Mmm,' I murmured before moving on hurriedly.

Guy had clearly left out some key details in his story, his wife's potential for wanton behaviour being high on the list. He should have seen this coming. The blame for this turn of events could not be laid at my door.

I was soon holed up in my office.

My postbag that morning was certainly mixed, with the usual unprintable rubbish, and a number of so-so problems that I would bother to answer should I need to fill space on the page. One of these, much to my dismay, was from a woman complaining that her husband refused to let her wear short sleeves in the summertime. Just what was wrong with the women of London? I thought to myself. Had the suffragettes worked so hard for nothing?

It was the drippy hat-wearers letter all over again, and not worthy of a reply.

Into the bin it went.

I placed five letters to one side on what had become my "reserve" pile for potential future use. Three letters went aside my typewriter for tackling in the current column, and one letter, which referred directly to an unwanted pregnancy, went straight in my waste paper basket.

For much of that morning I beavered away in Honoria Bett's little office quite happily, once again being visited by an inquisitive pigeon on the window sill outside.

However, this was not dear old unruffled Fitzherbert, but another pigeon. Where Fitzherbert had stood proud and full-breasted, this thing was stooped and unkempt. A dirty pigeon. A vile, raggedy, dirty pigeon. I did my best to ignore him.

I should, perhaps, have needed nature's warning. The diseased thing was surely a portent of doom.

It was almost lunchtime when a melodic knocking from Beryl Baxter tore me from my desk and into the hustle and bustle of her office once again. She began by whipping out the cheap scotch whisky without comment and presenting me with a question.

'Payton, I require your opinion. Have a look at those two photos on the side there and tell me what you think. Which shall we use this Friday?'

I cast my eyes down to see two snapshots of the same couple taken on seemingly different nights. The man was good looking in a smooth sense but otherwise unremarkable in a dark dinner jacket. The young thing on his arm carried the simple elegance of youth but in one photo wore a rather ghastly shiny gown that had caught the camera flash a little off, making her appear to have grown an extra arm. The gown also billowed out in a most unattractive manner at the shoulders.

'Who are they?' I enquired.

'I was waiting for that' Beryl replied drily. 'He is a television announcer with the B.B.C., so well-known that I'd have thought even you would have heard of him. His father is an archdeacon, of all things. She is a nobody, a rich-daddy type. The question, Payton, was which photo shall we use?'

I studied the pictures for a moment more.

'The shiny dress with the shoulders is appalling,' I stated, 'makes her look like a pantomime dame.'

Beryl joined me at my side and slid a drink into my hands.

'Yes, I can see that. Funny - that's a De Groot dress, you know. Yes, we'll use that one,' she snatched up the picture and thrust it out of the door, where an unseen hand tore it from her grip.

'Anita! Use this one!'

'But the girl looks worse!' I protested.

'Quite,' Beryl replied, a wry look on her face. 'That sly young kitten is stepping out with a married man, Payton. Wife and kids at home, you know. We don't want her to look good.'

'Quite a scoop,' I muttered.

'A scoop? A scoop? We can't actually say anything about the whole blasted affair, or there'd be hell to pay. No, Payton, in my business you soon master the art of implication. It will have to be a "so-and-so with friend", type piece. Those in the know will understand what we mean. We can't be seen to be criticising the very people who give us business, darling.'

'Of course not,' I replied, a little bored.

My colleague took a swig of her drink and proceeded by enquiring about my houseguest.

'So you have had it out with her, I take it? Does she deny it?'

I told her all about young Grace's weary response, and of her mysterious sadness.

'Talk to the girl,' advised Beryl in an uncharacteristically motherly tone, 'she must have had a pretty rotten ride, having mad old De Groot for a mother. Poor little Pim. Talking of which, it is the Fashionista this weekend.'

'The fashion—what?'

Beryl Baxter set down her glass with a thump.

'Payton Edgar, you never cease to astound me! How long have you lived in our capital? Please tell me you know about what is probably the most important event in my calendar, the De Groot Fashionista?'

'No,' I confirmed, a little irked by her outburst.

'You simply must know about it!' she exclaimed in disbelief, glaring provokingly.

'Well I don't Beryl. We all have our own areas of expertise you know!'

'Even so, I would have thought-'

'Tell me, Beryl,' I raised my tone. 'What do you know about brining meat?'

This was the first thing that came into my head, but it made my point.

'What has that got to do with it?'

'You tell me about the fashion-wotsit, and one day I'll tell you about the process of brining, alright?'

Beryl took this in good grace.

'The Fashionista, Payton my darling, is the best...well perhaps not the very best, but certainly the most swinging fashion show in my diary. It's the boss, it really is. It's been going for years now, every first Saturday in March. The word fabulous doesn't even begin to cover it. This Saturday night the Mayvere will be crammed with anyone who matters, believe me. And in the fashion world, it marks the launch of the summer season. Now, where is that thing?' She was poking through her top drawer, and then pulled out a pamphlet and handed it over.

The name De Groot was printed in far larger letters than the name of the event, and inside were sketchy images of pencil skirts and models in unusual beachwear. It was indeed at the magnificent Mayvere Hotel, Park Lane. A list of designers was on the back, with De Groot first and foremost. And then another name caught my eye, albeit in much, much smaller print towards the bottom.

Capstick's Catering.

I said the name aloud.

'Oh yes, they do the Fashionista bash every year, Capstick's. Not bad. We had them for our Christmas buffet the other year, do you remember?'

I would never have graced a workplace Christmas buffet with my presence, and told Beryl as much. If pushed, I would perhaps attend a sit-down meal with my colleagues, and even then only under considerable pressure. One cannot bear the indignity of eating from a buffet - akin to cattle eating from a trough.

But here was fate's finger, pushing the Capsticks towards me once more. If I could just get alone with Miss French, there was the chance I could get more evidence to prove Irving wrong about Capstick.

'I have to go to that function! How much are the tickets?' I stated seriously, at which my friend sniggered.

'Darling! Why do you care about fashion all of a sudden?'

'How much are the tickets?' I repeated resolutely, wondering to myself if money would be no object in my pursuit for truth.

'Hundreds, darling!' laughed Beryl.

'Beg pardon?'

'What I mean is that you won't get one, not now, it'll have been long sold out. Talk about gold dust. I don't think even a plague of diseased locusts descending upon the city would stop some people from going!'

'But you are going?' I persevered, feeling a familiar burning frustration in my chest.

'Of course, but I get my ticket well in advance, darling. I'll be reserving next year's ticket just after this one is over, believe me. It's the only way to get in-' She stopped short. Clearly something had dawned on her.

'Unless.'

'Unless?'

'Unless you know a De Groot, that is,' Beryl exclaimed with an arched eyebrow.

It took me a minute, but I got her meaning. She was nodding furiously.

'Yes, they'd never turn away Pim De Groot at the door, believe me. Oh, go on, Payton, it would make my night! That's what you have to do. Get the girl to take you!'

I reached in my pocket for the bottle of sodium bicarbonate. The most appropriate turn of phrase in such cases would be "easier said than done."

When I got back to Clarendon Street late that afternoon I had hatched no plans to entice Grace Kemp to take me to the Fashionista. Impossibilities such as this take time. It was with this in mind that I rapped on Irving's door.

It was not that I was seeking his wisdom as such, more seeking a forum in which to muse over my options. As it happened, we didn't even begin to discuss my dilemma, for I was to receive a shock inside the house that cast all such thoughts from my mind. Irving appeared a little distracted as he opened the door, and I followed him through to his living room where, to my horror, spread across the table was two thirds of a completed jigsaw puzzle.

A jigsaw puzzle!

My friend said very little and simply sat himself back at the table and began ruminating over the pieces. The picture, Van Gogh's Sunflowers, was near completion. Seeing the man like this simply broke my heart – the are no other words for it. Gone was the ambivalent but passionate artist, the bohemian intellectual I had grown to respect, and here in his place was a sad little man mindlessly and methodologically completing a jigsaw of five thousand pieces! I should have put my foot down at the crossword puzzle,

I thought to myself in remorse. But now, after the trip to the swimming baths as well, something had to be done.

This shock made up my mind -I had to act, to bring back the Irving I once knew.

I grasped the man's arm.

'Irving,' I said, 'I am going to do something now that will upset you, but it is for your own good.'

And with that, I swept my hand across the table top and sent each piece of the wretched jigsaw ricocheting onto the carpet. My friend sat staring at the now bare table top where his work had been, too stunned to respond. His eyes followed down to where pieces of the Van Gogh lay scattered on the floor. I clamped a firm hand on his shoulder and slammed the other down with a thump on the now empty surface.

'I have a plan for you, far better than wasting your time on silly puzzles. I can't sit by and watch a great artist like you stew in his own juices like this any longer. A lost soul needs you, Irving. And we need to awaken the artist within! I have had a letter, and I need your help...'

This blatant lie passed my lips with surprising ease. I was becoming a very, very good liar.

'I have received a plea for help, and a commission for you. I won't take no for an answer...'

Once I was outside Irving's house I mulled over my latest subterfuge. A plot formed in my mind; a plot to squeeze the artistic juices back out of my friend. I would need a stooge, and what better than a vulnerable old lady? One sad, wrinkled old face came immediately to mind. I had to get to Mrs Clay and throw myself at her mercy, beg her for a favour. I was sure that the timorous old thing wouldn't dare to decline my request.

I headed home with a renewed vigour.

I had not trusted Irving not to gather up the jigsaw and start the pointless exercise all over again in my absence, and so I had made a point of taking two random pieces away with me, raising each into the air pointedly before sliding them into my jacket pocket. He had watched me leave from the window with an air of dejection, yet I walked on.

That evening I would sit down at my typewriter to do the one thing I had told myself I would never do. I would pen a letter to myself. To my other self.

"Dear Margaret," my letter would begin...

CHAPTER 4

In which Payton Edgar braves the leftover stew

Dear Margaret,
I am hampered by old age and the feeling that I have done nothing in my life. I have no legacy to pass on, no wise teachings to leave behind of me. I feel entirely alone, even though I live in the city. My husband is dead. I have a son, but he is troublesome to say the least. I feel like everything I have worked for has gone, and that I have made no impact on life whatsoever. I have always been frightened that I will die alone and be forgotten, and now that appears to be just what will happen.
Mrs C, Farringdon

Margaret replies; it is natural for us to look for validation in life, and to seek some sort of ratification for all that we have done. I think that your inkling to leave the world a piece of yourself is not unnatural. You must scratch that itch; it is never too late to be immortalised! I have arranged for you to have your portrait painted by one of the most renowned artists London has seen in recent years. It may be a small step to give you what you need, but I believe that it will help. If you take me up on my offer, you will be forever displayed for all to admire and to appreciate for generations to come.

I solved yet another problem before I even took off my hat at my door that evening.

Just a few doors down from Irving's place, my beautiful Lucille sat on a wall looking at me pointedly through the slits of her eyes as I approached. Unusually, she allowed me to pet her a little.

'What's up, puss?' I uttered idly. She glared up at me frostily. I knew that if the cat could speak, she would be complaining about the invasion of her space by Aunt Elisabeth's evil new moggy. As it was, Lucille's cold accusing gaze was enough. But what could I do? My aunt was a force to be reckoned with over the silliest of things, and I knew that she would never relent over her hateful new mouser.

Lucille cooled off before I did, disappearing into one of her secret pathways behind the wall. What could I do?

By the time I had reached my door, however, I had the answer. It was painfully obvious. Titty wasn't my aunt's cat but a stray or neglected pet from the neighbourhood. Aunt Elizabeth had said that she came in through her window. She didn't use Lucille's cat flap, of that I was certain; Lucille wouldn't have allowed it. Besides, I made sure that the door to my aunt's room stood closed at all times, and so the moggy's only way in would be that window.

What if I could put a stop to that?

I slid on past my doorway and doubled on back around to the backyards of Clarendon Street. I had to use my stick to beat aside a number of weeds growing skywards in between the cracks in the old cobbles out the back. My aunt's window was set fairly high on the wall, overlooking a small dead-end alleyway that reached around the side of my building. Darkness had fallen quickly, but I did not let this deter me. I hooked my umbrella over my forearm and surveyed the scene. An old rain barrel was fixed in one corner and beneath it lay a stack of rotting planks. Heaven knows how long they had been there.

It was clear that, after stepping on the planks, jumping up to the barrel and across to the flaking windowsill of my aunt's room, any savvy cat would find it easy to invade the house through the open window. Thankfully that evening was considerably parky and the window was closed. This meant that my aunt did not hear anything as I pulled back three of the planks, easily obliterating the first step of Titty's pathway. Just to be on the safe side, I pushed my weight against the rain barrel, which was thankfully under half-filled and sat on moist ground, for it moved with fair ease to rest good foot or two away from the window.

I stood back and cast my eyes over my handiwork. No cat, no matter how agile, could get themselves up to my aunt's high window now. I had banished an unwanted intruder. Lucille would be proud of me.

Another problem solved.

'There's some leftover stew in the pot if you want it, Mr Edgar.'

These words sent a wave of revulsion creeping through my body. Grace Kemp had issued the comment from over a steaming cup of something brown she had just made in my kitchenette at the back of the house. She delivered me a tight-lipped smile and settled down onto my chez-lounge with one of her picture magazines. I steadied myself, plopped my stick into my bronze lattice umbrella stand, hung up the jacket I had just removed on my deer-antler coat hanger by the door and took in a deep breath.

It was no use trying, I simply could not fight my irritation.

'Must you consistently taunt and ridicule me by offering me leftovers, Miss Kemp?' I stated grimly. She did not lift her eyes from the page of her magazine.

'I don't know what planet you come from, Mr Edgar, but on this planet, planet Earth, that kind of gesture is what we call a friendly one.'

'Must you refer to the meal as leftovers? Could you please simply say "there is some home-cooked stew available" or some such thing? To offer Payton Edgar, a respected restaurant and food critic leftovers-'

'Alright then! There is some home-cooked stew in the pot if you want it, Mr Edgar. Is that better?'

I had my fists clenched but forced myself to back down. I would have to make sacrifices if I were to get closer to the girl.

'Home-cooked stew? That sounds delightful,' I replied having summoned up the will, 'are you sure?'

'Of course,' she muttered, 'it'll only get thrown away. I have to chop the veg up small because of your aunt's teeth of course, but it's nice enough.'

This was information I could have done without.

However, within a quarter of an hour I found myself seated at the basement kitchen table with a steaming bowl of stew before me. I had eked out one of the two remaining dumplings and cut off a hearty slab of bread as well, and I was loathed to admit that the whole meal wasn't bad at all. The stew had a meaty richness that ran throughout the dish without overpowering the whole thing and the dumpling was one of the best I have ever tasted, not too floury and beautifully seasoned.

Grace Kemp, it seemed, had another string to her bow. Perhaps I would eat at home more often from now on. As I ate, I mulled over just how I could get her to take me to her mother's ridiculous fashion show in order to get some more information on Miss French.

To my surprise, it was Grace herself who initiated conversation that night. It was as I was rather improperly mopping up the last of the stew with my bread that she padded down the steps into the kitchen, two hot steaming cups held out before her.

'I have brought you a tea, if you'd like it?'

And now I was suspicious.

She even retrieved my dirty plate, switched it for the drink and took the plate over to the sink. I watched her suspiciously as she placed herself with an air of caution at the table opposite me.

'Mr Spence came to see me today,' was all she said at first, but it was enough.

So, Irving had paid a visit and had surely gone out of this way to ease the friction between the young woman and I. I supposed that I hadn't given him a chance to tell me earlier, so enraged was I over his jigsaw-puzzling. Perhaps I should have been infuriated that Irving had taken this on himself, but the fact remained that he had done me a great favour if he had succeeded in softening her up.

Miss Kemp sat before me with an amiable smile. It seemed that Irving had worked wonders. She sipped at her drink before continuing.

'He is a good friend to you that much was clear. We had a nice chat, a very pleasant afternoon...'

'I'm glad to hear it,' I said, 'Irving is a very good friend indeed.'

'He seems to understand people,' said Miss Kemp.

As do I. My comprehension of human behaviour is second to none. My superior understanding of human nature must have rubbed off on my friend.

'And he is a terrific listener,' she continued.

A skill Irving had clearly learned from me.

'Although I have to say he was a little suborn.'

That trait was entirely his own.

'He said some very nice things about you,' Miss Kemp continued with ease.

'And he is a very good judge of character,' I was quick to chip in. She went on.

'He made me think that perhaps I have read you wrong. I've never been good with first impressions. Now, I have got to know your aunt a little better now, I know her ways, her tricks-'

'Yes?'

'I know what you're thinking, but I am not going to say that she is the ogre you think she is. Have you tried getting to know her? To spend some time with her?'

What had started as an unusually amicable conversation had soon veered back into familiar territory, much to my displeasure. Miss Kemp must have felt this too, for she relaxed her shoulders and bowed her head before shocking me with an apology,

'I'm sorry, Mr Edgar. It is just a little frustrating to see the good in both of you that neither will see in each other.'

'I try, Miss Kemp. I have always tried. Again and again and again.' I looked into Miss Kemp's eyes. They were firm but kindly, with a face that one could only admire.

'You are very good with her,' I uttered, truthfully. 'I think you are the only person she has ever had a good word for. I don't know how you do it.' Miss Kemp bit her lip and then a smile crept over that perfect face of hers.

'Let me tell you a story, Mr Edgar. One of my very best friends, years ago, had been a nursemaid to an elderly lady. She was our scullery maid, but said she always missed the old dear after she was gone. And she told me the secret, Mr Edgar. The secret of good nursing.'

Miss Kemp leaned in to the table.

'Each Friday was washday, and Agnes - that was my friend's name - would lug the bags of dirty washing down to the laundrette on the corner. Now although this old lady she did for was poor, she was also extremely proud, and always insisted that Agnes tape a linen dishcloth over the front of the washing machine, to ensure that nobody could see her smalls as they rinsed in the drum, you see?'

Well, each washday the old dear would remind her to do this, and when she returned Agnes would always say she had, of course, done just as she wished and covered the drum with a dishcloth. But she never had. Agnes didn't want to waste good tape, and said that when the washing was going you couldn't tell pants from sheets. But the point is, the old dear was reassured. And that is the secret to good nursing....'

'What?' I scoffed, 'Telling lies to old ladies?"

'The application of the mind, Mr Edgar. No matter what you think, no matter what ridiculousness your patient insists upon, you listen with respect and reassure. That is the secret.'

'I see.'

I said this with some hesitation, for I didn't "see" at all. What was she telling me - that all good nurses are pathological liars and to be mistrusted? I cleared my throat.

'May I change the subject?' I enquired softly, 'I have a situation that I need to discuss. I am in a tricky position.'

My desire was to make her see how much I needed to get to the fashion do, and the only way to achieve that was surely to get her on side. And so, over steaming mugs of tea I told her all about the death of Helen Capstick, of my work on Honoria Betts's agony column and of my belief that a murder had taken place. I told her every detail, including my need to find out more about the family, not to mention my prime suspect - the dreadful ingrate – young Frank Capstick.

Miss Kemp listened with a blank face, and once I had finished took a moment to digest what I had told her. Then she leaned forwards and spoke with a very straight face.

'So you are telling me, Mr Edgar, that you-' she licked her lips, '-that you are in fact Dr Margaret Blythe?'

At this her face crumpled into barely suppressed laughter. I set down my drink loudly.

'That is hardly the main focus of my story, my dear. And it is something that my Aunt Elizabeth must never ever find out about, alright? Are we agreed?'

'We are agreed,' she replied, still grinning. 'Your aunt would just-'

'I know. So she must never find out. Now, this is a very serious situation.'

The bemused creases at the corner of her eyes did not leave her face for some time, despite my best efforts.

'Besides,' I continued, 'it is nothing to be ashamed of. I have spent the past two months helping people, solving their problems, and it has been a most rewarding experience. Now, I took on that job in good faith and have been the victim of a particularly nasty fraud, not to mention that I believe a grave miscarriage of justice is occurring in which an innocent man will suffer greatly. A young mother has been murdered! And it seems that only I have the perception and the savoir-faire to acknowledge all of this. I need to continue my discreet investigations, Miss Kemp, and to do that I need your help.'

'My help?' she asked swiftly and with some surprise.

Had I played my card too quickly?

'That is, if you would see your way to helping me. But you need to understand the seriousness of my situation. My request is not an insignificant one, I know.'

Grace Kemp looked back at me with a familiar distain.

'Mr Edgar, why must you say a hundred words when only a few are necessary? It is like talking to a court jester, speaking in riddles. A girl needs a compass, a map and a dictionary to get through a conversation with you!'

Needless to say, this comment angered me considerably. I felt that familiar fire blazing in the pit of my stomach. I composed myself as best I could.

'I am a wordsmith, Miss Kemp. It is my trade, it is who I am.'

'Oh yeah?' she chuckled, 'well you don't get paid by the letter when you are talking to me. Keep it simple, and I might think about helping you. What is it you need me to do?'

Keep it simple, she had said.

'I need you to get me into the Fashionista next week.'

I barely had time to draw breath.

'No chance!'

'Miss Kemp, I know that you are the daughter of the organiser, and I have to get in-'

'Why?' she spat back with a force that stunned me to silence. She continued with only a slightly lighter tone. 'To check up on this catering family? Why can't you simply ring their doorbell and have a chat?'

'My dear, until the other week I was practically a total stranger to them and I have already appeared at their house once, unannounced, never mind attending a family funeral in which I delivered a eulogy. What do you suggest I do next? Dress up as the chimney sweep? Put on a frock and claim to be a long lost auntie? This bash is a perfect opportunity for me to innocently bump into them once more, and to observe them in their natural working habitat.'

She inspected her fingernails for a moment, clearly deep in thought. I reached out a pleading hand and rested it on the table top between us. It was to sit there for longer than I had anticipated.

I persisted.

'There is another aspect to this, one that I think may help you.'

'How can going there possibly help me?' she snapped.

'Your mother. I have heard how hard it has been for you. How you need to rebel-'

'You don't know anything!'

'-but what is the point of rebelling if she is unaware of it? Think about it. At the moment, she is none the wiser, happily going about her jewel-encrusted business. What if she were to see how her daughter was living? In a box room. And what was she doing? Scrubbing, sluicing and preparing shepherd's pie for an old lady. What would she say to that? Wouldn't you like to know? And I would be with you, all the way. To be honest, I'd love to meet the woman-'

'Oh yes?' Grace was quick to chip in. 'A fan of hers, are you?'

'Quite the opposite,' I said, 'she sounds ghastly.'

'She is.'

'Then show me,' I answered, lifting my hand up a little. 'And help me out, too. Please?'

She watched me and my best pleading expression for a minute before speaking. When she did, she was calmer, almost meek.

'Do you know why I chose the name Grace? All my life I've been called Pim by Mother. I hated it. I was christened Marianne, but Mother always liked Pim. It's a Swedish thing. And she knew I loathed it. It was Pim-Pim-Pim all the time. So when I managed to escape her and to become whoever I wanted to be I chose Grace. And do you know why?' she asked, without waiting for an answer.

'Grace Kelly.'

The name was unfamiliar, but I remained tight lipped as she carried on.

'I'll always look up to her. Such style, such poise. That is who I wanted to be. Did you see The Swan?'

There was nothing else for it but to shake my head. Was this ballet?

'She was so elegant in that picture, and I understood her at once. Like a swan on water, and a goose on the land. That's how I felt, you see. And I often think to myself what would Grace do?'

'And?' I said softly, 'What would Grace do?'

There was a moment's pause, and then Miss Kemp smiled a beautiful, genuine smile. My heart leapt.

'Never turn down an invitation to a party,' she replied slyly.

CHAPTER 5

In which Dr. Margaret Blythe attends a function

Dear Margaret,
I find it so difficult to make friends. I am only twenty-three, and yet I find it very hard to keep on top of the latest fashions. Everyone seems to have so much fun except for me. I live with my Mother, who encourages me to go out and meet young men, but I am never asked. What can I do?
Penny, Hounslow

Margaret replies; Your letter made me very sad indeed. I picture a girl who is a little wider around the middle then she would like to be. Am I right? Pig tails and an oily complexion? Am I right? My dear girl, the first lesson you must learn in life is that you cannot be someone who you are not. A thoroughbred is a thoroughbred and a mongrel is a mongrel. Remember how birds of a feather move – sooner or later a similarly unfortunate soul will fly your way.

Miss Kemp wouldn't dress up for the Fashionista, and I couldn't blame her.

It was quite true that I was using the girl to get where I wanted to be, and that she had no desire to attend the bash. The last thing she wanted to do that evening was to sparkle and draw attention to herself. Dear Irving has very little time or taste for haute couture, but even he looked on in surprise as Grace Kemp stepped first into the taxi in her plain little black dress and jacket. She had chosen not to adorn herself with accessories in any way, as if she were attending a funeral instead of a party. Still, she carried the look with her own natural style.

I, on the other hand, had worn a brand spanking new navy three-piece especially for the occasion, with a sky blue shirt underneath and an attractive cobalt blue silk pocket square peeking tastefully from my top pocket, folded in a reverse puff. My friend had fingered my lapel momentarily and said a few words of approval before slamming the door to the taxi. He then leant in to the window and mouthed one short sentence at me.

'Remember, the husband did it! Keep an eye on the husband!' He grinned and proffered us a royal wave through the window.

'What was that about?' Miss Kemp had asked as we drew out.

'Guesswork,' I replied, 'amateurish guesswork.'

As I had predicted, the Fashionista was the worst kind of pretentious function jam-packed with the worst kind of pretentious moneyed rabble.

The Mayvere ballroom looked more garish than I could have believed possible, striving to achieve something resembling the exotic, oriental sophistication of the nineteen-twenties, but actually hitting the mark nearer "The Show Bar" at Butlins, Bognor Regis. If I never had to see another fake Roman column or golden palm leaf in my life I would have been quite happy after this experience.

At the far end of the hall sat a large orchestra belting out a fox trot with considerable gusto. Across the far left of the dance floor, a long raised platform had been erected upon which stood a number of pretty young things in oddly flouncy frocks. I was to learn more about the nature of fashion according Olga De Groot that evening, the sum of which seemed to be that it was suddenly fashionable to be short sighted and to sport bizarre glasses with coloured rims and curly corners. It was also considered stylish to think nothing of adorning a hat akin to a fruit basket on one's head.

Perhaps it was of benefit to be visually impaired so one did not dwell on the unsightly details of one's accessories.

The dresses themselves were no better, some of which were cut just above the knee and most inappropriate for any normal respectable young woman to wear. I dreaded to think of the prices.

I entered the hall in in the glow of self-congratulation, for I had been exceedingly cunning in getting us into the place.

Having asked my escort to wait aside the bay trees on the pavement out front, I had swept into the building and with an air of insolent buoyancy announced to the doorman that young Miss De Groot was present, but that she insisted there be no fuss or fanfare on her arrival.

I flattered the man with what Irving would refer to as a "crispy handshake" and a telling nod, to which he pocketed the note, brushed up his jacket at the name and, with eyes cast downwards, ushered us both down the hallway, through the cloakroom and finally out into the ballroom with the noiseless haste you would offer to an imperial visitant.

To my delight, Beryl Baxter was one of the first familiar faces that cruised out towards us from the glittering crowd gathered at the reception area. I suspect that she had been lying in wait for us. Beryl looked resplendent in a purple sequin net evening gown that was halter neck and rather daring, given her advanced years. She covered a tanned and wrinkled sternum with a fine rhinestone necklace, and the wig of the evening was a brunette affair, swept back from the forehead and fastened at the rear with what looked like tiny chopsticks.

This was a look which suited her well, despite the questionable addition of what resembled a dressing-up-box tiara pushed down within the synthetic hairpiece and a pair of over-long cloth gloves that resembled purple Marigolds.

She greeted us both with her usual gusto, lavishing some effusive attendance over my young partner. She was clearly thrilled that Miss Kemp had attended, and I'm sure was champing at the bit to get out her pencil and pad and make some notes. There was no doubt that my companion would make a number of the columns in the following days papers should her presence be advertised. However, Beryl soon calmed herself and I was relieved to see that she was cleverly playing her cards close to her chest.

We grabbed drinks from a tray that was held rather high by a passing waiter, Miss Kemp opting for champagne and I for a disappointingly pedestrian red wine. We then edged carefully through the crowd to settle by a large French window that overlooked the car park. Beryl chatted mindlessly at us for some time, offering a diversion for which both Miss Kemp and I were grateful. Then, mid-way through an account of a charity ball she had recently attended, she caught sight of someone through the crowd, snapped her head upwards and cursed to the sky.

'Blast! Proxy made it!' she grunted through gritted teeth. Upon seeing our surprise, Beryl felt it necessary to explain. 'Germaine Proxy from the Messenger is over there at the bar, damn her! I had heard her mother was on her death-bed, but that doesn't seem to have stopped the old witch from coming tonight, unfortunately. Miss De Groot, I have a request if I may be so bold. When she comes over – and she will - keep in the shadows, will you? If you announce yourself to her the whole room will know it in a matter of minutes. Do you mind?'

I knew that the last thing Grace wanted was to announce herself to the room, and she nodded before leaning in to my ear.

'I'm starting to hate you for this, Mr Edgar. I had no idea we'd be swimming with the sharks tonight. This was a bad, bad idea.'

I gave a short sharp shake of the head and was about to reply when an extremely tall and large-framed woman in some unmistakably outrageous clothing bustled up to our little group. I had met Germaine Proxy previously, but thankfully only in passing at a tea party. I cannot remember the details of that day, only that it was outdoors and the afternoon had been horribly overcast and blustery and I had feared for my Hound's-tooth suit against the spotting rain.

Miss Proxy herself was not a figure that one could easily forget. That night she wore a burgundy red cocktail dress that was surely two or three sizes too small for her, with an unidentifiable auburn fur curled around her shoulders. Her hair was a shock of white pulled back by a thick red band, and her lips had been heavily painted despite the extreme paleness of her skin. She resembled an out-sized porcelain doll that had been squeezed into the burst remains of a red rubber balloon. It gave one a sensation of alarm and shock simply by looking at her.

'Well! If it isn't the purple peril!' she exclaimed loudly in Beryl's face, clearly starting as she meant to go on. 'Delightful gown!'

'Good evening, Germ,' Beryl replied with surprising control, 'and it is grape, my dear, not purple. Grape. The colour of the summer season, I assure you.'

'Really, my darling? Well if you say so.'

'I had heard your mother was ill! ' Beryl continued, matching her rival's sneeringly judgmental tone with some aplomb.

'Not anymore,' replied Mrs Proxy abruptly, although whether this was because the woman was now deceased or recovered she didn't elaborate. I wouldn't put it past any of these ruthless gossips to put a function ahead of mourning a loved one. Germaine Proxy sucked in her cheeks and leaned in again on Beryl.

'You've seen what Lady Freeler's wearing this evening, no doubt? Certainly de rigueur on a younger model, but most unbecoming on her, wouldn't you say? And got the mockers on the Van Deursens over there, have you? Heard about the mother, of course? Shame! But I've just got some really quite enlightening juice regarding the children, especially that little fat one. I ask you - who wears lederhosen to a party like this? But I won't stop at the Van Deusens or the Freelers tonight, my dear, even if you do. I am privy to some particularly interesting nuggets that would keep your substandard column's word count up for weeks. But you know me, never kiss and tell, oh-no.' She smiled a yellow-toothed smile over us all, before throwing a question into the air.

'And who are we all?'

Beryl took her cue and began to introduce us. I had been mulling over how to handle such a situation, and surprised even myself as I leapt into action with an outstretched hand and a beaming smile.

'I am so very pleased to meet you once more, Mrs Proxy. We have bumped heads together before but I do believe you were somewhat inebriated at the time, despite the early time of day. This is my fresh-faced young friend Miss Grace Kemp. A nobody, but a very pretty nobody nevertheless. I firmly believe that a girl on the arm is as vital an adornment to a man as a bow tie to a dinner jacket! I am introducing her to the cream of London's society tonight, as it were.'

Before I could continue, Germaine Proxy tightened her gaze on my silent companion.

'You are a tad familiar! Have we met before?' she boomed, her words dripping with curiosity. I leapt back in to the conversation before Miss Kemp could reply.

'You mentioned the Van Deusens, Mrs Proxy? Well you must have heard who else is here tonight, have you now? The latest name on the scene. A real surprise!'

My two companions looked at me with a fair measure of alarm in their eyes.

'Who is here?' Beryl and Proxy chimed in unison.

'None other than Dr. Margaret Blythe!' I announced in a conspiratorial stage whisper.

Beryl gave a sharp cough.

'Dr. Blythe is here?' she asked with a quiver, gasping over her gloved hand. Her disbelief only added authenticity to my charade. Germaine Proxy drew up to her full considerably towering height and was looking down at me with thin eyes.

'Goodness yes,' I continued, 'You remember that Dr. Blythe, has done a little work on the side for the Clarion of late? Bilborough was thrilled to have her, even if only for a short stint. Well, with her background and social standing you'd think that even the Fashionista was beneath her, but no! The rumour is that she is in with the De Groots! I do believe she's looking resplendent in a marvellous De Groot creation tonight, or so I'm reliably informed. You must keep our eyes open for her, Beryl darling.'

'Indeed I must! I can't quite believe she is here,' replied Beryl with twinkling eyes. She turned to her rival. 'Well, don't let us keep you, Germaine. I'm sure there are a number of truffles worth sniffing out tonight. And if you do insist on mentioning me in your column, remember that it's grape. G-R-A-P-E.'

'Darling, if I mention the likes of you it will be because I have been granted five hundred pages rather than five hundred words. Well, it seems that the cream has really risen to the top tonight. Good luck.'

She left following a quick glance at me, clearly still digesting my news.

'Margaret Blythe is here?' Beryl exclaimed once Mrs Proxy had melted away into the crowd. 'Are you mad?'

I gave a hearty shrug and sipped on my wine.

'Just a little bit of fun,' I replied.

I had lit a fuse, and was curious to see how much it would fizzle. From the corner of my eye I caught a cloud of grey smoke rising in the darkness outside of the window, where young Frank Capstick stood with his eyes to the sky. He looked, as usual, sullen and shifty.

I said a few words of comfort to Miss Kemp and slid through the French doors, leaving her in Beryl's secure company.

It was time to confront one of my prime suspects.

CHAPTER 6
In which Payton Edgar steals a pork ball

Dear Margaret,
My husband collects stuffed animals, and now they are taking over the house. My bedside lamp has a squirrel swinging from it, and we even have a zebra in our lounge. I am a member of the Women's Institute but am far too embarrassed to have a group meeting at my house. How can I control his obsession?
Housewife, Clapham

__Margaret replies;__ What on Earth are you frightened of? They cannot bite back! They are dead, and dead things should be disposed of. Simply bin the squirrel and, if you have no bin big enough for the zebra, give the rag and bone man a surprise. Taxidermy is a macabre pursuit and his unnatural obsession suggests to me that you have made a poor choice of husband.

Young Frank Capstick did not appear particularly surprised to see me, and continued to inhale deeply on his cigarette as we spoke.

'Hie, Mr Edgar,' he said casually.

'Getting some fresh air?' I quipped, yet received no reply. 'Are you here with your Father?'

'And Aunt Jenny, yes. We're on the catering tonight.'

'I haven't seen any food going around.'

'Buffet's out back, opens at eight.'

'And you help out? That's good of you.'

'For a bob or two, yes. Just the lifting stuff, none of the cooking or waiting on people or nothing like that. And I won't wear no uniform. Dad let me drive the van tonight, though.' For the first time I saw the large white van of Capstick's Catering parked some way off in the direction of his nod.

And then he turned to me with an expression that I hadn't expected. A serious expression.

'Listen, thanks for reading my bit out at the funeral. It was tougher than I thought, that day. You read it well.'

'Well, thank you Frank,' I answered his smile with one of my own, albeit one brought on by surprise. What was his game? To dissolve any instinct I had had to question him or to pry in any way with this gentle amiability. To make me think that surely this fine, polite young lad had nothing to do with the death of his mother? Did he think I was a fool? I sensed he was preparing to leave, and stopped him with a gentle question.

'How have you been getting on?' I asked. His answer took a minute to come, and when it did he spoke with a much slower, darker tone. It was not hard to sense his anger.

'Better now that bloke's been locked away. This was all his fault. I knew something bad was going on with Mum. She wouldn't tell me anything, of course.'

'Mothers do tend to keep things to themselves where children are concerned, ' I uttered, channeling Margaret Blythe with remarkable ease.

'Maybe. Those last few months she barely spoke to any of us. As if her head was somewhere else. I think that, perhaps, she was thinking of leaving us anyway.'

'Frank, you don't know that,' I chipped in despite myself.

'Well she wasn't happy. She wasn't there - wasn't herself, if you know what I mean? Did you see it, at the drama group? Was she different?'

'Can't say we noticed,' I replied uneasily, and then I ventured forth, softly. 'Do you have any idea why she was different, as you say?'

'Can only have been because of that Clay bloke, can't it? Well, it's over now. For him anyway.'

'How can you be sure he had anything to do with your mother?'

'I saw enough. Mum was acting all shifty, and then this old woman came to our house. I saw her talking to Mum in the front garden, said something about her son. Didn't know who she was then, but I know now. It must have been Clay's old mother. Then Mum and her were arguing-'

'Mrs Clay? Arguing? What about?'

'Who knows? Adults never tell me anything. Like Aunt Jenny. She and Mum had a huge falling out, just before Mum died. Bet Aunt Jenny didn't tell you that, did she?'

'What was that about?'

'I just told you, nobody bloody tells me anything!'

And with that Frank ground his butt into the ground with the ball of a foot and offered me a hand unexpectedly.

'I'm sorry, Mr Edgar. I didn't mean to yell at you. Thanks again, for the other day. I'd best be off, got the last of the plates to get out of van. Have a good evening.'

'Good night, Frank,' I replied as I watched him move away into the darkness.

Something of a live wire, that lad, I thought to myself. And yet despite his childish outburst, there was a maturity about him which was admirable. If he was putting on an act to persuade me of his innocence, he had done a good job of it. Perhaps I had been wrong about him.

I digested what I had just learned.

So there were arguments all around the Capstick's house, were there? What had that been about? And what on earth was Richard Clay's mother doing talking to Helen Capstick in the garden? The old woman had kept that one quiet. This all seemed very bizarre, and made me even more determined to get to the bottom of the whole affair.

By now my glass was empty, and I slipped back inside the ballroom to rescue my escort and garner a top-up.

It was a good half hour later when we bumped into the caterers, accidentally and entirely by chance, of course. I had seen Jenny French from afar, beavering away at the end of the ballroom to the right of the orchestra, and had guided our little group discreetly ever closer. Unsurprisingly, Beryl stuck with us much of the night and it seemed that nobody else were aware that a junior De Groot was in our midst, much to my relief. We would have to tackle the senior De Groots eventually, but I wanted to get as much snooping done as possible beforehand. I am sure that Grace did not mind delaying the inevitable, either.

Dressed as a French maid, Miss French looked much younger and perkier than on our previous encounters. She was, however, clearly under some strain in preparing for the opening of the buffet. She came and went through a swing door behind a fake palm tree like a cuckoo in a clock, her arms laden with cake tins or napkins or some such thing. I had expected her to at least flash me a weary smile as I approached, but was left wanting, and was instead greeted with something of a surprised scowl.

It was hard not to show alarm at the dark rings around the woman's eyes. They had not been there before.

'Mr Edgar! You do keep popping up!' she sang darkly. Suddenly, John Capstick appeared through the swing doors, looking very smart as maître-de. He greeted me loudly. Behind him Miss French busied herself away.

'Mr Edgar! Good to see you again,' Capstick boomed. I could not help but be pushed backwards some feet by the man as he approached. 'Here to pick up some fashion tips, are you?'

If he were asking me to justify my presence, I was ready.

I swiftly introduced him to Miss Kemp and Beryl Baxter, and as he was asking them politely about thoughts on the show so far I muttered a quick excuse with a promise to return, and moved quickly away. I wished to search out Jenny French once more.

I caught her just as she emerged once more from the swing doors. This time she held something of a smile for me. Was it my imagination or was the smile just a little more fixed than before? Was Miss French suspicious of me? If so, what did she have to be nervous about?

Behind her, the doors closed just slowly enough for me to catch a sight within that interested me; the glistening buffet table.

'It's quite a surprise to see you here, Mr Edgar. Are you with the fashion set too then?'

I replied swiftly, rambling a little about accompanying a friend, but it was clear that she was barely listening. In fact, she cut me off a little.

'Yes, it's been a busy night for us so far, and set to get worse before it gets better.'

'Miss French, I have to ask you a quick question,' I stated carefully, at which she straightened and looked me in the eye.

'Oh, yes?'

'I heard that you were at Onslow House the other day. May I ask why you were there?'

She hadn't expected this and I immediately saw something in her change as her guard went up.

'Why do you want to know?' she demanded unexpectedly sharply.

'Just curiosity,' I replied truthfully. 'I had been there to meet with the drama group, and Mr Claremont informed me you had been there. I just wondered-'

Miss French began fumbling with the ties on her apron mindlessly. After a thoughtful pause she pulled on the strings, undid the apron and lifted it over her head before holding it in a ball tightly at her middle.

'Without wishing to sound rude, Mr Edgar, I don't see what business it is of yours. My sister died there. I just wanted to see the place. To remember her. Now it is very nice to see you again, but I have to go!' She was lying, I was certain of it. And I had made her nervous.

'Just one other thing, before you go. You had an argument with your sister just before she died. Can I ask what that was about?'

I had pushed just a little too far.

'No, you most certainly cannot! Who do you think you are, Mr Edgar, to be asking these deeply personal questions? Now, I simply must get on. Do let John know what you think of our spread, won't you? He strives for perfection.' She glanced at her wristwatch and flapped her hands unnecessarily.

'Golly, it's a quarter to. I need some fresh air.'

And with that she pattered away, gathering up some tins from beside the door before she went, clearly heading for the van outside. I had caught a fleeting glimpse of the food on a long buffet table through the doors, and could not fight my curiosity.

I think that it is worth repeating that I have never been partial towards a buffet. The idea of eating food that has been sat out for hours, having been fingered, sneezed upon or coughed over by some stranger does not appeal to me. What does appeal, however, is perusing the buffet before any of this contamination can occur, when the food is freshly laid and unspoiled.

I found myself in a long tidy room, the only feature being the impressively lengthy table in the centre, stretched practically wall-to-wall. At the far end of the room there was a small door which led out to the car park. Taking some steps alongside the buffet I took some time to admire the Capstick's handiwork. The presentation was well judged and well suited to the ostentatiousness of the venue, with the occasional floral arrangement or sculpted figurine sprouting up at the rear of the display. I had started at the sweet end and I moved slowly along, appreciating the pastries, macaroons, trifles and cheeses. Further along my eyes feasted on sausage rolls, pork balls, scotch eggs and delicious looking terrines, not to mention the bountiful salads and breads surrounding these items.

With my mouth watering, I took a look around the room furtively before seizing one of the pork balls.

I barely had chance to taste the thing, for as I chewed on my sample voices grew louder as somebody approached from the outside. These voices were followed by the fumbling of a lock at the rear door. I can only say in my defence that I was startled and panicked and, being too far from the doors through which I had entered, I found myself diving for cover under the crisp white tablecloth. There I crouched furtively like a fool with half a pork ball still in my grasp. I swallowed as quietly as I could.

Two people had entered the room, and I placed their voices quickly.

'Here we go, Jen. That'll save us some bother.'

'Where did you find the key?'

'Cloakrooms, in the end. Better late than never,' said John Capstick.

'Well, it will be quicker packing at the end of the night, so that's good. So long as it hasn't set off any alarms,' said Jenny French, sounding more tired and far less animated than only a few minutes ago. There was a curious pause before she went on.

'Ooh, I'm so nervous, john,' she breathed.

'It will be fine. We've done this many, many times before,' he replied.

'It's not that. I just-'

There was a curious moment of silence.

'Kiss me, John.'

These three terrible words were followed by a telling silence that lasted a good minute- or-so. I clutched my pork ball tightly in disbelief. I knew it! She was in love with Capstick. How long had this been going on?

'More,' she said delicately, and somewhat sluttishly it must be said.

'There's no time, Jenny. And what if somebody would see us? Frank's just at the van you know.' John Capstick spoke softly but firmly. 'I do love you, Jen.'

'I love you too, John. We have to tell him, you know that.'

'Not yet. It's too soon, Jen.'

'Mmm. Well, I'll go and round up the girls in the changing rooms and check their uniforms. You get those last boxes out, will you?'

I remained on all fours for a good minute after I had heard the back door bang shut. Having lost my appetite I abandoned the remainder of my pork ball under the table before backing out from under the sheet on all fours. It was only as I heaved myself up with some difficulty that I realised I was not alone.

John Capstick was still in the room.

He stood, a box under each arm, watching in astonishment as I appeared from under his buffet table.

'Good evening, Mr Capstick,' was all I could think of to say.

'What are you doing? Just who are you, Mr Edgar?' he stammered in confusion.

'I am Payton Edgar, restaurant critic and food lover. I must say, I am impressed by your buffet. Excellent pork balls. Do excuse me!'

And I ran.

CHAPTER 7

In which Payton Edgar squares up to a fuming dragon

Dear Margaret,
I struggle to make friends as I am no good at conversation. My colleagues seem to be able to chatter away about everything and nothing, but I find myself tongue-tied and at a loose end. I can start up about the weather, but never know where to go from there. Can you help?
Speechless, Charing Cross

Margaret replies; Talking about the weather cannot be regarded as intelligent conversation, it is merely idle chatter that can be performed by the most brainless of souls. What you struggle to do is to make exchanges at a more academic level. I should give up hope on this immediately. The art of conversation is an art indeed, and the poor sentence structure and grammar of your letter serves to prove that you are an unintelligent soul who is clearly aiming above his or her station.

Following my bizarre declaration in the buffet room I was through the swing doors like a whippet on fire. My perusal over the pork balls had not gone well at all. I hastily located my friends once more, grabbed a fresh glass of wine and joined them, forcing a grin as if nothing untoward had occurred.

'Where have you been?' asked Miss Kemp with a sideward glance that contained more than a hint of irritation. Beryl was distracted, gesticulating to someone in the crowd.

'Tell you later,' I replied rather breathlessly, wondering if indeed I would tell anyone about my misadventures under the buffet table. She could ask no further questions for we were beckoned closer by Beryl with some urgency.

'Hold on to your trousers, Payton, here comes Jane! You remember her, Payton? My friend, Miss Burden; the man-eater? I tell you honestly, Miss Kemp, you would be hard pushed to find a more sweet and timid person from the look of her, but believe me she is a force to be reckoned with when it comes to the male gender. I said to Payton, she gets through men like I get through scalp adhesive. She-'

Beryl cut herself off as the bird-like lady I had met briefly before at Thistle House approached us. She wore a simple grey dress with a lace shawl over her bony shoulders. There was no hint of the floozy about the woman, and we were forced to take Beryl at her word. Beryl made the introductions once more, remarking that Miss Burden was high up in some fashion house of which I had never heard.

Beryl introduced my escort simply as Miss Kemp. Miss Burden did perhaps set her gaze on me for a little longer than the others, but then regaled us in a short and uninteresting tale about when she had met Beryl through her second husband. My colleague was a fine one to talk about the predatory nature of other women. Beryl had eaten her way through three husbands and there were rumours about a forth on the horizon. I had never quizzed her outright about this, and she had never told. We were quite happy keeping our private lives to ourselves. Other people, though, were fair game for Beryl. She picked up a nugget of information about some actress who was present, apparently dressing in something rather risqué.

And then Jane Burden issued a statement which delighted me beyond words.

'Of course,' she twittered, 'the real story of the night is that medical woman who's here. Dr. Margery Blythe...'

'Margaret!' I interjected.

'Sorry - yes - Margaret! Have you seen her?'

'Can't say that we have yet,' Beryl replied with a wry smile in my direction. Her friend continued.

'Nasty old Germaine Proxy's got her high on the radar for tonight, she has. Quite the distinguished guest, apparently, although nobody really knows what she looks like. I've never seen her.'

'Oh, I have met her, on the odd occasion,' I declared, revelling in the moment and happy to completely forget my embarrassment in the presence of John Capstick just minutes ago.

'You will know her when you see her. She is quite marvellous, really. Very, very striking to look at, and so very academic. Quick with her wit, too. She often has a troupe of hangers-on trailing behind her, always with a pad and pencil to document one of the many delicious bon mots the lady frequently issues. I believe she is in a De Groot dress tonight, with something of a nautical motif.'

'So I heard. How fitting!' Miss Burden chimed, 'I shall keep an eye out for her. Perhaps she is with Olga De Groot. Well, we will see when they enter.'

'Are they not here yet?' I asked. Beryl filled me in.

'The De Groots always arrive at the same time every year, usually bang on eight just before the buffet opens, and often with some fanfare. It is a bit of a bore, actually,' she looked at her watch. 'Any minute now, I suppose.'

Miss Burden caught the eye of a passing gentleman with a square jaw and shoulders to match, and swiftly bade us farewell, flittering away through the throng after her prey. Beryl watched her go with a grin.

'She really can't control her urges, that woman. You just wouldn't believe it, would you?'

In the end it was a full ten minutes past eight before the De Groots made their entrance. The orchestra struck up some plodding piece right on cue. As they did I cast my gaze to Miss Kemp who stood beside me watching the spectacle with barely concealed disgust. The contempt she held for her parents was all too easy to see.

There were no announcements, but the crowd launched into an apparently spontaneous round of applause that rippled through the huge room as the star couple appeared from the reception area and made their way across the ballroom to the platform where even the models stood clapping like performing seals. Lars De Groot was a crusty old thing, clearly a good few decades older than his wife. He must have had some sort of military record as he stood tall and straight-backed in a beautifully tailored dinner suit, his complexion a similar colour to his speckled grey hair. He had no smile. It was apparent that the man had clearly had lived a fine life, and he reeked of an ancient nobility known only to an exclusive few.

Had they been hanging in a museum, the gentleman would be a dull, robust old frame, and his wife the vibrant but surreal canvas within it.

Olga De Groot had clearly designed her attire around the image of a peacock, and – quite frankly - it looked simply dreadful. A shiny sequin dress in turquoise was adorned with billowing green and blue taffeta pleats. A cyan feathered shawl was draped over her shoulders, and on her head sat a feathered hat which at first glance could have been mistaken for a perched pheasant. She too held no smile, but nodded slowly at the crowd as she passed by as if we were privileged to be in her company.

Once they had stepped onto the platform, the orchestra allowed the tune to fade and a squealing microphone appeared from nowhere. Olga De Groot spoke into it as the applause died down.

'Thank you so very, very much for coming,' she said with a growl. This horribly obvious statement was received with unwarranted adulation from the crowd.

'In a year in which what you put on your head is almost as important as the dress you wear on your shoulders, you will be interested to know that I have banned any of my models from top hairstylists this year. Hair is out! This year and right through to the end of the winter we will all be talking straight lines and accessories. That is all I have to say to you. Please enjoy yourselves and enjoy my art, and make sure to tell your friends.'

The audience applauded this drivel as though the woman were some sort of prophet. Beryl was scribbling into a pad. I watched the scene in quiet disbelief for a minute, before turning and taking Miss Kemp's hand.

'Come on,' I said, 'let's go and see your mother.'

She pulled back, overcome by reluctance.

'No time like the present,' I said with a confidence I barely held myself. 'Come on. Let's go see the De Groots.'

A firm grip on my wrist stopped me in my tracks. Grace Kemp pulled me in close to her as the crowd hummed around us. Her expression was one of naked fear.

'No. I can't do it,' she whispered, 'I can't go to her.'

'You can and you will,' I replied with gusto.

'You don't understand, Mr Edgar, you don't know what she is like.' Her grip remained tight. The girl really was frightened. For the first time I saw Grace Kemp as that shrinking violet, Poor Pim De Groot, skulking in the shadows cast by her domineering parents.

'I can imagine, from what I have seen-'

'She treated me like a dog. Worse than a dog. It'll be Pim-this and Pim-that. Do you know how hard it's been for me coming here? At every function I must wear what she told me, no matter how foolish I looked. I must never speak. I must walk exactly three strides behind her and Father, eyes down at all times. They schooled me at home, I had no friends, no free time to myself. It was always school, chores, bed, school, chores, bed, and then at the weekend endless functions and launches. You'd think a girl would love it, but I wasn't allowed to speak a word. Mother would hit me with a rule if I so much as said a few words to another person on the outside. She didn't want me there - she hated me. And I hated her. I can't see her now. I have lived in fear that she will find me. I can't sleep at night. I thought I might feel different, coming here tonight. But now I can't do it. I don't want to ever see her again!'

Her speech was delivered with a cold strength, however, I wasn't dragging her this far to let her run away now. I freed my hand and then grasped both of hers together. They were small, smooth and cool to touch.

'All the more reason to do this now. You have been running from the woman for too long, and she is clearly not worth the time nor the energy you give to fretting over her. Come with me, show her that you are an adult and that you are living an adult's life quite happily without her. It needn't be a fight. I will be with you all the way. Now come on!'

Olga De Groot saw us approaching before her husband did. They had not yet alighted from the platform and so, rather unfortunately, they loomed ominously over us as we reached them. Grace stepped forwards.

'Mother-' she began, weakly. I stepped up.

'I suggest we go somewhere private to talk,' I said loudly, at which Olga De Groot turned her astonished gaze from her daughter to me, and then back to her daughter. Her sharp eyes were a cold, penetrating grey.

'Pim? Pim? What are you..? And who is this old man?'

Old? I was surely decades younger than her husband! I felt my fists clenching at my sides, but kept my cool and saw that the nearest exit was by the changing area where numerous models were streaming from. I pulled Grace along with me.

'Come on everybody, in here. De Groots! This way now!'

Within a minute I had shooed a couple of scantily dressed young lovelies away and had the four of us in what turned out to be a rather dilapidated and draughty cloakroom. They had followed me silently, Grace with a worried look and her mother with the wide eyes and flaring nostrils of a fuming dragon. Throughout all of this her husband remained mute and expressionless, so much so that I wondered if he spoke a word of our language at all.

We got off to a poor start, for unfortunately Grace had lost her tongue. She allowed her mother to enter into a tirade punctuated with huffs and snarls.

'What is all this, Pim? What are you doing here? And what on earth are you wearing? Don't let them see you like this. You know who's here tonight, and you dress like that! You silly girl! What have they done to you, Pim? You look like the ghost of a peasant girl drowned at sea. And you! Old man!' A long finger wavered in my direction. 'Is this your doing? Who the devil are you and what are you doing with my daughter? You! I'm talking to you! Standing there in your cheap suit!'

I struggled to fight my fury at this unbelievable barb, and spoke through gritted teeth.

'I'll have you know, Madame, that it is a handmade bespoke suit from Savile Row. The man designed for Churchill, and-'

'Oh, really?' she drawled loudly, feigning boredom. 'A designer for the fuller gentleman, no doubt. Well, the casing may be glittery but that doesn't make what's inside gold. So then - underneath your suit - who are you and what are you doing with my daughter?'

'Mother,' said Grace, thankfully finding her tongue, 'I am here to tell you that I am no longer running away. I am settled and happy. I have a job-'

'A job!' the woman screeched, 'A job! Not again, please! I feel quite, quite faint! What is it this time? A flower stall in the Covent Garden? Sewing rags to make skirts for orphans? Licking stamps? Heavens preserve us! Well? What is it?'

She had asked the question outright, and I watched her daughter, awaiting the reply. It was Miss Kemp's moment to shock her mother, and I have to say I willed her on. But my new young friend was worth more than that.

She took some time to answer.

'It is just a job, a simple job. You don't need to know what it is.' Her eyes flittered to meet mine for a moment before returning to her mother. 'But what you do need to know is that I enjoy it, and that I have found a place where I am welcome. And I am happy. You won't see me again, Mother, so I'll say goodbye to both of you, and perhaps just a small part of you, however deep down, will be pleased for me in my happiness. Goodbye Mother, Father.'

And with that Miss Kemp turned and vanished through the cloakroom door I held open for her. The De Groots stood open mouthed like a pair of fancily dressed trout. Grace had melted into the throng outside. She had said her piece, and I felt a warm pang of pride for the girl.

That said, she may have said her piece, but I hadn't. I had begun to follow her out, but stopped myself. I turned in the doorway.

'You have a wonderful daughter there. You should be proud.' I issued a knowing smile. 'And if you're not, it really doesn't matter. Because I *am*.'

CHAPTER 8

In which Payton Edgar is perhaps just a little bit cruel

"Germaine's Gems"
The Evening Messenger
Friday March 5th 1962

Yet again Olga De Groots Fashionista proved to be the place to be for anyone who is anyone on London's fashion scene last week. Olga De Groot (pictured below, left, in feather hat) continued her domination of fashion with an army of accessories, some of which broke the mould in their simplicity alone. Straight lines on hems and skirts were present in abundance, and it is clear that polka dots are the thing to be seen in. Olga also announced daringly that "hair is out", as I am sure one of my fellow gossip columnists who spends so much of her income on threadbare hairpieces to accompany her purple rags will be gratified to hear. But I am not here to talk about the fashion, dear readers. Forget the Shapells, the Freelers and the Van Deusens, the face to spot was a relative newcomer to the fashion scene, yet one who has been a good personal friend of this correspondent for some time; Dr. Margaret Blythe.

Dr. Blythe is one of the new wave of powerful and intelligent women who can show men a thing or two, believe me! She looked marvellous in a strapless De Groot cocktail dress with sailor-inspired collar, and almost stole the show from the lady herself. Unfortunately, the De Groots were only able to attend the function to launch the buffet at the start of the evening. Any gossip that a skirmish occurred which caused our hostess to flee has not been substantiated. Should any kind of dispute have happened, your correspondence at the Messenger would have been the first to know. Watch this space for more gossip on the inspirational Dr. Blythe later this week.

Germaine Proxy

Monday morning trundled along and to my horror I was greeted by Cockney Guy at the front desk.

How the man had returned to his post I did not know. Bilborough was a notoriously soft touch. I shook the rain drops from my umbrella, said a quiet hello and requested my post. Guy stared out at me with tired eyes for a moment before turning and flicking his blackened fingers through the pigeonhole. He tossed a few bundles onto the counter. At a glance I could see that I had more letters than usual and was thrilled, but carefully maintained my composure, took up the letters and went to leave.

'Incha going to ask how I am?' grunted Guy over my shoulder like a sullen child. There was no escaping this one. I turned and held out a hand.

'Guy, I'm so very sorry about what happened with your wife, but you did ask for-'

'Nah, save it, mate' he droned, much to my relief, 'I asked for advice, and you gave it. Can't always be winners can we? Probably be better off in the long run, eh? Anyhow, I've found myself a floor at a mate's house, and met myself a new girl already.'

'Really, Guy. That's fast work!'

'Well, much as I'd liked my old missus, she was always a bit too brazen for me. Now I know her for the hussy she is. Proved it by running off with Alan, didn't she? No, I need a girl who I can rely on. Now I've met myself a calmer, much more down to earth woman who'll stick by me. Works at a fashion house, does Jane. Dead sweet she is.'

'Jane..?' I enquired thoughtlessly. The man-eater!

'Jane Burden?'

'That's her!' exclaimed Guy, 'do you know of her?'

I found myself with some more sage advice to offer the man, but swallowed it. I had interfered in this particular affair enough.

'Through a friend, that is all. Well, enjoy yourself Guy!'

While it lasts, I thought to myself sadly.

I had indeed received sixteen letters for Margaret Blythe, and I enjoyed a morning of judging people and fussing over their problems. As it happens, it was to be my last such morning, for Bilborough cast his head around the door at a ten to eleven to inform me that Honoria Betts would be returning to work the following week.

The news, which would have been most welcome at one time, gave me pause.

'Are you sure I can't persuade you to stay on it?' Bilborough asked once more, 'I can stick Honoria onto the Green Fingers column without too much fuss...'

'No thank you, Mr Bilborough, I replied firmly. 'This is her job, and I'm sure she will do you proud. I would, however, appreciate your consideration on extending my own column as previously discussed.'

Bilborough rolled his eyes in false resignation.

'It's in the bag, Payton. I cleared it last week. Starting next month you can go to fortnightly reviews if you wish. I'll bring you down the contract. But I do have one condition, and you may not like it.'

'Go on,' I replied warily.

'You know how much I love your reviews, Payton. But we need more scope, more variation. I would like you to do a good review, with praise and delight, every now and then, just for a contrast. Boost a local business, that kind of thing.'

More scope and variation? Praise and delight? How dare the man dictate how I run my column! I bit my lip and, although he had appeared to have finished his speech, he loitered suspiciously in silence. There was something fishy about all this.

He went on.

'Now my cousin has a place up near Kings Cross, very British, very en vogue-'

I was right about the new contract. It was fishier than a gill of picked shrimps.

'Mr Bilborough, I accept your offer and will gladly write some glowing reviews where it is warranted,' I thought of Harvey's restaurant instantly. 'But I will not offer praise where it is not due, whom ever happens to own the establishment. That is my stance, and I shall never change it. Is that understood?'

The man was obviously not used to being spoken to in this forthright way, but he took my point and nodded his understanding reluctantly.

'If you give me the details I will gladly put the place on my list for review, but cannot make any promises as to the outcome.' I said.

It was always fun to stand my ground, and after Bilborough had departed I typed out my final draft and set it aside to be handed in. I took up my papers and notes from the past few months and slotted them into my briefcase, leaving a pile of potential letters for Margaret's page for Honoria to sift through.

As a final act, I opened the bottom draw of the desk and took out the horrendously tasteless little ceramic boy in dungarees, still holding brightly-coloured flowers coyly to his chest. I examined it momentarily, turning it over in my hands and marvelling at how little taste in décor some people have. I would be glad to get away from the thing. I replaced it on Honoria's desk, just where it had sat on my first day as Dr Blythe. I should have done her a favour and dropped it into the waste paper bin.

Fitzherbert the pigeon was nowhere in sight. I had hoped for a leaving party to see me off. Suddenly the raggedy bird I had seen before fluttered clumsily down to the window ledge. It was streaked in dirt and dust. But was it another bird? He was as fat as my friend, but far less friendly. He carried city dirt without shame. I looked closer and saw familiar rings at his neck. It was indeed Fitzherbert, but he had fallen on harder times.

I said my goodbyes, but he had closed his eyes.

I left the room tidier and more organised than I had found it, and made my way to Beryl Baxter's office. She was seated at her desk with her head in her hands. Her hairpiece that day was a dark red affair that was plonked more carelessly than usual on top of her head. It was more than a little askew.

'No whisky this morning, Beryl?' I asked with a generous portion of cruelty. A dark eyed glare was all I received on this one. Beryl was famous for her late nights and I was sure she had been partying long after I had left the Fashionista and probably well into the Sunday too.

'It is, Payton my dear, a glorious morning despite my two-day hangover. Did you see this wonderful piece?' She tossed me the Messenger and I perused poor Germaine Proxy's lamentations over the elusive Dr. Blythe.

'And what is your take on the night?' I asked warily. I had made Beryl promise to go easy on young Grace Kemp and begged her not to spoil the illusion of Margaret Blythe.

'I have composed a beautiful piece, washing over the frankly monotonous fashions of the evening to focus on the story of young Marianne De Groot, praising the girl on how she held herself with a quiet decorum all night and stood up to her domineering Mother and Father, forcing the pair to flee the party at a ridiculously early hour. Believe me, young Pim comes off as a heroine of our times, and the De Groots, so far as I am concerned, are headed for the "has-been" dustbin, whatever old Proxy says. The reception to her latest designs was tepid at best, and if I see another polka dot I swear I will vomit.'

'And Margaret Blythe?'

Beryl laughed. 'Don't fret, Payton. There's no mention of her, or her absence I should say, in my piece. I chose to make this a personal victory. Once I had read Germaine's fantastical piece, I gave her a discreet phone call and informed her of the true nature of our make-believe comrade. As you can imagine, she was not best pleased. She won't be writing about Margaret Blythe again, but her comments in that rag today will do wonders for the profile of our beloved agony aunt.'

147

I resisted telling her that this Friday's Dr. Blythe column would be my last in print, knowing how much she would disapprove. I didn't have the strength to fight against Beryl as well as Bilborough. Beryl went on at length about her plans for the evening, culminating in a late-night session of Bridge. I have only been subjected to Bridge once or twice in my life, and in my opinion it is a game for dullards and fanatics only. I said as much.

She went on to tell me in no uncertain terms that Bridge was "in" and that it was not the game one played but the people one played with. After this overlong and unnecessary lecture Beryl stood and excused herself, heading for the ladies room, but not before I asked if I could use her telephone phone.

'Knock yourself out,' she had replied in her shrillest tones, and I assumed that this was meant as an expression of her consent.

Irving took only three rings to reply, making me long for the days when it would take a good twenty or thirty rings before he would even consider setting down his easel. He sounded fractious and I told him as much.

'And well I might be!' he snapped, 'I have that old woman coming around in half an hour for the first sitting of her damn portrait. I could wring your neck, Payton, I really could. I have never been a portrait painter! I am prostituting myself-'

I smiled to myself as he went on, picturing how I had cornered Mrs Clay with the offer of a portrait and won her over with flattery and charm.

'Just keep calm and remember why you are doing this. For this poor sad woman - and for me too. Even if you don't enjoy it, just get through it. Irving, you have a natural talent that needs exercising.'

He took my advice with little grace, grunting and tutting and making me wonder why I had called. As if he had read my mind he asked curtly what I had wanted.

'I have a free afternoon and predict a degree of boredom. I wondered if you wanted to meet for tea, but obviously you are busy-'

'-no thanks to you!' Irving rattled.

I allowed a stony silence to settle on the line. If only I had the confidence to move forward in my investigation, some more diverting prying would have filled the afternoon quite nicely. I had been horrified at my behaviour under the buffet table at the Dr Groot Fashionista and had risked mockery by telling Irving a little about it, carefully leaving out the more humiliating details. And now he offered me an opportunity I had missed; the opportunity of sniffing around the Capstick's house once more. He explained his idea with frustrating simplicity, lacing his words with sarcasm.

'If you are bored, Payton and you really are desperate to carry on with your absurd investigations then just go to the Capsticks' and bother them some more. Apologise for your snooping at the Buffet table. Knock on the door, say you are sorry, they invite you in for a cup of tea and there you are. Inside the house again to snoop around and get yourself into even more trouble. Like a moth to a flame!'

If he had meant this to dissuade me then these words would surely just do the opposite. I was on the brink of replying when I reminded myself that he'd need to be calm and ready to enjoy his portrait painting that afternoon, and so I stopped myself from butting in. I merely issued a mild response and terminated our call.

'Perhaps you are right,' I had said, the words almost choking me.

As it was, I did not go near Bloomsbury that afternoon. By the time I left Thistle House the sun had broken through the clouds and it looked to be a pleasant afternoon. I took the morning newspaper to Lincoln's Inn Fields and passed the time quietly. Unfortunately, boredom hung over me that afternoon like a dark cloud, a cloud which I then took home with me.

Perhaps I should not have taken out my frustrations on my Aunt Elizabeth, but then what are family for if not to do just that?

I popped into her room on the way to my study.

'Good evening, dear Auntie,' I said with as much merriment as I could muster. She had informed me on many occasions that she hated it when I called her this, and was now glaring at me sourly.

'There is nothing good about this evening,' she growled, 'it is just yet another long evening of empty nothingness. I sit alone, left to rot. Decaying-'

'That's nice!,' I smiled, feigning obliviousness. As she continued on with her moaning, Grace Kemp entered the room with a fresh pile of clean towels and flannels in her arms.

'Oh, Mr Edgar, hello. How are things?'

'Fine for him!' Aunt Elizabeth cut in, 'swanning around like the Lord Mayor of London. Leaving his decrepit old aunt to fester in a bed of lonely misery.'

I purposely misunderstood and turned to Miss Kemp.

'How often do you change those sheets, Miss Kemp?' I asked haughtily. Her lips had been pursed and she dropped the towels onto a chair. She was clearly concerned.

'Those sheets are fine, Mr Edgar, as you well know. It is the cat-shaped hole that's causing a problem. Her Titty's not been around for ages now. Your aunt's taken to sleeping with the window open, and it's not good for her chest.'

'Oh dear,' I proclaimed with mock dismay, 'have you lost your pussy? Well, I would like to remind you that it was a stray, and not yours to begin with.'

Aunt Elizabeth plucked at her blankets idly.

'Sometimes I think I can hear him calling out,' she mewed childishly.

'That is probably Lucille. Or perhaps poor Titty's ghost,' I added.

'He is dead,' my aunt shrieked, 'I know it.'

'Now you come to mention it,' I waggled my finger, 'I did see a heap of ginger fur at the corner of Lupus Street just the other day. '

I left my aunt's room feeling a mixture of delight and remorse. Delight at the success of my plan to stop the mangy stray from entering my house and remorse for my chosen words. Had I perhaps been too cruel?

Once alone in my bedroom I chastened myself for my words. Aunt Elizabeth didn't deserve to suffer, just because I had gotten myself tied up in an unsavoury state of affairs. I sat for a while, deep in thought, and then I quickly threw on my rain mackintosh and took myself outside.

I cut around the house and approached my aunt's window with care and then, in silence, I replaced the barrel and plank in anticipation of Titty's return.

The week trundled on.

My aunt's ginger cat made no appearance, and her mood grew blacker by the day.

I cogitated over visiting the Capstick's house for a number of days, and also avoided seeing Irving for fear of his wrath. I could only pray that the portrait sitting had gone well. It was not until the Friday, the day of publication for my final Dear Margaret column that I decided to pay him an overdue visit.

I was left waiting for a good two minutes after ringing the bell, and when the door was finally answered it was with a sharp click as the lock was slid back, but nothing more. I gently nudged the door open and I could just make out my friend's shadow moving back along the hallway.

I could not have had a better sign that Irving was back on track. How many times I had told him off for such lax security, not to mention the rudeness of such a welcome? Yet on his doorstep that morning I could not have been happier. I followed him in, but did not remove my coat. The hallway smelt musky; a delightful mix of paint and incense. Passing through into his studio I found my companion in his painting casuals, his hair a mess and smudges of green and black paint smeared across his forehead.

It was just what I had hoped to see.

'Can't stop, Payton, this is good, this is good,' was all he said. I asked him carefully about the portrait I had commissioned him to paint and he gestured carelessly to the far corner of the room. Moving over to study the canvas, I was again pleasantly surprised. In reality Mrs Clay was aged and had an interesting face, but this canvas displayed a funny looking creature, with a green tinge about the jaw and wide searching eyes. One could see remnants of the person within the picture, but much more besides. There was no denying that the painting was striking, and I was to stand appraising it for a good minute. It put me in mind of a Picasso, although I would never dare say this aloud to my companion, and the sitter's facial features were more or less in the right place.

'Was she happy with it?' I enquired. Irving took a long minute to answer.

'Very,' he said hesitantly.

Good old Mrs Clay. Polite and gracious as ever.

'But I want to hold onto it for now. She didn't mind."

I'm sure she didn't. I left him at his canvas, knowing that in this frame of mind there would be no chance of conversation or tea.

And thankfully no chance of a jigsaw puzzle.

CHAPTER 9

In which Payton Edgar receives a tip-off

Dear Margaret,
I am in my late thirties and have been engaged now for over five years. My fiancée is a good man from an affluent background who works hard in the City. My problem is that I don't think he will ever get around to marrying me as he is so busy all of the time. He won't even talk about children until after we are married. We seem to have the same conversation almost every week, and it is always me who starts this up. He says that he feels married to his job. My friends tell me I should be more insistent. What do you think?
Patient, Ealing.

Margaret replies; There is patience and then there is patience. It may help to look at it from an outsider's point of view. Here we have a woman who has a rich boyfriend with excellent prospects and a good nine-to-five job, who could marry her practically any weekend of the year if he chose to. She has brought up the subject of marriage week after week for five long years, to no avail. Indeed, the man rolls out that hoary old chestnut about being married to the job. What would you say to this woman?
Take the hint, my dear, and forget it. Have you ever considered taking up Bridge?

It is most probably a crime to pose as a police inspector, but any sensible jury would surely understand my rationale.

I hadn't intended to do it, there was no plan to deceive, but I was rendered helpless by the cruel twists of fate that can appear out of nowhere and when one least expects it. The misunderstanding was yet another reversal of fortune that pushed me into absorbing another alias for the sake

152

of getting to the truth. In my defence, I didn't actually state at any point that I was a member of the constabulary. This was all assumed.

It had been a quiet, uneventful weekend, and having enjoyed a Sunday afternoon stroll I found myself in Bloomsbury, not entirely by accident.

I had been greeted at the door by Jenny French, who blushed furiously within seconds of clapping eyes on me, a wordless act which only confirmed that Capstick had informed her of my being caught loitering under the buffet table during their embrace. Her usual sunny disposition was long gone, having been replaced by a cool suspicion.

She did not invite me in.

'I came to apologise,' I began, mustering up as much courage as I could.

'Everyone else is out, Mr Edgar,' she replied simply. 'And I have company.'

As if to confirm this I heard a rustling from within the house and a bushy haired woman appeared at her side, buttoning up a grey overcoat with fat painted fingers.

'Well, I best be off, Jenny. You have company.' This was said with a smoker's growl, a quick nod and a distracted half-smile. 'Let me know if the rat gets in touch. Even at night, I'm getting so worried.' She pulled out a rain hood and fastened it under her rounded chin. 'S'not like Tom, this, pain in the neck though he is. I'll kill him when I get hold of him. Thanks for the paté, love.'

And with that the stranger eased past me clutching a large blue tin and stomped away down the pathway.

'Who was that?' I could not resist asking. Miss French had adopted a distracted, troubled expression.

'That's Mr Limestone's ex-wife. Our lodger's done a runner, or so it seems. He was meant to pick up his children yesterday but he didn't appear. Nobody has seen him.' She allowed her words to trail off and watched until the visitor had disappeared out of view. Miss French was obviously concerned, or troubled, by Limestone's disappearance. But why?

Then, as if a spell had been lifted, she snapped her attention back onto me.

'I will tell John that you came around, Mr Edgar, but he will say the same as me I know. I trust this will be last we will see of you now?'

The uncompromising question was said with a certain forcefulness that I had not witnessed in Miss French before. She did not wait for a reply, and I found myself face to face with the door. Fair enough, I thought to myself.

Again I had come away with more questions than I had answers. Where was Thomas Limestone? The last I had seen of him was at the funeral, and that look on his face as he practically fled the scene was fresh once more in my mind. Something had happened, I decided, and it wasn't good.

I was just closing the gate behind me when a piercing hiss cut through the birdsong.

'Psst!'

This unexpected emission made me jump, and when I looked around I could see nobody. I stepped out onto the pavement uneasily and after a moment of silence began to move away.

'Psst! Psst!'

The noise was unmistakably being made to attract my attention, and now appeared to originate from behind me. I turned to see a pasty face peering nervously around the side of the privet. A little hand beckoned me over.

It was the Capstick's next door neighbour, a rather dried up woman in a dusty pinafore dress. She wore thick milk-bottle glasses and no make-up on a weather-beaten face that must have seen the turn of the century while in her prime. Her hair was a tired brown and set in tight curls. She scrutinised me with amplified sparkling eyes that carried something resembling excitement.

'Making enquiries, were you, officer? I saw you the other week, getting into that police car with the inspector. Well I have new information for you. Important information! But not here!' She glanced around as if wary of onlookers. 'Come around the back, that way round, bottom of the garden by the garage. I'll meet you there.'

And with that, she was gone.

I did indeed meet her around the back at the bottom of the garden by the garage.

I hadn't quite appreciated just how well set these houses were until viewed from behind. Each had a pleasant stretch of garden, which was rare for somewhere so central and, in the Capstick's case, enough room for a fair-sized garage. I was not jealous, however. I have no garden, and am all the better for it. A garden is something that can only cause one stress and frustration with its ever-growing stalks and weeds, forever demanding attention. Not to mention the loitering vermin within.

I didn't have so much as a window box at home, and was quite glad about it. St. James Park was my beautiful garden, and I didn't have to so much as pull a weed.

The stranger was standing behind a thick wooden gate at the bottom of her own garden, and with her hands clamped on top of it peering over she looked like a perched owl.

'Are we alone?' she whispered conspiratorially. I could not resist glancing around us.

'I believe so. And you are?'

'Mrs Hedge,' she replied with some surprise, 'You're quite new, aren't you, officer? I'd have thought your colleagues would have told you all about me!'

'Of course, of course. I just wanted to clarify things, positive identification and all that. What is it you wanted to say to me, Mrs Hedge?'

'Strange doings in the middle of the night!' she declared, her eyes growing ever wider behind the thick lenses. 'You need to ask, why would a catering company need to be taking their van out at two o'clock in the morning? Mmm? I was up at two, see. I often am, due to, well - for personal reasons. And I saw, out of my bathroom window, and heard, with my ears. Yes, yes. And the question is why?'

'Who was it?' I enquired, somewhat hypnotised by the passionate conviction that was in her voice. 'Who was driving the van?'

'Well, that I didn't see. Frosted glass, you understand? Can't have every Tom, Dick and Harry watching me at my toilet now, can I? But I heard it. The van went out. It did!'

'And did you see at what time it returned?' I asked.

Mrs Hedge pushed her glasses back up the bridge of her nose and issued a grimace.

'Why on earth would I wait up to see how long they were out for? In the dead of night? I am not a complete nosey-parker, you know. And besides, I need my sleep.'

'Of course...'

'It was more than an hour, though. I gave up and went to bed after that.'

Her mission completed, Mrs Hedge bade me a cautious farewell that practically dripped with intrigue and padded away up her garden path in her pale pink slippers. I mulled over what I had just heard for a short while, and then I did something very, very naughty.

As I was there at the garage anyway, I could not fight the desire to take a look.

Without doubt or hesitation I tried the Capstick's garage door. It was unlocked. The inside was dark and draughty, but I dared not turn on a light. The dim sunlight cast in through the one filthy window was just enough for me to see by. I stood for a minute and moved my eyes over the junk piled around two sides of the room. The far wall was neater and cleaner and had all the storage paraphernalia for their business stacked high.

At my feet sat a sad-looking sausage dog, a tin toy that had once probably been pulled lovingly on a string but now lay on its side, rusted and earless in the debris of the garage. The Capstick's van sat cold, taking up most of the space in the small building, and I squeezed myself with some difficulty around to the boot. It was locked. Peering through the window I observed that it was empty. Large squares of cream-coloured carpet made up the flooring of the vehicle, which caused me to pause and examine the insides more closely. There was one square of carpet missing close to the window. I had seen a square just like it elsewhere in the room.

I don't know precisely what was egging me on, but I had to squeeze myself around to the far corner of the bonnet to see that I was right. Pushed down against the far wall was a cut of the carpet. Was this the missing piece? I don't know what I had expected to find, and I experienced some difficulty reaching over the rubbish piled about, but eventually my fingertips had the corner and I pulled on it gingerly. It came away, heavily at first and then something fell from it with a clatter to the floor and I had the carpet square in my grip. It was indeed the same carpet as on the floor of the van, but this piece was very grubby and there, in one corner, was a dark red stain.

It took me a minute to prize my eyes from this. Was it a bloodstain? I was looking down at my feet in thought when a second item caught my attention and I bent down to retrieve it. It was a large spanner. This had fallen from amongst the carpet as I had pulled it out. Grasping it by the handle I lifted the tool to the light, where I could clearly see blood-red smears across the head of it.

A murder, a missing man, and now a blood-stained weapon. The stuff of crime fiction indeed. And yet here it was in reality, sending a cold shiver down my spine.

CHAPTER 10

In which Payton Edgar reports a crime

Dear Margaret,
My husband wants to take over my life. He dislikes the fact that I dye my hair Autumn Copper, and has even hidden my bottle to try and stop me. He also wants me to give up my market job on a fruit and veg stall in the Covent Garden. I love my work, and don't think I should give up my job for any man. What are your thoughts?
Mary, Lambeth

Margaret replies; in the interests of research I attended Covent Garden and bought a bunch of bananas from your stall. I can certainly see why your husband disapproves of your vulgar hair colour choices (more Summer Sunburn than Autumn Copper, I fear). Also, you were heavy handed with the fruit and most impolite when challenged over the fact that you had short-changed me. To top it off, the bananas were bruised, over-ripe and entirely dissatisfactory. If you ask me (and let's not forget that you have) I think you should give up your job too.

Inspector Standing kept me waiting once again.

The desk clerk had put up a mild show of resistance, it being a Sunday and all, but my loud and wordy demands to see Standing had eventually won through and I had been led into a small interview room. It was not the same room as I had visited previously and there was no pleasant view of the river. In fact, there were no features at all except three wooden chairs and a rectangle table with a noticeably scratched and scuffed surface. I was drumming my fingers on the table top with some vehemence when the Inspector entered, red-faced and with an unmistakable curmudgeonly air about him.

To this man I was obviously nothing but a pest.

'You are lucky to catch me, Mr Edgar. An unexpected development brought me in. So, what is it? What is so important?' he grumbled, putting me in mind of a particularly hostile teacher I had once loathed at Sunday school. It was difficult to remain calm.

'I have some fresh evidence,' I began, summoning a firm confident stance, 'evidence that will prove Richard Clay's innocence once and for all.'

'Oh, yes?' he sat before me and looked pointedly at the clock on the wall, 'you have two minutes.'

One could almost hear the tapping of a crucifix against a desktop as he spoke. Nevertheless I would not let this exhibition of blatant discourtesy put me off my stride.

'Mr Limestone, the Capstick family's lodger has gone missing. He failed to collect his children at an allotted time, and has not been seen since. Despite his stringent persona the man is clearly intelligent, and I believe that he had worked out who murdered Helen Capstick and perhaps confronted the murd-'

'Perhaps?'

'The man was penniless, distraught following a costly divorce. I believe that he confronted the perpetrator and demanded payment for silence.'

'Blackmail!' rumbled the inspector, with a strange glint in his eye. I continued.

'I believe that Limestone was bludgeoned over the head with a spanner and concealed in Capstick's catering van. The van was then driven out in the middle of the night in order to dispose of the body. I have spoken with a witness who indeed confirms that the van was taken out at two o'clock yesterday morning. I have examined the van and found traces of blood upon the floor of it and on the aforementioned spanner. This can now be found concealed behind a tin dog in the Capsticks' garage. So you do see, don't you, how this clears Clay? Add to that the fact that one of the van drivers - young Frank Capstick - is suspicious in the extreme, I insist that you investigate immediately!'

I sat back in my chair in triumph. Inspector Standing studied me quietly for a minute and then stood, his chair scraping loudly across the floor.

'A wonderful story, Mr Edgar, worthy of Christie herself. But a pile of tosh, none the less.'

'Tosh?!' I coughed out in surprise.

'Mr Edgar, I appreciate that you fancy yourself something of a private investigator, but your ideas are most peculiar. You are embarrassing yourself. A case such as this one involving Richard Clay cannot be approached without method. Now, I do not know what it is that is driving you to prove young Clay's innocence, although I have the feeling your fondness for his dear mother may be a part of that-'

Just what was he implying?

'-but I have to tell you that we have firm evidence of Clay's guilt, and the fact that he is guilty means that he cannot possibly have disposed of Thomas Limestone as you claim, for he has been with us at the station, hasn't he?'

'That is further proof of his innocence!' I chimed, 'I-'

"And while I agree with you that young Frank is something of a scallywag, he is no murderer. Now, you mention a witness who observed some goings on in the dead of night? Would we by any chance be talking about Beatrice Hedge, John Capstick's next door neighbour? Round face, thick glasses?'

My face must have given it away.

'I thought as much. Mrs Hedge is well known to us here at Scotland Yard. She has apparently witnessed more crimes than all of my officers put together and is ever present in an investigation such as this with her opinions and experiences. She has been particularly active over this one as you can imagine, it being so close to home and all. So far in this investigation Mrs Hedge has made numerous claims, as we had expected. Among other things she reports having seen what she describes as a suspicious dark-skinned man watching the house from the bushes at night, and has personally informed me that young Frank Capstick carries a knife which he keeps in his back pocket, a la *Rebel Without A Cause*. I had thought that an apparently sensible gentleman like you would be above spreading petty lies and wasting police time, but it seems that I was wrong.'

I saw red. My fists clenched tightly under the table I glared at this buffoon of a policeman and struggled to control my breathing.

'How dare you!' was all I could muster. Standing must have seen the violence in my eyes, for he softened a little and returned to his seat. After a quiet pause he leaned forward and adopted a surprisingly gentle tone.

'Mr Edgar, I am going to tell you some things now that may be a surprise to you, but I feel that it is important you are given all the facts in order to see what really happened to poor Mrs Capstick. I would, however, ask you not to repeat any of this to anyone else, as they are facts known to the police and the police alone. Is that understood?'

If this was a tactical move to get me on side and keep me quiet, I have to say that it worked. I nodded, reluctantly.

'The first thing that I will admit is that your missing man, Thomas Limestone, telephoned me the day before last. He called through for an appointment, and that afternoon he attended this very station, sat right where you are now and informed me that he wished to take a holiday. A holiday, Mr Edgar. He said that he appreciated that he was involved in a murder investigation, but that the past few months had been so taxing, what with his divorce and the death of his friend, he needed to get away. Considering that we have the murderer locked up here already, I granted him his leave and asked where he planned to go. I believe that your absent Mr Limestone is now relaxing under the sun and sucking on an olive somewhere in the South of France.'

'I can't-' I began, not knowing what to say. This made no sense. How could the man even afford a holiday? Standing went on.

'As for Clay, who has as good as confessed to murder-'

'As good as?' I put in, 'but not actually confessed?'

'Mr Edgar, we know for a fact that Clay and Helen Capstick were having relations. Clay admits as much. You yourself have the evidence of the letter written by Helen herself to your agony column, telling all of us that she is scared of him and telling us all about his violent nature. Now I grant you, the lad looks pathetic and like he couldn't harm a fly, but in this game you soon learn that looks can be deceptive. For example, a man can have the outward impression and reputation of a gentleman of discretion and learning, but actually be a bumbling fool with a loose grip on reality beneath the facade.'

Exactly what Standing meant by this I was unsure, and would have enquired had he not blustered on. The man certainly adored the sound of his own voice.

'So we have a couple in love, but an adulterer who has no intention of leaving her husband. There is no evidence to say that she would be leaving her husband, and indeed our interviews with those close to her provide evidence that it was quite the opposite, that Helen would never consider divorce or any such thing. One female friend at her theatre group tells us that Helen confided in her all about her love and affection for her husband and son. Hardly the words of a wanton woman with divorce on her mind! And how would Clay feel about all this? Angry? Resentful? Murderous?

'We have in one of our evidence bags perhaps the most damning clue, Mr Edgar, and one that will tip the balance in the law courts. In Clay's attic we found a short note, handwritten by Helen Capstick – and yes, we have had it verified – written on the very morning of her murder. I will show you.'

Words can never convey just how much I hated this man, a man who adored the sound of his voice, and there I sat feeling robbed of my own as he pulled over a clear bag and pushed it gently across the table to me. I leaned in and read out the scribble.

'*Feb 1st. No milk today, thank you.*'

Standing issued a harsh irritated grunt and turned the note over with a discontented mumble. On the back was scrawled a short note. It read:

Richard, please meet me on the roof of the Onslow building at 6pm. We have to talk. Helen

'That, as you know Mr Edgar, is the building from which she was pushed, and it was at a few minutes to six that she was indeed pushed. And as if that weren't enough, we have two eye witnesses that saw Clay standing at the corner of the building just by the entrance, watching as crowds gathered around her body. And do you know what he did then? He turned and fled, Mr Edgar. He turned and fled.'

It certainly did look bad for young Clay. I clutched wildly at a straw.

'And what of the stain? What of the blood in the back of the van?' I demanded.

'A red stain in the back of a caterer's van. What can it be, I wonder?' Standing licked his lips. 'Did you taste it, Mr Edgar?'

'Certainly not!'

'Then perhaps you should have, for I'll bet my hat that the bright red stain was nothing but jam or some such foodstuff, spilled in transit.'

'Jam?" I muttered.

'Jam,' said the Inspector firmly. 'Now, I think we can safely say the case is closed, can't we? Good evening, Mr Edgar.'

Over in the little house nudged up against Farringdon Station, a crime had been committed overnight that would prove to be a blessing in disguise of sorts. This crime would lead me to finally sniff out a murderer.

In that house at Farringdon, dear old Mrs Clay huddled close to the fire, her knitting on her knee, listening to the gentle music from her wireless. And then came the almighty crash that exploded through the room. She must have thought the heavens were falling as a heavy object hit the carpet, sending shards of glass flying all around.

The poor woman must have clutched her wool in terror as icy wind poured into the place through the violent break in her window…

CHAPTER 11

In which Payton Edgar revisits a terraced house

Dear Margaret,
Please help me. I have been married to my husband John now for almost sixteen years. He is a good man, and we were very happy together. We have one boy, Frank, who is growing up quickly. But now I have fallen in love, even though I daren't admit it to myself. I have been going to an amateur dramatic group now for a year, where I met Richard. He is unmarried and works at our local hospital, portering. I have been able to keep our affair a secret so far as we had many auditions throughout the week in the run up to our shows. Richard comes across as gentle and friendly, and he is at heart. He is clearly in love with me, but as we have gotten closer he has become more and more jealous of my family I have told him in the past that I won't leave my family, but now I'm thinking that perhaps I should. I think it may be best if I leave, as sometimes Richard has been so angry he has threatened to beat me, or even to hurt my family. I am sure he is capable of it. I think that he could be dangerous if I don't follow my heart and run away with him. I am frightened of Richard, but he is a fixture in my life now. We have our production of 'The Merry Widow' starting in a few weeks. What can I do?
Bothered from Bloomsbury.

I had stood for some minutes on the forecourt of Scotland Yard, gathering myself steadily in a futile attempt at getting a grip on myself. I closed my eyes and drew breath. The Inspector's case had been a sturdy one, that could not be denied. It seemed that young Clay would indeed be found guilty of this murder after all, but despite this I could not shake my annoyance at the Inspector's superior tone.

Jam, indeed!

I took what Standing had said to me to heart, and sulked down to the Thames. By the time I reached the water I was cresting upon a fresh wave of anger and frustration, laced with the certainty that something in the Inspector's case was missing. I watched the sweep of the tide for some time. The water of the river was strong that day, with violent undercurrents pushing the water from deep below.

That Limestone had run away was a possibility. What didn't make sense was how Limestone could possibly have afforded a pricey holiday abroad, as he had suggested to the Inspector? The man said himself that he had no funds, that his wife had bled him dry. And that dark red stain on the spanner head haunted me. Jam? I think not!

I could not let this lie.

I decided to return to Scotland Yard and demand an audience. I had to at least persuade the police to search the Capstick's garage, that much was clear.

I had only been out of the place for just under three quarters of an hour, and yet I was informed that Inspector Standing had left the building. I coaxed the desk sergeant as much as I could, convinced that the idiot Inspector was loitering somewhere in the building, possibly diving for cover after spying my return. Unfortunately the desk sergeant stood firm and once again I found myself at a loose end, pacing outside the police station, frustrated and angered.

There was nothing I could do.

Suddenly a familiar white van careered around the corner and parked haphazardly across two spaces. John Capstick bundled out in something of a hurry and made for the police station. He was almost at my feet when he saw me standing there and I caught more than a flicker of irritation pass over his face.

'Mr Edgar, what are you doing here?' he asked shadily.

'I have been helping the police with their enquiries,' I replied mysteriously, putting on my hat firmly. The man was clearly agitated; he stood with a clenched jaw and strands of his hair stuck to his forehead with sweat.

'Is that why you are here?' I enquired.

At this he visibly shrank with shoulders slumping.

'I'm here to pick up Frank. He has done something pretty stupid, I'm afraid.'

'Oh, really?'

'Well, it's been such a trial for him, these past few weeks, as you can imagine. He was arrested in the night for attacking Clay's house, threw a brick through the window. He's upset, that's all.'

'Of course,' I said with an empathy that was not entirely unfelt. 'Is there anything I can do?'

Capstick reacted with a jolt, as if my words insulted him.

'I think you've done enough already,' he responded before issuing a curt nod and moving off into the station. I took this information to a bench at the roadside, where I sat and mulled things over for some time.

Understandable, I suppose, that the boy should need to vent his anger in some way. His mother was dead, after all. I thought of poor old Mrs Clay in her house, alone and afraid as the youth tossed bricks through her window. Who would she have to console her with her son in prison? Young Frank seen her arguing with Helen Capstick in the garden of their home that day. What had that been about? This was a question I had not yet answered.

There was something I could do.

I caught a cab to Farringdon Station.

The cab drivers of London Town are curious creatures. Their knowledge of the roads is admirable, however in my experience I have found that efficiency is often outweighed by the pull of the pound. My driver this time, however, took a surprisingly direct route and I was in Farringdon in no time at all.

After looking over the hastily boarded-up window at the front of the house with some shame, I knocked gently. Richard Clay's mother put up a small defence initially, and one cannot blame the poor old woman for her trepidation. And then she had let me over the threshold wearily, as if she had resigned herself to allowing strangers into her house. I would like to think that she was relieved to see that it was Payton Edgar at her door, a kind and friendly gentleman calling to check on her welfare, for that was exactly what I intended to be.

She refused to allow me to make the tea, and after walking me through a gloomy corridor to the back room she commanded that I sit in one of her threadbare armchairs. The one nearest to the fire was far more tired and worn, with knitting piled high aside it. This was clearly her perch, and so I sat on the opposite side of the fireplace. The rumble of passing trains was ever-present. Like me, my host had no television set, but that was where our similarities ended. My homestead is simple yet decadent, with each piece of furniture and nick-nack carefully chosen and thoughtfully placed. The Clay residence was nothing more than a miserable terraced box, disorderly and yet – I suppose - homely. The room reeked of comfortable pursuits; knitting, reading or listening to the wireless. I found myself wishing that my mother's home had been like this when I were a boy; a safe haven. Richard Clay was a lucky man.

If it wasn't for being accused of a bloody murder, that is.

I was not surprised to receive tea with all the trimmings on what was surely her best china, and was soon nibbling on a Garibaldi biscuit as Mrs Clay talked about helping "that poor artist friend of mine".

'I could have fallen asleep, sitting there,' she chirped, shaking her head. 'Mr Spence made me very welcome I have to say, poor soul. It was nice to be able to help him. He seemed to enjoy himself.'

'And you did me a great favour,' I put in.

Without enquiry on my part she went on to give me her account of her sleepless night. She showed no anger towards the Capstick boy who had attacked her home, only regret over the death of his mother.

'But, just like the police,' she sighed, 'the boy is wrong. My Richard did not murder anybody.'

'I spoke with the Inspector this afternoon. The evidence does seem to be very strong against him,' I said delicately. Mrs Clay showed no bitterness at my words and even nodded slightly.

'It is unfortunate. I suppose I have always known that it would end badly with Richard at some point or another. Even as a young child he had a very, very vivid imagination. This is what I tried to explain to the police. A clever boy, but with a wild mind, you see? I don't know, maybe he would have been different if he had his father around. Bill never put up with Richard's stories. He was always a naughty boy, but after his father died Richard got much worse. The problem for me is that there is always some reality in his fibs, always some grain of truth in amongst the lies-'

'Your son is an adult, Mrs, Clay,' I reminded her gently.

'Oh, I'm well aware of that, Mr Edgar. I've long since stopped trying to sort out fact from fiction. But he still needed telling. When the girls come knocking on my door, Mr Edgar, well then it becomes my business.'

'Girls?' I echoed her words as she sipped at her tea.

'Since he's been older all Richard's fibs have been around girls. If they are nice to him, he thinks they are in love with him. If they are off with him, he usually doesn't seem to notice. Occasionally, when a girl makes him notice, he takes it very hard. There's never been a real courtship, ever.'

'Up in the loft Richard told me that Helen Capstick had been his first true love-'

'Fiddlesticks! And you believed him?' Mrs Clay issued a dark chuckle. 'There's been a slew of girls - a good four or five before her. But the problem is that I don't think they were courtships, not to the girls, that is. Sadly, my boy believes it all happens, in his mind, like.' She sighed. 'Richard, in his love for them, tends to be, well - a bit of a pest, to put it nicely.'

I picked another biscuit, avoiding the plentiful and dreadfully dull Rich

Tea and plumping this time for a delicious custard cream. I was careful to cup my hand under my chin to catch any crumbs as I had been given no plate.

'Are you telling me that he makes these relationships up?'

'Of course he does. And then they come knocking on my door shouting at him to leave them alone. One girl even claimed never to have even set eyes on Richard before she started receiving flowers and cards. He'd just spotted her across the road and that was it. I knew that it would not be long before some poor girls fiancée or husband would come banging on the door. Perhaps this…this shake up will put a stop to all that.'

'But he was in love with Helen Capstick?' I said in confusion, spitting biscuit crumbs about a bit, much to my horror.

'So it seems. But I'm sure she didn't love him. Well, at least she knew who he was, though, being at the drama club together. Richard's quite a good actor, you know.'

'I'm sure he is,' I replied, nibbling at the last of my biscuit. So they hadn't been lovers after all. What did this mean? Every detail of my investigation was turning upside down, and everything felt like it was getting less and less clear. I reached into my pocket and pulled out the letter to Margaret Blythe, the letter which had started all this, and held it out to Mrs Clay.

'Can you shed any light on this?' I asked. 'It was sent to the Clarion's problem page, by Helen Capstick - in theory.'

She read the letter carefully in silence. The steady ticking of the carriage clock on her mantelpiece was the only thing that cut through the silence, and I struggled to ignore it. It took me away momentarily to my aunt's musty bedroom. What was this fancy that old ladies have for irritating clocks?

Eventually she set the letter down on her lap and shook her head. Her expression was one of tired resignation.

'Yes,' she said, 'it is.'

'Is what?' I asked, unaware that I had posed her a question.

'I mean,' Mrs Clay went on, 'that this wasn't written by Mrs Capstick.'

'I thought exactly the same thing' I replied. 'I believe it was written to frame your son, to make us believe that he is guilty of Helen's murder. I think that our murderer wrote this letter-.'

'No, I don't think so, Mr. Edgar. It is obvious who wrote this letter.'

'It is?'

'It is written by Richard. He has always been a letter writer. Poems, journals and letters. Damn letters!' His mother issued yet another deep sigh and slapped the note against her knee.

'Your son wrote this?' I gasped, taking the letter back from her. As she retrieved her cup my eyes scanned the page. 'Why would he do that?'

Mrs Clay appeared to be summoning up strength from somewhere within. She took a long drink of tea and then set her cup aside once more.

'Richard told me some months ago that he was in love with a woman he met at his theatre group. Much as I might caution him, even beg him not to tell his mother untruths, he insisted that they were in love. Well I knew better. This time I decided to act before it all went wrong, more fool me. I found out the address of this woman in amongst his things and went around there-;

'You spoke with her in the garden!'

'That's right. You seem to know everything, Mr. Edgar! But I had intended for it to be a diplomatic visit. I meant to ask the girl about Richard, and to work together to see what we could do. Well, Helen Capstick was no angel, that much was clear. She barely gave me time to say my name before she bawled me out like some common fishwife! Yes, Richard had clearly been up to his tricks, and things were a little worse than I had thought.

'Helen Capstick said that she wanted nothing to do with him, that I was to tell him to send no more cards. It all got a bit messy then. Her husband came home and heard us talking. Helen Capstick had to explain to Mr Capstick just what had been going on, and I did feel for the poor man.'

'John Capstick was there?'

'Yes, and that only seemed to make the woman more determined. She made threats. Said that if Richard wasn't careful, her husband would take action. She said her husband was ready with his fists, but I tell you, she was no weakling herself. Mr Capstick just stood there looking perplexed. Helen Capstick began poking me with a sharp finger and I found myself being pushed down the pathway and through the gate most disrespectfully. Suffice to say that I didn't want Richard associating with a woman like that, even if it was an imaginary relationship. I took myself home and told Richard to stop the foolishness straight away. Day or so later, he told me that he had.'

She looked sadly at the letter in my hands.

'And then he must have written that.'

So John Capstick had known about Clay all along. What had he said to me at the funeral? "The husband is always the last to know."

He had lied to me. Why? And if he had lied about this, what else had the man lied about?

Then another thought distracted me.

'But in the letter, if it is indeed written by your son, he says some terrible things,' I stammered, trying to understand, 'some terrible things that make him only look worse. The beatings-'

'They are a threat,' said Mrs Clay simply.

'A what?'

'A threat. Read the letter again. Richard is saying to Helen if you don't love me, I will do this. I am ashamed to say it, but it is true.'

I hastily reread parts of the letter.

'So your son sent this expecting it to be printed as a threat to Helen Capstick? How cruel!' I caught myself. 'I'm sorry.'

'No, you are quite right,' Mrs Clay said sadly, 'it is cruel. Cruel and calculating. I don't think Richard sees it that way, but it is. I just don't think he knows any other way to get a girl than by writing lies and silly threats. And yet my son is no murderer, Mr Edgar. I know exactly what he is, and what he isn't. A mother knows.'

'Indeed.'

We were interrupted by a stern knocking at the door. Mrs Clay shot me a weary glance and then stood and made for the door. I finished my tea and felt a wave of lethargy blow over me. A flutter of anger was brewing deep in my chest as I thought about John Capstick and his lies. Suddenly the man was cast in a different light. I shuffled in my chair. I had grown keen to get away.

A familiar voice ran out through the hallway.

The murderer of Helen Capstick was at the door.

CHAPTER 12

In which Payton Edgar sees the truth

Richard,
Please meet me on the roof of the Onslow building at 6pm.
We have to talk.
Helen

'Hello again, Mrs Clay. These flowers are for you. I came to apologise on behalf of my son for what happened last night.'

Mrs Clay had twittered some response and apparently invited the man in. I stood firm as she brought John Capstick into the room and his eyes fell on me. I thought for a minute he would have a seizure. The look Capstick gave me, a blend of surprise mixed with something else, gave me a start. I immediately saw something new in him.

Fear - and guilt.

'Mr Edgar!'

'Of course, you know each other. Well, jolly good. Please do stay for tea-'

'And you know Mr Capstick?' I parroted in confusion. Mrs Clay replied brightly.

'Oh, yes indeed. Mr Capstick was kind enough to come see me after that dreadful row with his wife.'

'I think I should be going,' I muttered, far too meekly. Mrs Clay had taken a dripping bunch of chrysanthemums from Capstick and was cooing softly.

'My! These are fresh, aren't they? You must have got these from the Sunday market on the corner, am I right? You really shouldn't have. I'd just better pop them in a vase. Sit yourselves down, both of you. I'll pop the kettle on.'

She left us alone together.

Capstick did not sit as instructed, but instead stepped in closer to where I stood. In his eyes I saw a fierceness that had not been there on our previous encounters. The man was obviously enraged that I kept popping up unexpectedly, but within the anger there was confusion. He did not understand why I was everywhere, and this surely gave me the upper hand. And now I knew that he was a liar.

We stood sizing each other up like wrestlers before a fight. Capstick's lies had all unravelled, and it was now clear to me that he was capable of murder. The look in his eyes told me everything. He loathed me, that much was clear, and here I was again, two steps ahead of him. Before he could speak I squared up to him and, much to my own surprise, spat out an accusation.

'Why did you lie? You knew all about Richard Clay, didn't you?'

'What?' Capstick grunted.

'You said at the funeral that you had no idea about the relationship between Clay and Helen.'

'Did I?'

'Yes, you did. And yet, you were there when Mrs Clay paid a visit to Helen, weren't you? You knew all about Clay pestering her. She told you, didn't she? So, why did you lie?'

From the kitchen I could hear Mrs Clay assembling a new cup and saucer as the kettle rumbled and began to whistle. I took a chance.

'Where is Thomas Limestone?' I asked gravely. A flicker of rage passed over John Capstick's rugged face. There were a fair few details that still eluded me, but suddenly I was certain.

'It was you!' I breathed, somewhat thoughtlessly. "You went with Helen to the roof. You got Clay in the frame for it. It was you.'

We didn't need to say anymore. John Capstick's expression said it all. He didn't jump to deny anything, but instead allowed a subtle, smooth smile to pass his lips. I studied his face with my fists clenched at my side.

I have to say to my shame that my overriding feeling at that exact moment was one of irritation that Irving had suspected Capstick all along. Once again my friend had backed the right horse.

Richard Clay's mother entered the room, a fresh teapot in one hand and a rattling cup in the other. I spoke quickly, before I could be committed to any further beverages.

'I'm sorry, Mrs Clay, but I have to leave, and I have to, erm, go to work.' It was the first excuse that popped into my head.

'Work?' Mrs Clay screeched, 'on a Sunday?'

'I am a journalist, we never tire,' I replied uneasily. Capstick was watching me with a dark stare. 'Thank you for the tea, Mrs Clay, it was lovely as always. Goodbye!'

And with that, I was out the door quicker than a horse at Ascot.

I was dizzy with the shock of it all. It seemed that I had unearthed a murderer! And yet there were so many questions left unanswered.

I staggered through the streets with only half a mind as to where I was going. It was not long before I was on Fleet Street. I had not told an untruth, I was indeed going to work, where I could call for help immediately. Although most of my colleagues from the fifth floor would be at rest, Thistle House itself never slept. For the news-hounds on the lower floors, Sunday was just another working day.

The weekend porter was asleep at his post. I took the lift as usual to the top floor, only to find it unnervingly quiet. The fifth floor of the building was a curiously baron place on a Sunday, and the rumble of the presses far below was the only sign of life. I pressed on across the floor and took myself to the nearest offices which happened to be that of Beryl Baxter. The room seemed oddly stagnant without Beryl cackling and throwing herself about in it. I sat on her chair, took a deep breath, and then reached out for the telephone. With my free hand I pulled out the scotch and tumbler from the top drawer and poured a shot to calm my nerves.

The phone rang for five rings, and then was picked up.

'Irving, it's me!' I spat, hardly able to contain myself.

'This is Mr Spence's line, he is busy at present, can I help you?' rang out a female voice. For a second I was stupefied.

'Who is this?' I demanded.

'Mr Edgar? Is that you? This is Grace!'

'Miss Kemp? What the Dickens are you doing answering Irving's phone? What are you doing there?'

'Would you believe it?' she tittered, 'I am having my portrait painted! Irving is off cleaning his brushes. Oh, I'm so excited. I-'

'Shut up! Just please shut up!' I spat, altogether losing my social grace. I threw down the scotch and let it burn my throat. My hand was shaking.

'I beg your pardon?'

'Listen to me, Grace, this is very important. Tell Irving that he was right, John Capstick killed his wife! There are some things that I don't understand, but he as good as admitted it to me!'

'Really? Where are you, Mr Edgar?'

'Fleet Street, at the office. It was the closest place I could run to. I am going to call the police...'

'But you called here first?' said Grace drily.

'Naturally, I had to let Irving know. Tell him that I will see him later.'

'But where is Mr Capstick?'

I told her all about our stand-off at Mrs Clay's house.

'And you told them where you were going?' said Grace with surprise.

'I only said "to work". Capstick doesn't know what that means-'

'He does, Payton. He does.'

'I beg your pardon?'

'Remember when you left us with Mr Capstick at the Fashionista, Beryl and I? We ended up talking about where we worked, and Beryl told him all about Thistle House and your offices. Mr Capstick knows exactly where you work.'

'I had better go.'

'Call the police.'

'Yes, goodb-'

A dark shadow appeared through the frosted glass the adorned the interior wall of Beryl Baxter's office. The presses rumbled on ominously. The figure moved steadily over to the door way. In my ear I heard Grace Kemp hang up at her end of the line.

John Capstick stood in the doorway. His expression was grim.

CHAPTER 13

In which Payton Edgar has something of the Samurai about him

'Capstick!' I said, more as a release of air than anything else.

Instinctively I drew my stick closer, clutching it tightly. The man looked down on me menacingly. Various manners of address flashed through my mind as I stammered to speak. Should I opt for innocence and ask the man what on earth he was doing there? Or should I choose to respond with haughty distain and demand he leave the premises immediately? As it was, Capstick himself decided the mood for me.

'Mr Edgar, I came to explain a thing or two to you. We are alone?'

The words may have been natural and enquiring but the tone was one of dark ferocity. His large frame filled the doorway, and I knew that I was trapped. I sat, wordless, gawping up at him, at the eyes sunken into dark sockets and the bared teeth. The man was the very picture of a shadowy murderer. How had I thought he was anything else? His fists seemed about as big as my head. I found myself nodding.

'Did you ever actually meet Helen, Mr Edgar? Are you really from the theatre group?'

My head was shaking itself.

'I thought not. Lies from the start, eh? And for what? Why do you have it in for me? For your information, Mr Edgar, Helen was a dragon. She got worse and worse with every passing year. A bossy, controlling dragon!'

'She didn't deserve to die!' I exclaimed, my tone sounding not unlike that of a mouse in a trap.

'Yes – yes, she did. I need you to understand why I did what I did. You didn't know her, Mr Edgar. Even her own father doesn't miss the woman. She stormed through everything like a mad whirlwind. Yes, she was

173

attractive in a matronly kind of way, but she used her ways to get what she wanted, with any man she met. She was a tyrant, ruling us all with an iron rod. It's no wonder Frank has turned out the way he has.'

'Frank seems alright to me, a bit sullen perhaps,' I said in defence of the young man.

'He is a weak-willed pansy!' Capstick spat fiercely. 'He should be beating up strangers in the street or starting house fires to avenge the death of his mother, not throwing stones through a feeble old lady's window. Helen made sure that she killed any sign of the man in him, just like she tried with me. But I am stronger than she thought.'

'And Miss French?' I asked, interested, 'what does she think about you killing her sister?'

He didn't even flinch at my words.

'Jenny had long since given up on her. Compared to the storm-cloud that was Helen, Jenny is the warmth of the sun. My angel. She knows how hot and bothered Helen was in the last few weeks, and thinks it only natural that her sister should take her own life. When Helen found out about us, Jenny gave as good as she got. They stopped being sisters that day. Jenny tried, but I wouldn't let her feel guilty over any of it. It was all Helen's doing.'

So that was what the sisters' row had been about. Helen knew about her husband and her sister's affair. Then why stick around? I asked as much, and Capstick sneered.

'Helen wasn't about to let me go just like that. Stubborn 'til the end, she just sank her hooks in deeper. She was happy to make my life a misery. I had to shake her off.'

I pondered for a moment on just how much Miss French knew, and considered the reason for her visit to the roof of Onslow hall.

'But Miss French is suspicious,' I said casually. Capstick growled.

'She'll never believe it was me. I won't let her.'

And now he moved from the doorway, but just a little. A hat stand to the left of the door had caught his eye and he mindlessly smoothed his hand over a hanging fur for a minute. I surveyed the vacant doorway, but knew that the man would surely catch me had I made a run for it.

Bide your time, Payton, I told myself, gripping my stick ever tighter.

'It was you that did all this, Mr Edgar. If it wasn't for you, Helen wouldn't have fallen from that building you know.'

I certainly hadn't expected this.

'How so?' I hissed. The indignity of his words gave me a new strength. How dare he imply that I was in any way to blame!

'I knew that she had to go, and if she wouldn't go of her free will, then she needed a push, so to speak.' The man had the audacity to smile at his nasty little pun. 'I had learned about Richard Clay, and it seemed like an opportunity. The man obviously had a screw loose. That's why I went on round to Mrs Clay's house, made sure he was listening, and gave him hope, hope that our marriage was crumbling. I needed to keep him in the frame, and then I just needed the right time. And it came in your letter.'

'My letter?'

'Well, the one from this Margaret Blythe woman. I hear that this is you in a dress and a wig, Mr Edgar? How apt. Helen came to me with the post that Wednesday morning, enraged by a letter she had received from this woman at the Clarion, a letter she knew nothing about. She told me more about Richard Clay and his pathetic declarations of love over the past few months. Helen was furious at this little worm. She wanted to set me on to him, like a rabid dog. And so I took the opportunity and suggested to her that we hatch a plan.

'She wrote the idiot a note and dropped it round at his house, and I was to be there to threaten the man when he turned up at the meeting place. It all seemed too good to be true. Helen really thought she was stoking my fire. She read Clay's letters to me, the ones she had kept, and the man was obviously even more deranged than I had given thought to. It was a perfect opportunity.'

Capstick was practically bragging now, seemingly enjoying sharing his ingenuity with me. I could not allow the man to go on thinking he was so clever when what he had done was murder, plain and simple.

'And so you took Helen up there willingly and pushed her. You killed her in cold blood.'

He actually laughed.

'She was so angry at him, so ready to frighten the guy, so certain that we had Clay cornered. I made sure we got there a little early. The look she gave me when I had her backed up to the edge! It was a picture. The last thing I saw on her face was pure rage, and she didn't even have the humility to scream as she fell. I was out the building like the clappers, leaving Clay to take the credit. And he did. The perfect murder.'

I could not let this go on. Capstick had moved over to the desk and sat at the desk opposite me, as if reporting to a senior. Now it was my turn to stand, and I carefully edged towards the door.

'It wasn't the perfect murder though, was it?' I declared, getting a little more comfortable with the melodrama now. I cast a glance out into the hall, praying that a cleaner or some such person would be ambling about. The place seemed mercilessly devoid of human life. Capstick must have caught my glance, for leapt abruptly to his feet with a loud scraping of the chair. I lifted my stick feeling for all the word like a lion tamer with his pet.

My hands were shaking even more, and yet I had the strength to continue.

'Mr Limestone got onto you, didn't he? He knew something was wrong, and he came to you, didn't he?'

'You don't know what you're talking about!' Capstick grumbled, his cheeks flushing a crimson red.

'I know that Limestone had worked it out and that you coshed the man with a spanner and disposed of his body using your van. I know it all, Capstick.'

I was taking a chance, but I could see by my adversary's countenance that I had hit the mark, or close enough to it. Suddenly his face cracked and he laughed as if I had made the funniest joke he had ever heard. This cackle chilled me more than anything else he had said. The man was clearly insane.

I kept my stick aloft.

'And I thought it was the Inspector I had to keep an eye out for!' Capstick licked his lips and went on.

'Limestone was a fool, claiming to be all clever and professor-ish when really he didn't have the savvy to blackmail anyone. He only worked out what had happened because of something you said about driving her about, and a letter. You see, it was you again, Mr Edgar. Limestone always had a thing for Helen, lord knows why. And she knew it. Had him under her little finger, she did. The stupid woman got him to taxi her over to Clay's place to deliver her note that morning. I hadn't considered this, that she would have him drive her. She said a few things about us composing a letter to sort out a problem, and Limestone only worked out what it was all about when you spoke at the funeral. Then he came to me with a price for my silence. That's the kind of man he was, Edgar. Desperate. I wasn't about to give him a penny, but then he played games with me.'

'Games?'

'Lording it over me, saying he would go to the police. The man was spineless and petrified of me, and I knew it. I dared him to do whatever he liked. And he did. He tried to frighten me, left me sweating outside the station in my van the other day while he went in, threatening to spill the beans to that Inspector. I knew he daren't do it. He just gave the Inspector some tripe or other, I'm sure.'

The supposed holiday, I thought to myself.

'All that just to back me into a corner. After that little show, I agreed to pay him, and made a rendezvous in the garage that night. I think he was planning to go away somewhere with the cash. He was desperate for that money. He put up a pathetic fight, he really did. I was too strong for him.'

'And the spanner helped too, I'm sure,' I replied dryly. I backed a few steps to the doorway and issued an ominous question.

'What did you do with him?'

Capstick chuckled. 'Let's just say he's gone for a swim,' he replied.

The Thames, I sighed to myself, always the Thames.

'And now there's you, Mr Edgar,' said Capstick with a theatrical relish. He moved silently closer.

'The police will be here any minute, Capstick!' I lied.

'Right, of course they will. I don't think so. I heard you on the phone, gossiping to your pals!'

'Well they know it was you,' I replied, sweating, 'I told them everything!'

'The ranting fantasies of a deluded man!' Capstick declared confidently. 'The police already think you are a joke, Edgar. And if you had been drinking alone here in the office, getting yourself all worked up, it's no wonder you had the accident.'

The scotch bottle sat tellingly on the desk and the manner in which he said the word "accident" sent a chill right through me. There was nothing else to do but make a run for it, and so I took a deep breath and made my move.

In a swift movement I pulled on the hat stand with my stick so that it fell between us, and turned and fled. The hat stand must have held Capstick off for a second or two, but not for long enough, for as I cantered across the open space heading for the stairway I felt a crushing force on my back as if I had been kicked by a mule and I was sent sprawling forth onto the cold dusty floor.

I had been projected some way, for I had time to stand and turn, breathless but still clutching my trusty stick, and yet by the time I had done so Capstick was on me. He grabbed me by my lapels and practically lifted me from the ground. It was only the superior material and the skilled stitching of my tailor that kept the collar from ripping. I realised with horror where we were headed as the rumble of the presses far below grew almost deafening. My back hit the iron railing with such force I thought it would certainly give and send me tumbling backwards, but it didn't. The rail simply groaned ominously at my rear.

Capstick dropped me and prepared to punch hard.

Now, I happened to learn a number of things while I was at sea during the war, admittedly mostly about catering for large groups and the difficulties of food hygiene in preventing mass poisoning in a camp full of miserable, hungry men. But I had also, perhaps inevitably, learned a thing or two about brawling. Never having been the principle instigator of a fight, I had however found myself caught innocently in the midst of one or two in my time, and had learned a little practical self-defence. This knowledge stood me in good stead, for as Capstick came at me with a fist, a sharp upwards jab of my stick to his groin sent him on a different path entirely.

I am no martial artist but I dare say an onlooker would have likened me to the swiftest samurai as Capstick dropped to my side and I sent a second blow with the stick around the back of his head with as much force as I could muster. The brass owl handle met with his skull with a nauseating crack, and Capstick collapsed forth into the iron railing. I followed at his back with the momentum of my swing, losing footing as I turned. Shouts of alarm that could be heard from below were immediately drowned out by the railing as it issued a last terrifying metallic squeal and gave way under our combined weight.

We both went over the edge.

Cheating death was to become something of a habit of mine.

I am sure that many noble and heroic people have died with their great accomplishments going unsung, however I was determined not to be one of them. I emerged from this particular fight to the death with nothing but sore and bruised arms. I had dangled for some minutes over the fearsome printing presses, my left arm hooked painfully over and into the hanging iron railing, flakes of paint and rust crumbling down into my hair and onto my shoulders.

I didn't dare to look down.

The deathly thump of John Capstick landing on the presses some five floors below was a sickening sound. Had I glanced down, I would probably have followed in the plunge. This sickening crunch was immediately followed by a violent grinding and groaning of the presses as Capstick became caught up in the mechanism.

I clasped my hands together and prayed for the ancient ironwork to hold, and it seemed like an age before panicked footsteps thundered above me and a strong hand grabbed my forearm.

As it was, I did not have strength to pull myself upwards, but the combined muscle of the basement lads was enough to bring me up and over the edge. I didn't even have a thought for my jacket as they hauled me up to safety. I laid on my back gazing at the domed ceiling high above for some time. The silence in the place as the presses ground to a halt and men stood over me, speechless, was oddly surreal.

I had very nearly died.

It was barely an hour later when Irving sharply asked me for a second time to stop reminding him of this fact. But I had indeed nearly died, and could not stop mulling this nasty thought over and over in my mind.

My friend had arrived at the fifth floor to find me downing a second undiluted Scotch whisky in Beryl Baxter's office, a kindly constable at my side jotting down yet more details of the afternoon's events. I only allowed myself to be vaguely aware that my actions over the past few months had, to some extent, led to both the death of Helen Capstick and Thomas

Limestone, not to mention the gruesome wrangling of John Capstick.

I reminded myself that my involvement in all of this was both indirect and unpredictable. I was careful to leave out any details that pointed a finger in my direction, no matter how indirect or unpredictable they were.

To my horror, Irving had arrived at Thistle House in his painting casuals, forcing me to reprimand him for allowing himself to be seen in public in such rag-tag attire. Thankfully, Bilborough did not clap eyes on him, although he was lurking around the place, most probably assessing the damage done to his precious printers. I had been more than a little irked at his apparent concern for the wretched machines over my personal welfare.

Irving had taken the scolding over his attire kindly, and at first he was full of wonderment and gentle words of support for my nightmare experience. After a half hour, however, he was ready to call a taxi and head home.

Inspector Standing was loitering near to the main exit, leaning stiffly and peering down into the basement at the mess on the presses. I left Irving at the doorway and made for the Inspector's side. He had not been to see me up on the top floor, and had offered no comment on the events of the day.

The cretin knew I was at his side, but did not take his eyes off the spectacle below. He wore an expression of pure dissatisfaction, the thick moustache pointing southwards as usual. I peered over the edge, took in the dripping mess of newsprint and blood-red matter, and turned to the man.

'Well, Inspector, a rather unnecessary spillage of jam, wouldn't you say?'

It was strange not to venture out to Fleet Street on that sunny Monday morning to collect the week's batch of letters, however it was not an unwelcome change. It had been a fun few months all in all but I was not sad to see the end of Margaret Blythe. She had caused me a considerable amount of trouble, and it felt right to be handing over the baton.

Beryl was clearly missing my presence at work too, for she telephoned through to my home mid-morning and we arranged to meet at Mario's for tea at four. It was only when I was on my way there that I realised it was perhaps not that she missed me, just that she wanted all the dirt on my bloody squabble with a murderer over the weekend.

I was right. Over a steaming cup of tea I gave Beryl what she wanted, a juicy account of my heroics of the previous day, and she listened with admiration and awe. At the end of my tale, she tapped my hand lightly.

'Yes, I heard you'd asked Billy not to name you in the story, but I was thinking about that. What if we got him to report that Margaret Blythe caught the murderer? It would be true in the main part, and excellent publicity-'

'I don't think so, Beryl. She's played her part now, I think it's time to let it rest. She is Honoria's responsibility from now on.' At my words Beryl gave a start.

'Oh my goodness! I didn't tell you! Seeing Honoria clearing out her desk this morning was quite a surprise.'

'Clearing her desk?'

'What a transformation! I wish every grisly old crone I know could have what she had done to them. Whatever she had surgically removed, it did the trick, and she is a different person altogether. Her skin and hair were immaculate! She said she has been living with pain for over twenty years and now it's all gone. The wonders of gynaecological surgery! She practically floated into my office like a butterfly this morning, with a smile on her face, her arms full of letters to Margaret, thanks to you. Now, these are for you-'

She unceremoniously dumped a large stack of letters onto the table top, each one for the attention of Dr. Margaret Blythe, following it with a large paper bag.

'And she asked me to be sure that you got this too.'

Inside the bag were two cards and a carefully wrapped present. I opened the first card, which was an unpleasant blue floral affair. Inside, Honoria had written;

To dear Payton Edgar,

Over the weeks I have become an avid reader of Margaret Blythe and her acerbic wit, and shall continue to be so. I will not, however, be returning to my position at The Clarion, and shall instead be touring the Himalayas by goat in the coming months. I insist that you continue your good work as Dr. Blythe, and shall be telling Mr Bilborough this first thing on Monday morning.

All the best, Honoria.

(PS, a little gift to inspire you!)

I did not allow myself time to digest this information, but reached for the present and second card. This was more tasteful and carried a picture of two small ducks huddled together in the rain. I opened it and read it. It was still in Honoria's hand, and it plastered a broad smile on my face.

Finally I unwrapped the present with the smile still stuck to my face. My mouth dropped. There in my lap stood a garishly-coloured ceramic little boy in dungarees holding a bunch of flowers to his chest.

CHAPTER 14
In which Payton Edgar leaves the room

Dear Mr Edgar,
Thank you for giving me life,
With love,
Dr. Margaret Blythe

I was instantly infuriated when I arrived home the following afternoon.

An ugly doll sat on top of my mantelpiece staring out at me with one glassy eye open. As I hung my coat and hat on the antlers I could not take my eyes off of the thing, sitting innocently in all its porcelain horror. I stormed straight over to it and immediately noticed a second anomaly; my briefcase had been slotted down the wrong side of my armchair. Bony old fingers had been prying, that much was clear. It was with some alarm that I appreciated just what was inside the case - my handwritten notes on Margaret Blythe and some of the latest letters.

Within seconds I was banging on my aunt's door, wishing that I could enter without invitation, were it not for the fear of what I might see following an uninvited interruption.

'Stay out!' Aunt Elizabeth croaked from within as usual, and I entered briskly.

I shook the doll in the air at her from the bottom of the bed.

'What is this thing doing on display in my living room? I have told you where you are allowed these - these vile items! In this room only. And my briefcase! You have been in my briefcase!'

'I have done no such thing!' my aunt shrieked. Behind me I heard footsteps as Grace approached from her room.

'It never ceases to amaze me that you are so confined to that blasted bed that you can't get out to fetch yourself so much as a drink of water, and yet clearly you are able to plant things as vile as this in amongst my carefully chosen accoutrements.'

Grace took the doll from my grip as I continued to shake it in the air.

'Payton, calm down. I put the doll there,' she said softly.

'You did what?' I shouted, before tempering my approach for the sweet young thing. 'You did what, Grace?'

'I'm taking it to get the eye fixed tomorrow morning. I put it on the mantelpiece to remind me. The eye is in the bowl on the side.'

'In - in my antique Tibetan singing bowl?'

'I suppose so, yes. The poor thing needs it fixed, look.' She held up the unsettling figurine which, sure enough, was missing an eye, leaving a deep blank socket which only made the thing even more disturbing than it already was. Speechless for a moment I returned my eyes to Aunt Elizabeth only to observe a new detail that gave me pause. The rancid ginger cat sat in her lap, its eyes like slits.

'What on earth is that moggy doing back in here?' I coughed, suddenly wishing I hadn't encouraged its return. Grace clutched my arm.

'Yes, I meant to tell you about that, Payton. The cat came back of its own accord, thank goodness. And I have been doing a bit of investigation of my own, and I found out that Titty belonged to an old man on Lupus Street. His wife died last year and he was lumbered with the cat, and he's only too glad to be rid of it.'

'So he's here to stay,' my aunt put in with a sneer, 'isn't that nice?'

I knew that I had to leave and find my bicarbonate of soda, urgently, but Grace stood in my way.

'Now apologise to your aunt, Mr Edgar, for falsely accusing her about moving this doll' she commanded gently, her eyes wide and with a small smile. I felt the burning bile rise up in my throat but steadied myself and wet my lips.

'I'm sorry, Aunt Elizabeth, if I was mistaken.' I looked to Grace. 'Okay?'

'Okay,' she answered and moved out with the doll. Aunt Elizabeth sat grinning a toothless grin. One pencilled eyebrow raised, slowly. I turned and clutched the door handle.

'Goodbye, dear Aunt,' I murmured, closing the door.

'Goodbye, *Margaret*!' she cackled pointedly from inside the room.

THE END

29323064R00105

Printed in Great Britain
by Amazon